THE DRAGON KIN

CAROLANI DAY

THE DRAGON KIN

Dark Fairy Publishing

Connect with the author at:
www.carolaniday.com
Twitter @CarolaniDay
Facebook: Carolani Day, Writer

Artwork by Hannah Rodgers: diphosart@gmail.com

First Printing, 2020

Thanks so very much to everyone who supported me in my author's journey. To my husband, a constant love and support, and my two beautiful girls who I love more than anything in the world.

A special shout out to my beta readers. Thanks for giving my work a shot, taking the time, and giving me invaluable feedback. My book is better because all of you helped me get here!

And of course, thanks to my readers. Truly.

PROLOGUE

Ken glanced over at his superior, trying his best not to let his excitement show. He'd found her. *He'd found her!* Just an apprentice second class, out on his first official assignment, and he'd been the one to find the most valuable energy source their organization could hope for. An energy source that seemed to be more and more scarce as the years went on, especially in America, and that girl had it. The only one in his lifetime, easily. That had to be worth getting him into first class apprenticeship, which was just a step away from Novice Adept.

"Stop gripping the steering wheel so tightly," Adept Hodges said. Ken thought he might be amused, but a quick look at his face showed otherwise. "You'll leave dents."

Ken gave out a small chuckle, as he was supposed to, and forced his fingers to loosen slightly. "When will you call in the others?"

"When I am sure she is the one. Here, they're finally pulling over. What is this? A lake?"

"Yes, Sir. It's a popular lake amongst the teenagers,

and she's come here before. It's called Pine Cove Lake."

"I don't care what it's called. Who's with her?"

"Her best friend. Friends since elementary school."

"Pfft. Friends..." Hodges stared at the two girls as they got out of their car and went to set up their blankets on the lake shore. "Well, if you're right they won't be friends for much longer. They're getting complacent, stupid even, to let her stay here for so long. I'm astonished we didn't find her sooner."

Adept Hodges turned slitted eyes on Ken. "And why is that, Apprentice Moore?"

Ken felt his skin go cold, even as a hot spike of adrenaline lanced through his spine. His suddenly sweaty hands squeaked on the steering wheel as he gripped it even though they were parked.

"Uh, Sir, I just got here three months ago, and it's a wide, very wide, territory. I o-only got to this school a few weeks ago, but I could feel it, so I set up a marker at the schools until it pinged. When I figured out who it was, I did the required background and family checks, then contacted you straight-away."

Hodges eyes narrowed even more. "I see." He returned to looking at the girls, one of which was now putting on sunscreen. "And your supervisor? Did he never circuit the schools?"

Ken knew what it would mean to tell Hodges who had failed, for years, to identify the girl, but it wasn't as if it wasn't deserved. Hodges would be able to find out on his own anyway.

"Adept Richardson, and I'm not sure, Sir. I do know he's been here for over ten years and that Apprentice Connor was here before me for at least two years."

"At least..." Hodges tapped his knee absently and Ken was sure Richardson, Connor and every other apprentice under Richardson who'd been here before him would be repudiated if he was right, and he knew he was right. It was that girl, he was sure of it.

"Get out, it's time to test her. All we have to do is get her in the water."

"And if she's the one?" Ken asked, scrambling out of the car in his excitement.

"Then we'll call in the others, take her, and kill whoever else is with her."

Ken looked over at the two girls as one hugged the other.

CHAPTER

1

With the sun bearing down I could feel the inevitable bane of summer warming my shoulders. Every year it stalked me, prodding at me once the New Year passed, and this year it was approaching exceptionally fast, the evil thing. Lia, as always, was blissfully unaware of the evils warm sunshine brought. She just leaned back with a smile on her face.

Glaring at her happy complacency, I started lathering up on the sun block. "You really should put on sunscreen. Skin cancer is one of the most deadly things out there."

Lia looked over at me. "I don't burn, Dani, you know that."

I rubbed the white junk onto my upper arms, using the remnants on my fingers to get the areas around my eyes. If I didn't know her better, and I knew her better than anyone else, I'd have called her tone haughty, but since it was Lia, I knew she was just playing around.

"Doesn't mean you won't get cancer. Don't think that golden skin of yours is immune." She laughed as I held out the tube to her, which she took, but then just put some on my back where I couldn't reach.

"Thanks," I said as she covered me.

"Gotta protect your precious porcelain skin!"

She snickered as I did a mock-backhand at her. Porcelain, sure. As if permanent light tan skin was a standard porcelain color.

It was nice out. A not too cold, not too hot kind of day, which was unusual considering it was typically pretty chilly all the way through May. We were out, prematurely celebrating high school graduation, which would take place in three weeks and apparently we weren't the only ones with that idea. Ten to fifteen of our fellow classmates were here in various groups, but it wasn't that surprising. Our town didn't have many things going for it, and Pine Cove Lake was popular all summer long. I scanned who was here; I knew all their names and they knew me, but none of us were friends – hazards of growing up in a small town.

Once I was all sun-protected, I sat down on my towel, and propped my head up on my knees, pushing my brown hair out of my eyes with a mental note to get it cut again. Sighing, I looked out over the water and at the trees beyond. I wouldn't miss much about the town when I got out, but I'd sure miss this lake. It wasn't the only one around, but it was by far my favorite.

My mind drifted to the only thing I'd really, really miss. Lia. She was the only family I had, blood relation or not. My foster fam was fine, but it was like a roommate sort of deal. Lia, though, actually cared about me. About what I thought, how I was, and everything a family member was supposed to. Honestly, she was the only person I cared about. Why'd I have to lose her again? And this time, it would be forever. Stupid summer. Stupid graduation. I hated it all.

But, I also knew it was coming, and so it was a dull ache deep within that I was mostly resigned to. I sighed and tilted my head to the side to look at Lia. I tried to keep my voice light. "Has your family decided when you're leaving yet?"

Lia reclined back on her elbows, her long auburn hair pooling its waves onto the ground behind her. She was soaking in the sun rays I'd just spent fifteen minutes trying to prevent on my own skin.

"I'm not sure. Mom and dad would never go for it, but I mentioned to Westen about letting me stay longer this year and he said we could talk about it."

I snorted and turned back to the water. Westen was a stick in the mud who tried way too hard to be a responsible adult; he'd never change his mind. He showed up two to three times a year to tell me to buzz off so Lia could have dedicated family time. If he wanted family time so much, maybe he could, oh, I don't know, live with his family or something? Instead, he was always popping in for breaks and the summer to take Lia on vacation and leave me by myself.

"Hey," she said as she nudged me with her arm, knocking me out of my melancholic revelry. "We'll still see each other. Just because we don't have high school anymore doesn't mean that's it. You know that, right Dani?"

She could always read my moods, and usually tried to pop me out of the more depressive ones. I swallowed, and did my best cheery, but not over the top neutral voice to convince her of my sincerity.

"Of course. Did you choose which college you're going to? Once you have that settled we can figure out how long it'll take to drive for a visit."

She adjusted her bathing suit top, going for nonchalance; I could tell.

"I don't think it'll be too long of a drive. Heck, we could probably see each other every weekend."

I snorted a laugh. "Sure thing, Miss Ivy League." She wasn't really going to an Ivy League school, though it wouldn't have surprised me if she'd applied and been approved, but she had been accepted to over ten super nice universities, while I was simply going to the "local" community college Flathead Valley. It was at least the most local one we had, even though it was nearly an hour down route 93 from our little town of Janesville, Montana. I didn't know who Jane was or why she got a ville, but she sure picked an out of the way place to settle down in.

"My parents want me to go to the family college, of course, but Westen's convinced them I can get more life experience by letting me choose my own."

"Huh." I never would have expected that. Westen always seemed to be the upholder of the family rules. "That was unexpectedly nice of him. So, did you pick one? I hear UCLA is pretty nice. Think of all the sunscreen you could not wear down in sunny Los Angeles. California is all the rage, after all." Please be nearby, please be nearby...

"Hardy-har-har. No, I was thinking something closer to here."

Hope surged through me – I might not lose my only friend after all! University of Montana was only a couple of hours away from Flathead Valley. I could drive down every weekend if that were the case. It would mean I'd have to take a full load of classes while working during the week to have those weekends free, but I'd do it.

"Ya, I was thinking I'd start out small before going big time." She was deliberately teasing me, her blue green eyes twinkling at me.

"Where, Lia?" She smirked and I got up on my knees to loom over her as she laughed. "Where are you going! Come on, tell."

"Oh, just a little college known as Flathead Vall-"

I screeched and laid a hug onto her, cutting her off. "You're joking! No, you'd better not be!"

"Get off." She pushed me as she laughed. "No, stupid, I'm not joking. I applied and just got approved. Got an acceptance email yesterday and everything."

I sat back down. "And you didn't tell me?"

"What? And ruin this lovely surprise for you? I found out last night."

And probably had to spend the rest of the night talking to her parents or Westen about it. Plus, I was working last night, so I couldn't begrudge her the wait. A huge well of relief kept bubbling through me. *I wasn't losing her!*

"You know," she said in a conspiratorial manner even though no one was near us, "I bet we could find a nice apartment just off campus. I don't think we're sorority material."

I laughed at her naiveté, one of her most persistent defining qualities. "Ya, pretty sure community colleges don't even have sororities."

She crinkled her nose. "Fine, dorm room material. Whatever. I see us having our own place. No rules, no sharing with other people. It'll be awesome."

And then she'd move on to her brighter future, but that would be years down the road now, instead of weeks. I'd have my pretend sister for at least two more years; I could hardly believe it. I'd been preparing myself for her to leave me behind this entire year, and now I had more time.

"This is the best surprise I've ever been given!" I

couldn't help but squeal again and give her a tight hug that made her squeak in laughter.

"Let's look at apartments tonight. You're not working, right?" Lia asked, squeezing me back.

"No, I'm not." I noticed two senior boys walking toward us from behind Lia, and it distracted me. I let her go and pulled back with a smile. "Ya, we can totally look for apartments. I need to get a job down there lined up."

The boys were definitely coming to us. I had a feeling I knew why, and it had nothing to do with me.

"Lia, you didn't have a meet up scheduled with Braden or Mitchell, did you?"

"Huh?"

I nodded my head toward the two who were twenty feet and closing.

"Oh, no, but hey, the more the merrier right?"

I snorted. "Or, the exact opposite."

Lia let out a laugh and gently shoved my arm as the boys made their final approach.

"Hey ladies," Mitchell spoke up, sounding extra friendly. "What's funny?"

"Dani is," Lia answered.

"Oh, really?" He seemed to be genuinely interested, but I knew how good of actors most of the guys at our high school were. "What about?"

"Nothing," I said, before Lia could answer.

She looked at me, got my cue and turned the conversation in the natural way a lot of people that weren't me could do.

"So, what brings you two fine gentlemen over here?" She smiled up at him, dazzling him with her pearly whites, I was sure.

Mitchell was all eyes on her, but Braden kept his gaze moving, on her, me, the lake, the other kids around, off into wherever.

"I was gonna go for a swim, and thought you ladies might want to join."

Mitchell gave his own toothy smile in response and shifted his stance, in a way I assumed was for us to notice his well sculpted abs. Apparently it worked as I saw Lia get that glint in her eye. She was a big flirt, boys, girls, whoever, and enjoyed every minute of it. I glanced up at him through my sunglasses; he'd recently dyed his hair blonder, too. The boy was pulling out all the stops. I tried to remember if Lia and him had gone on a date yet, and couldn't place anything specific. I gave a small snort of laughter, hidden by turning my head. Just because I didn't remember certainly didn't mean it hadn't happened. Lia was highly social.

"Sure!" Lia stood and slid out of her towel wrap skirt thingy to show off her two piece in all its glory. She wasn't overly voluptuous or anything, but she looked great and she knew it. "You coming?"

"Nah." I waved her off, still comparing her curves to my straight boyish frame. That's what I get for being a runner. "Go have fun. Don't drown."

"Spoilsport," she teased, then ran toward the water with Mitchell not far behind.

I blinked, realizing Braden hadn't gone with them. I looked up at him from my perch on my knees. "So, uh, what'cha doin'?"

That's me, smooth as... smooth things. Lotion. Smooth as lotion? Whatever. At least I hadn't said all that out loud.

Shaking my head I went back to watching the lake. Lia was swimming out, kicking water up in Mitchell's face.

"Mind if I sit?" he asked.

Confused, I looked back at him. He wasn't glancing around at everything anymore, just at me, but when I looked he flushed and looked out at the water.

"I don't really want to swim," he answered my unspoken question. "It's too cold for me still."

"Ya, me too." He seemed to be waiting for my answer. Why the heck not? "Sure, you can sit."

He smiled and took over Lia's seat on the beach blanket we had down, sitting crossed legged and far enough away I didn't have to worry about him bumping me "accidentally."

"So... were you guys planning on going to the bonfire tonight?"

Ah, that was his game. "Where is it this time?"

He smiled at my words. I guess he'd been expecting me to flat out reject it.

"Out at the abandoned Johansen Barn. Starts right after dark. I hear Tyler's gonna raid his dad's liquor cabinet."

"That's not exactly an achievement," I said dryly.

"No, well, I mean, I don't drink, much, I mean-" He'd started to stutter a bit in trying to find his words.

I couldn't help but laugh. He seemed to actually care what I thought. "Don't worry, Braden, I don't-"

A giant boom sounded off from the lake and I whipped my head around, Braden and his semi-asking me out completely forgotten. The water had blown upward and outward, like a bomb had gone off, causing a huge circular tidal wave that was heading our way.

Braden shouted something as he sprang to his feet beside me, but I didn't hear it. I hadn't even realized I'd stood up, but he was grabbing my arm and pulling me toward the cars. "Come on, we gotta go!" That I heard.

"You go!" I pulled my arm out of his grasp and looked around frantically. I grabbed up my backpack and stuffed Lia's purse in it just as the water splashed over my legs, almost knocking me back with its force. "Here, drop this at my car."

He looked at me like I was insane, but he caught the backpack when I tossed it and ran toward the parking area, trying to keep out of the water as much as he could.

I ran as much as one could run in calf deep water pushing against their legs, trying to find Lia. Mitchell popped out of the water to my left, and I switched directions to him. The water started receding back into the lake and now was pulling on my legs instead of pushing.

"Mitchell!" I yelled, trying to get his attention.

He was spitting out water and trying to stand up. I got to him and helped him steady himself in the sand.

"Where's Lia?"

"What?!" he shouted.

"Lia!" I yelled louder.

He groaned a bit and shook his head, one hand at his ear. "I don't know!"

"She was back there," he shouted, still looking around. "There!" He was still yelling. His ears must have gotten messed up being in the water when that thing, whatever it was, went off. He looked back at the lake, whose water was resetting into its bounds as much as it could.

As I looked around, I saw Lia break the surface, close to where the epicenter must have been. She started treading water and seemed to be dazed by the way she was looking around. I hoped she didn't get as messed up as Mitchell had. He seemed way out of it.

He moved to go back into the water, probably to get Lia, and I shoved him toward the shore.

"No, go get help," I yelled. He looked confused, so I got louder. "Help!"

"Ya, ok," he shouted back, then started walking a drunken line toward the cars.

I dove into the water as soon as I knew it was deep enough to support me doing so, ignoring my body's shock at the cold. Lia was swimming toward me, but at more of a doggy paddle pace than actual swimming.

"You ok?" I asked as soon as I was close enough for her to hear me over the water and swimming.

"Ya," she called back, but it seemed a bit weak to me.

I reached her and got alongside as she continued moving toward the shore. She looked exhausted and pale. "Here, hold onto me, I'll do the swimming."

On the plus side, she didn't seem to be having the same type of hearing issues as Mitchell, as she didn't need me to repeat myself in ever increasing tones. She put one arm around my neck and let her head rest on my other shoulder, tilted up so she could breath.

I started back toward the shore, moving much slower now that I had 95-ish more pounds to tread water with. Even with the water taking most of the weight, it was still difficult.

Since it was so slow going, I had plenty of time to see what everyone else was doing. Braden was putting Mitchell in his car, one of the few remaining. Most of the high schoolers had fled, but there was a small group still talking and making lots of horrified looks around, and some older guys I didn't know staring at us from their car.

"You doing ok?" I asked Lia, still steadily paddling. We were almost close enough to stand up in the water.

She nodded into my back.

"Do you know what happened?" I asked.

"Something... was... holding me under and then... the thing went off."

I tried to look at her, but couldn't. I had to keep swimming even though my mind was whirling with possibilities.

"I don't understand. Was Mitchell holding you under? Like, as a joke or something?"

She shook her head against my back. "No, I don't know... it wasn't a person."

We were nearly at the shore and Braden was running out toward us. I had to admit, I was mildly impressed. He'd seemed ready to bolt when it first happened, and here he was, coming back for us. Maybe I'd have to re-think my opinion of him. Not that I'd had a specific opinion on Braden; he was mostly grouped into the all-high-school-boys category.

My knees scraped the bottom of the lake and I slowed, sinking both knees into the muddy sand and lifting my torso up out of the water. I made sure to hold onto Lia's hand as I stood, pulling her up with me.

"Hey, are you good to get up?" I asked. "Can you walk?"

She stood up behind me. "Ya, I can walk." She sounded wobbly, and when I stood next to her I could see she looked wobbly too.

"Here, hold on to me."

We automatically moved into the standard support position when walking next to someone. We sloshed through the remains of the lake's edge. It was still rippling in and out of the shockwave.

"Hey," Braden yelled out to us. "You guys ok?"

I looked at Lia, who grimaced a grin in response.

"Ya, we're ok," I responded for both of us.

He stopped at the water's edge. "You need help?" He obviously didn't want to get in, and I didn't blame him.

"Could you grab the rest of our stuff?" The water had pushed the towels out and sucked them in a bit, so they were twisted around on the ground where they'd been deposited by the receding waters.

"Ya! On it." He hurried over to grab them, the beach blanket being more difficult as it was very heavy from all the water.

Lia stumbled and I had to hold her up. "We're almost to the car. Fifteen minutes and we'll be at The Clinic." It was actually a hospital, but it was so small we all called it The Clinic.

Lia shook her head. "No, just take me home."

"But you could have internal damage or something. Mitchell's ears got all kinds of messed up. Do you know what that thing was?"

She shook her head again, keeping her eyes on the ground in front of her. "I don't know what happened, but I don't want to go to The Clinic. I want to go home."

"But..."

"Dani, please. My dad will check me out. Just take me home."

I readjusted my hold on her arm. "Ok, but I'm telling

your parents what happened and if they want to take you, you're going."

A weak smile sprouted on her lips. "Sure thing, boss."

"You better believe it," I replied, getting a small, if pained chuckle out of her.

Lia wouldn't elaborate on what happened, stating she didn't know and didn't want to talk about it. She laid her head to the side and closed her eyes for the ride. I didn't want to push her, so I dropped it, but I worried the whole way. It only took us twenty minutes to get to her place because I sped just a bit.

I told her parents what had happened, only to be shuffled off and told they'd take care of it. They were nice enough, as always, but I shouldn't have expected any different. I'd waited in my car for ten minutes, watching to see if they'd take her to the hospital, but they all stayed in the house.

Frustrated, I'd gone "home," only to feel a strong distaste for staying there, which happened most nights. Except, now that it was getting warmer, staying out was a lot easier than during the winter Montana months. The Millers were alright. They left me alone and I left them alone. I hadn't even spoken to them all day today. Did I speak to them yesterday? Ya, I think I told Marianne I'd be out with Lia all weekend, so at least they shouldn't be expecting me or anything.

I didn't want to stay here tonight, anyway. If Lia's parents weren't going to take care of her, I'd at least be nearby in case she needed me. I'd get some fresh clothes, charge my phone while taking a shower, eat something and be out before the Millers got back from their weekly movie night.

In less than an hour after I'd left, I returned to Lia's house, but instead of parking on the front street, I'd turned down the dirt road that went around the back side of their property. About two-thirds of the way back, I turned in, drove over thirty or so feet of dirt and grass to park under the huge bur oak tree that held one small treehouse, courtesy of Westen, of all people.

Lia and I had begged him for a tree house when we were eight years old, when he'd come for the summer pickup of Lia. He'd stoutly said no, made us say our goodbyes, and had taken Lia on their family vacation the next day. But, when she came back in the fall and I came to meet her, there it was. Westen had denied being the one to build it, but Lia said her parents had no idea where it came from, so the only logical conclusion was him.

We hadn't played in it since we were kids, but I'd been using it for an alternative housing situation off and on for five years or so. It had started in the summer, when I was a young teen bored out of my mind and missed my best/only friend. It became a place to go to when I couldn't stand sleeping in my room at the Millers' house. They'd stopped caring about it after a month or so when nothing happened and I kept coming back. As long as everything appeared fine, then to them, it was.

I turned off my car and got the sleeping bag and

pillow I permanently kept in my trunk, along with my backpack of homework and bag of miscellaneous clothes and stuff, including an illustrious snack of Doritos and diet Dr. Pepper for tonight, and strawberry Pop-Tarts for breakfast.

I'd gotten really good at climbing the boards nailed into the trunk as a ladder one-handed while the other held all my stuff. I put the backpack on, put the misc. bag into my pillowcase and held onto it with an arm stuck through the middle of my rolled up sleeping bag. It was awkward, but I hated making two trips since it was something like fifteen feet up in the air.

Getting settled in didn't take long since I was so used to doing it. The room wasn't much bigger than my sleeping bag anyway, and I knew where everything went. Once set up, I texted Lia to message me when she could and got out my homework to finish it before I lost the light, but I kept glancing over at the house. It was just in view of the north facing "window." Window was a generous word, since it was just a rectangle cut out of the plywood used to make the walls. Pretty standard homemade treehouse stuff.

Homemade... I put my homework book down as the thought struck me that I'd always thought Westen had built the treehouse, but he couldn't have been even fifteen years old that year. If Lia and I were eighteen now, or nearly eighteen in my case, and Westen was in his early twenties... wasn't he? He was, what, five years older than us? Maybe a couple of more. We'd been eight, so there was no way...

He certainly hadn't looked older than twenty-five, at the most, the last time I saw him at winter break. Thinking on it, I don't think I've ever known his age, just that he was an adult and we weren't. In all my memories he always looked the same, but doesn't that happen to everyone as they grow up? They imagine people in the past as they know them now, for the most part, right?

It was bugging me so much, I put my shoes on and trekked down the tree to get into my keepsakes shoebox I kept in the trunk, tucked into a net bag strapped up so it wouldn't slide around or pop open. The light was starting to go, so I grabbed it and took it up with me to peruse at my leisure. I had a camping flashlight thing that could convert into a lamp up there. I was sorting through the photos, some of them Polaroid, when my phone lit up with a message. It was from Lia, and as I picked it up another one came in.

<im fine - took some meds bath and nap - good as rain>

<Sry i didnt message sooner – was dealing with parental concern – just got my phone back>

Before I could reply another one came in. <thks for gettin me hom sis>

I smiled at the phone. She knew calling me sis was a sure-fire way to lift my spirits. Here she was the one who'd been hurt, trying to make me feel better.

<No worries. Glad you're feeling better. You sure

there's no internal bleeding or anything?> I replied. I always used proper grammar when texting, to Lia's eternal annoyance and teasing. I just hated reading through all the errors. Whenever someone writes "ur" my mind reads it as "yuuuuuuuuuuur." It gets worse with other popular textese.

<ya – absolutamindy> Of course, Lia liked to abuse grammar and words as much as possible, as evident with every text. <dad did full workup – eyes head lungs – im all good>

<K, but if you wake up sick or your vision is blurry, you let me know. I'm chillin' in the treehouse tonight, so I can take you to the clinic no problems>.

<aww ur so sweet!> and she sent some candy emojis for emphasis. <brb – family, txt u soon>

<K>

Lia knew I spent nights out here, but her parents had kicked me out a few times for safety reasons, so she stopped telling them. We tried to do a sleepover a year or so ago, with parental permission, but the space was just too small and we'd given up to sleep in her room. She'd make funny signs through her bedroom window I could see, but mostly we texted.

I put my phone down and went back to my box, making my way down through the years. There was Lia and me entering high school, my locker combo written on the back. Being such a small school, we all had the same individual lockers every year. Lia had gotten a locker by mine by bribing the girl whose locker was originally next to mine with her homemade lunches for an entire month. They were some freaking nice lunches, too: homemade meatloaf, lasagna and the like. Totally worth it.

Smiling, I shuffled through some of my other stuff. The small notebook I'd tried to make art in during middle school, and failed miserably. The friendship bracelets we'd made in the fifth grade. Skipping down to the bottom of the box, I looked for the earliest photos we'd taken together and stopped when the photo I pulled out wasn't the one I was looking for, but rather one of my mother.

It was her holding an ecstatically laughing baby me with her beaming at the camera. I used to stare at this photo, trying to find myself in her. I always knew my hazel eyes and light brown hair came from her, as she had those same attributes in the picture, but as I'd gotten older I saw other things. The dimple on only the right side, the slight upturn of our noses. I missed her, but in a recovered soreness kind of way. In a, I wonder what could have been way. I didn't remember much about her, mostly individual memories here and there. Her combing my hair. Us baking cookies and eating chocolate chips while they baked. She'd died in a car accident a year before I'd met Lia.

Setting it back into the box, I went back to searching and found what I was looking for; the first photo ever taken of Lia and me, here at this house out front. We were seven years old, and she'd moved to town just a few weeks earlier. I was living in a state ward house at the time, and we'd met at the playground in the park. Some boys were teasing her, and I'd told them to knock it off. They'd hit my face with a stick and run. The stick was small enough to whip my cheek and break open the skin. Lia's parents had taken care of me by bandaging up my bleeding face, gotten me back to my caregiver, and set up a playdate for us to hang again a few days later. We'd been best friends ever since.

In the picture, I was obviously me, light wispy brown hair flowing in the wind with a stick like body I never really grew out of. Lia was obviously her, auburn hair, naturally wavy even as a child, and noticeably bright and light blue green eyes showing even in the old photo. My face still had the very visibly healing scab across my left cheek in the photo, but we didn't care, arms around each other as we smiled as big as we could.

And there, leaning against the house on the porch far behind us, was Westen. It was grainy, he wasn't in focus, the photo was over ten years old and not taken with the best equipment, but I could swear it was him. He crossed his arms the same way and held himself the same way. But there was no way he was a kid in this photo, much less a teenager. He looked the same age as he did now, which was impossible.

I heard a noise outside and my head snapped up to see a guy walking straight towards the treehouse from Lia's main house.

It was Westen.

I glanced around me frantically. It's not like I had a lot of hiding places. There was literally nowhere to stuff my things in the one room plywood wonder with no amenities besides a "door" and three "windows." I didn't even have time to grab my stuff and make a run for it. I'd been so absorbed in my memories I hadn't noticed him until he was basically here. Quickly, I put my keepsake box back together, except for our childhood photo, which I slipped under my pillow.

I leaned out the window facing him and shouted, "Fancy meeting you here. Aren't you a little early this year? School doesn't end for a few more weeks."

He looked up, locking eyes with me. My breath caught, he looked pissed. The kind of pissed where you wonder if the person is going to punch a wall, or your face. Not that Westen would. He'd never shown that kind of temperament since I'd known him, basically all my life. However, I hadn't done anything to deserve his ire, had I? Surely staying in their treehouse was a minor offense.

Then again, it was Westen... and his blue eyes were intense right now.

"What," he pronounced that word as a distinct emphasis on its own, "are you doing on our property Daniella?"

I scrunched my nose. He was antagonizing me on purpose. Fine, I could too.

"Bird watching."

He made it to the base of the tree. "It's dusk," he said flatly then started to climb up.

I had a moment of incredulity at him climbing boards nailed to a tree in business casual wear of slacks, button up, and nearly shiny shoes, but there he was doing it like it was normal. He even managed to look graceful climbing a tree, sheesh.

I moved to the door, laying down so my head was even with the floor, looking down at him. My hair fell down both sides of my head, but there wasn't much I could do about that without a hair tie handy.

"You guys have the most amazing nocturnal red chested quirtel birds here."

He paused to look up at me, over half-way up. "There is no such bird."

"Prove it."

He continued climbing. "Move."

"You can't come in until you say the secret password. It is our clubhouse, after all."

"Move!" He swished at my hair when he'd climbed high enough for it to touch his head. My light strands flicked against his dark brown hair as he swatted at it like I would a buzzing fly.

I sighed and levered myself into a sitting position on my pillow so he had some place to go to when he entered – the bottom portion of my sleeping bag.

"You're never any fun," I muttered.

He hooked his hands on the floor and lifted himself in, looking around at my cozy little space. Of course he was strong enough to just lift himself up with his arms, stupid Westen. I had to use a knee to lever myself in.

He wrinkled his nose and I bristled, thinking of all the mean things he could comment on. The fact that it was obvious I was staying here. My old, fraying back-pack. My pathetic excuses for food in the corner. He settled in against the far wall and I braced my elbows around my bent knees, the strain giving me something to focus on besides my best-friend's really angry older brother.

I stilled as I remembered I didn't know how old he really was.

While he took in the sights I quickly sent Lia a text. <traitor>

A jingle went off and my head shot up. That was Lia's notification tone and I'd just texted her.

"You confiscated her phone?" I closed my dropped

jaw when he raised his head to stare at me. Stare was a kind word, it was more of a vicious scowl.

His jaw flexed from his obviously clenched teeth. "I didn't want her to text you until I'd talked to you." He looked at the phone and saw my message. "Nice," he deadpanned.

"She didn't warn me." I narrowed my eyes at him. "You don't just take someone's phone. That's so rude!"

I dropped mine into my backpack. No point in me having it right now, obviously Westen was on a Westen-gets-his-way warpath, like what happens every single time he showed up. When I looked back at him, he was staring at something on the wall above me and I closed my eyes in embarrassment. *It wasn't what it looked like.*

"It's not what it looks like."

He raised his eyebrows. "It looks like a pair of binoculars. Bird watching, indeed."

My cheeks flushed against my will. Traitorous blood.

"They're for star gazing, actually."

He stared blankly at me, obviously waiting me out. It worked.

"Hey, your parents were the ones to buy them. They've been out here for years. We use them to look at the stars at night. Stop deflecting from the fact that you took your sister's phone, and don't be so creepy."

He was trying to hold back a scowl. "I am not being creepy. Stop being so childish.""Stop treating me like a child," I shot back.

He gave an exaggerated sigh of annoyance.

Fine, I'd play ball if it would get him to talk about something I wanted to talk about. I leaned back against the wall, my arms still hooked around my knees. "So," I spoke with exaggerated chill, "how ya doin'? Long time no see."

"Can we please have a normal conversation?"

"Sure, when are you going to start?"

He closed his eyes, obviously praying for patience. Westen seemed to be fraying around the edges, which meant I was winning. I gave an internal little smirk that probably showed up. When he reopened his eyes they seemed to catch on my cheek and I automatically altered my position so it rested hidden in my left hand, elbow propped up on my knee.

"Well?" I asked.

He took a deep breath. "We're leaving."

No. He couldn't be saying what he was saying.

I swallowed, making sure my voice came out even. "Explain further, please."

"With what happened, we're taking Kalia to a specialist to check her out in the city, then we'll go straight to our family summer home."

My head instantly filled with righteous anger, from him dictating our lives again, to him insisting on calling us by our full names, everything was pissing me off. She always told me she preferred Lia because it sounded normal, and Kalia seemed so old-fashioned and out of place. "Kah-Lia" she used to pronounce with a guttural spit put into the Kah part, and we'd both laugh. She'd always gotten her parents to call her Lia, but Westen never would. Mine either, I was always Daniella. Well, screw him! He didn't always get to have his way. I felt the tightness in my jaw as I unclenched it to speak.

"She said she was fine. She can go to the hospital here whenever she needs." He was shaking his head while I talked, which just made me more mad. "What about school? What about our graduation ceremony!"

"I'm sorry, it's not-"

"Don't pull that with me!" I shouted over him, cutting him off. "You've never been sorry in your life. Why are you doing this to us?" My arm swept out in an arc to incorporate me and Lia in the house.

His face went stony. "Stop being so dramatic."

I scoffed and turned my head away, trying to control myself. Just as always, Westen shows up and makes my life horrible.

"Why not try telling me the truth then."

"What do you mean?"

I scowled at him. "Why are you really taking Lia early? She can go to the hospital here, or specialists in the city, and still be back for graduation."

He narrowed his eyes at me. "We aren't taking chances with her safety."

"What does that mean?"

"What happened today at the lake?"

I blinked. "Didn't she tell you?"

"Tell me your version, please."

Ah, the good ol' Westen please that was more of a demand than a request. But he didn't look mad anymore, and he wasn't glaring at me.

"I'll tell you if you answer my questions when I'm done."

He looked at me for a second before nodding.

Sighing, I leaned back against the wall. "I don't really know what happened. Lia went swimming with a friend from school, and I was on the shore talking to someone when the lake exploded. At least, that's what it seemed like." I stopped, seeing in my mind the water shooting up again.

"Please elaborate."

I rolled my eyes. *Elaborate*, sure.

"Water blew up out of the lake and a big wave came out from it, nearly knocked me over. At first I'd thought a bomb went off." I scoffed at myself, shaking my head in remembrance of the strangeness that occurred. "Everyone started running away. I couldn't see Lia, so I started out into the lake. I found her and helped her in. Nothing else happened." I looked out at the house, imagining Lia in there huddled in bed, sick from whatever happened. I spoke quietly now. "When I asked her, she said something was holding her under, but that it wasn't a person. Did she tell you what it was?"

He shook his head. "What else did you see? What about the other people? Was anyone watching?"

I closed my eyes to remember the walk back to the car. "Most of the kids had gone. One was helping us with our stuff, some others were talking and gaping at everything."

"No one else was there? Other than the students you knew?"

I shook my head, eyes still closed. "Just some guys at their cars, but they were staring at the lake like everyone else."

Westen shifted and I opened my eyes to look at him. He seemed alert to something. "Were those adults dressed for the lake or did they seem out of place?"

"What? I have no idea."

"Please, try to remember."

I took a deep breath and closed my eyes to better picture it. Had they been wearing swimming gear? No, but not everyone who went to the lake expected to go swimming.

"I guess they were a little off. I think two guys? One was maybe mid-twenties? The other one was way older, at least fifty. No swimming or picnic gear or anything, unless they hadn't taken it out of their car yet. They were the only ones there not from the high school."

"And you've never seen them before."

I scrunched my face even though my eyes were closed, trying to remember if I'd seen them around town. "I don't think so, no."

"Were they looking at you and Kalia?"

I opened my eyes, giving up on envisioning it. "Ya, they were, but we were the last ones from the lake to get out."

He sat there looking at nothing as he thought it over. When he wasn't telling me what to do or asserting his authority of me and his sister, he looked kinda cute. Laughing internally at the ridiculous thought, I waited for him to continue, but he never did.

"So, any more questions?" I asked.

"What? Oh, no. Thank you."

I raised my eyebrows. There was something I'd barely ever heard from him. I tried to sound normal and non-chalant. "You're welcome. My turn?"

His look soured and I couldn't help but smile at him returning to his natural state of expression.

"Yes, it's your turn. Why are you smiling?"

I shook my hand in a negating motion. I was just going to ignore that question.

"Ok, first, how old are you?"

He looked taken aback. I couldn't remember him looking like that before. In all fairness, to him it was an entirely out of the blue question.

"I'm... twenty-two."

I glared the most glarey glare I could. "That is such bull."

"It is not." He looked like he was eating lemons.

"Then why did you pause when answering?" I grabbed the photo from under my butt pillow and held it in his face. "And why do you look exactly the same age as when I was seven?"

He stared blankly at the picture, taking it in his hands before looking back at me. "That's our uncle."

I rolled my eyes. "What uncle? I've never heard of or met an uncle."

"Yes, you have. You just don't remember because he only visited that once. He lives in Florida."

"What's his name?"

"Jack." He held my gaze, not blinking, I'm sure just willing me to believe.

"Oh, please. He's the same height as you. Same dark brownish, blackish hair. You need a new style, by the way. You even stand the same way! All arrogant and full of self-pride." He narrowed his eyes at me. "I bet if the resolution were better I could see that very same scowl. The eyes are even blue."

They were more of a grey tinged with blue right now, but he got the idea. He let me snatch the photo back as he glowered at me.

"What's more plausible, that you forgot meeting our uncle the one time he visited for less than a week when you were a kid, or that I'm really a forty something year old man masquerading as a twenty-two year old and no one else noticed?"

"So you built this treehouse when you were what, twelve years old?"

He gave me an I-have-no-idea-what-you're-talking-about look. "I didn't build it."

"Whatever..." I put the photo back in my keepsake box and tucked it in the corner, feeling really, really stupid. I wasn't going to get any other answer, and when he put it like that...

I cleared my throat, hoping my cheeks didn't flare up again. "Fine, why are you really taking Lia early?"

He gave me a long, considering look, and I just waited, trying to look polite and unconcerned. Even when I wanted to give the "Well?" look and wrist-rolling gesture to get him going, I didn't. After what seemed like ten minutes, but was probably closer to one, he finally spoke.

"We think someone's after Kalia and the incident at the lake was the beginning. We're taking her somewhere safe."

I blinked, trying to get my bearings. I just... someone after Lia? And how did they go after her in the lake? Trying to make her disabled enough to grab her?

"What do you mean after her? Like, trying to get her or something? Attack, kidnap, what?"

"Daniella, slow down."

"But, no one came over to us or anything. And how did they cause the explosion in the lake? Is it for money or something? Like a kidnapping for ransom?"

"Daniella!"

I looked at him, not comprehending. He looked mildly concerned, but if he were talking about people coming after his sister, I couldn't imagine how concerned he could get. He was tightly wound as it was.

"I..."

He got on his knees and leaned toward me, putting out a hand on my shoulder. I wasn't used to people casually touching me, except for hugs and such from Lia, so it caught my attention more than other things would have. It was because of that I realized how rapidly I was breathing, the shallow breaths shrinking in my chest.

"Deep breaths, Daniella, that's it."

I closed my eyes and forced myself to calm down, something I hadn't had to do in a long time. Lia was fine. She was in the house. I wouldn't lose her like I'd lost everyone else.

I finally opened my eyes. "My name is Dani," I said coldly.

His mouth quirked up to one side. "Of course."

"I'm fine." I felt the need to clarify so he would give me some space. He figured what I meant and went back to his "side" of the room.

Taking another breath, I said the first thing was on my mind. "I think that's the first time you've told me the full truth."

"That's not true." He looked mildly irritated. Suddenly, my world felt back in place with me ticking him off.

"Close enough. Ok, so, there's men after Lia?"

He looked out at the house, and I followed his gaze.

"Yes, we think so. That's why we need to take her away now, and why making the graduation isn't an option."

"Why can't you call the police and let them deal with it?"

He shook his head as he answered. "With men like

these, until they strike, there's nothing that can be done. We're not risking Kalia, that's why I came immediately."

I looked at Lia's bedroom window, trying to control my face as I knew it would give me away. I knew if I talked, that my voice would crack, so I swallowed and clenched my jaw instead. The fact that I knew this meant so much more than just the next three weeks, and right after she'd told me she was staying... To say I felt crushed just couldn't fully convey how I felt, but I would deal with it, like I'd dealt with every other super crummy thing that had happened in my life, and I would do it in private. Not in front of Westen, or anyone.

So, even though my throat burned and it felt like my insides were being pulled down into a vacuum, I got my emotions under enough control to speak. I kept myself facing the house, not even looking at him when I spoke. It helped.

"This means... She's not going to Flathead, is she?"

"No, she's not."

"And, and I'm never going to see her again, am I?"

"Not necessarily."

I don't think I'd ever heard him sound sympathetic before, but right now, it didn't mean anything to me. He was taking away the most important person in my life, the only family I had, blood relation be screwed. She was more my sister than his, I thought viciously. Tears threatened, but I refused to let them spill around other people. It was more of a habit to hold them in than let them out, so it wasn't too hard. My jaw ached from it all.

"Don't lie." My voice sounded pathetic, even to me.

"It's possible, and I'm sure with you two, you'll find a way to meet up. Once we know she's safe, I'll even help you."

I finally looked at him, sure my face was red and blotchy with my efforts to suppress the emotions roiling through me.

"Don't say that if you don't mean it." I did my best to look stern.

He reached out and took my hand. His hand was so warm, it felt nice covering my own chilly one. It also felt like he could crush my bones if he'd wanted to, but he just held it loosely in his own.

"I promise to help you and Kalia connect again once I've guaranteed her safety."

Clearing my throat, I nodded. "I'm holding you to that."

He smiled and patted my hand, making me feel like a toddler. Great.

"I would expect nothing less."

I gave a weak chuckle and took my hand back. "Well, this is awkward!" I exaggerated for comic effect, to good use as Westen laughed and backed up. Then I went right back into mushy mode when I asked, "Can I at least say goodbye?"

"Of course." He moved toward the door. "Let's go."

"Right now?" I didn't hold back my bitter sarcasm. "Sure. Why not? Why would I expect any different? Hold on, let me get my shoes on."

It was getting fairly chilly, but I figured I didn't need to put on my sweatshirt until I got back, so I just shoved on my tennis shoes, grimacing when the back of the left one folded in. The tape I'd put in to cover the holes I'd worn in them didn't do anything to help them hold shape, and I had to take my foot out to finagle it back to where it was supposed to be.

I paused, looking around. I guess there would be no more coming back after tonight. I'd get my stuff and go to the Miller's. I wouldn't want to stay out here knowing she was never coming back.

In my busy work, I didn't notice Westen looking over the treehouse again until he spoke up.

"How often do you stay out here?"

"Uhh... Not that often." I kept my eyes down on my foot as I tried stomping my foot into place on top of my sleeping bag.

"Now who's lying?"

I glanced up. He gave me a straight look, but I could see the laughter in his eyes. It dropped away when I didn't respond. I grabbed my car keys out of habit and swung my leg out the door.

"Let's get going, huh?" I said as neutrally as I could.

I rushed down the ladder, hopping off the last five steps. I considered running to the house to avoid talking to Westen. He may be able to crush me with his little pinky, but I bet I could outrun him. I went running nearly every day and was the top female runner on our team, not that it meant much. Our high school track team, well, really, all our teams were pathetic.

Westen touched down next to me, also hopping the last few steps. How positively youthful of him. My mind blanked out a bit as I stared at the house, realizing that this would probably be the last time I'd come here and visit Lia.

"Ready?" he asked.

My feet felt like lead now that I knew I was saying goodbye to my friend for not just the summer, but the indefinite future. Sure, Westen said he'd help us meet up, but that was when she was safe. What if these wackos never let up? I knew the Thompson family was loaded, considering they had a gigantic house and land, as well as their vacations, but kidnap rich?

"What are the chances-" I started to ask when Westen pulled my arm to stop me walking. "What?"

His eyes darted around, trying to see something. Instinctively I looked around too, but I didn't see anything. His grip tightened on my upper arm and I felt the heat of his hand.

"Westen, what is it?"

"Get your car, drive it up the lawn to the back of the house. Do it now." He was still staring out at the surrounding land.

"I- what?" I tried pulling my arm from his grip and couldn't. I'd never really thought about how much bigger than me he was, but I felt every inch of our difference right now. Even though I was tall for a girl, just over average height, he had to be nearly half a foot taller and had at least eighty pounds of hard muscle on me. If I didn't know Westen most of my life, it would have frightened me a lot more. As it was, I was getting annoyed at him holding my arm.

"Uhh... What the..." A deep tremoring noise seemed to be coming from around us, but I couldn't find a source. The noise suddenly stopped and I nearly tripped as Westen turned my arm to get me to face him. When I met his eyes I sucked in my breath involuntarily. He looked scary intense, so much so that it seemed all the blue had left his eyes to leave only the dark grey behind.

"The men are here. I need you to get your car and get Kalia out of here while I deal with them. Can you do that?"

"I..." I looked out, not seeing anything. I trusted him to not be messing with me though. I nodded. "Yes."

"Hurry."

Then he let me go and ran off toward the house, going faster than I'd have given him credit for. My breath caught. Was that an orange glow? I watched him for half a second, imagining the faint remnant glow that embers gave off coming from his neck and hands before realizing I was being stupid and wasting time. I turned and sprinted toward my car back at the tree, fumbled out my keys from my pocket and opened the door before looking up. There was no way he'd made it to the house before I made it to the car, but I couldn't see him anywhere.

Not having time to think about where he went, I got

in, revved the engine and started making my way over the grass at an entirely unsafe speed.

I momentarily regretted not putting on my seatbelt when I hit a rough patch of ground that sent me nearly into the ceiling, but I didn't ease up on the gas pedal. Westen had disappeared by the time I got to the car, and though I frantically looked around for signs of what he'd seen, I saw nothing out of the ordinary.

Until a fireball went off near the main road.

I swore, loudly, then corrected my driving as I almost went into the path of a bush. I kept alternating between looking at where I was going and trying to see what was going off over in the blast zone. It seemed as if an enormous flame had gone off, moved back and forth a bit, and held for a few moments before dissipating enough that I couldn't see it anymore. All I saw were some ground flickers of fire. There were shadows running around and I fervently hoped Westen wasn't over there.

I stopped trying to look when I saw Lia and her mother running out the back door toward me. Right before I reached them and stomped on the brakes. Mrs. Thompson was holding a sword, a freaking shiny steel actual sword in her right hand and some kind of short staff in her left.

"What is going on?" I asked as Lia got in my passenger side, but she ignored me.

"Janette! Get in the back!" Lia yelled it as an order and I stared at her like she was crazy. Who talks to their mother that way?

Mrs. Thompson did a final sweep and then slid into the back, telling me to punch it before she even shut the door. I didn't wait for answers to my questions, I gunned it. Fortunately, I'd angled my car in such a way that I didn't need to do any turns to get out, but when another stream of fire erupted near the front of the house, I veered away from my original goal of hitting the main road. Alrighty, we'll go to the side road.

"What," I enunciated every word, "is going on? Do they have flamethrowers?"

"No, that's Westen," Lia answered. She didn't sound so good, kind of winded. Then again, how would I react to knowing men were attacking my house?

"Are you ok?" I asked her.

"Dani!" Mrs. Thompson thwacked the back of my seat. She'd never not been sweet ever since I'd known her, but right now she was more like a drill sergeant. "Drive. You're going to the dirt road?"

"Well, since there's fire randomly going off on - holy crap!" There was an unquestionable explosion and my rear view mirror filled with red and orange so big I couldn't see anything else.

"Focus! Keep driving," Mrs. Thompson barked at me.

I didn't even have it in me to snark "I am" back at her. That had to have been their house. There was nothing else that big to catch fire behind us. I glanced at Lia, she looked waxen, staring out the window back toward the flames.

"I'm sure Westen and your dad are ok," I totally lied, but hoped was true.

"Of course they are fine," Mrs. Thompson answered from the back, but she seemed to be talking more to Lia than me, especially when she said, "They are trained for this, Kalia."

She looked pale and drained, staring out the back window. I wanted to ask why they were trained for this, and what that meant, but I saw the dirt road ahead of us, finally.

"There's the road."

"Turn left and go as fast as you can once you're on it," Mrs. Thompson ordered.

I looked at Lia, then at her mom in the backseat, with a halo of red filling the back window. "But what about Mr. Thompson and Westen?"

If I turned right we would go up near the front of their house, to possibly where the guys were. If I turned left, we'd go past the treehouse I'd just come from and out into their neighbor's land.

"They will take care of themselves. Our priority is getting Kalia safe." Mrs. Thompson kept alternating which window she looked out of, assessing and moving on constantly.

I kept seeing flashes of lights in the mirrors from behind us, but they were getting fainter the further out we got. We were well beyond the treehouse and into the Davis's property when smoke burst out from under my car's hood. Not prepared for it, I said some words I never spoke in front of adults, especially not Lia's parents.

"Sorry, Mrs. Thompson," I said automatically, while trying to hold the steering wheel steady.

She wasn't paying any attention to me, instead squinting out into the road. "Turn off the road. Get us as far into the land as possible."

"Into the Davis's?"

"Yes, go!"

I turned the wheel sharply, hoping there was no wire fences I couldn't see with my headlights, but the car was slowing down and the smoke was getting so thick I couldn't see much in front of it. Now I was worried the engine had caught fire and we'd all be consumed by flames.

"Uh, Mrs. Thompson?" I asked, flicking my eyes to her before putting them back on the black smoke billowing from under my hood.

She was checking something at her waist and adjusting the gear she'd strapped on. I hadn't really noticed before, but Lia's mom was decked out for combat in addition to the ginormous sword. She had on bracer things, and a thick, tough looking vest.

"Dani, keep going. When I tell you to stop, brake as quickly as you can. You and Lia need to run. Get as far away as possible. Hide in the woods. Westen will find you."

Lia turned to look at her, and I realized she had tears coming down her face. I hadn't even realized she'd been crying.

"Janette?" Her voice wobbled.

Mrs. Thompson reached forward and brushed her cheeks. "Hush, child. It was an honor raising you all these years. Now be brave, be a Lady of Eir." I had no idea what or who "eye-ur" was, but Lia seemed to take it very seriously.

"Dani, stop!"

I slammed on the brakes, jolting forward in my seat and nearly smacking my nose on the steering wheel. Lia had held onto her seat, and Janette had already opened the car door and gotten out before I realized we'd fully stopped.

"Come on," Lia said to me, sounding like she'd gotten some of her mother's bravery.

We scrambled out of the car and met just in front of my smoldering hood. I coughed through the acrid smoke, looking around for Mrs. Thompson, and not seeing her. Lia grabbed my hand and we started running through the vegetation.

Less than a minute after we'd left the car a boom shot through the air and I turned, gaping at the remnants of my car as it spewed bits of flame from its hood. I realized Lia was pulling on me as I stared at the burning wreckage. My heart throbbed at the loss, but I turned and we started running again.

We got far enough away I couldn't see my car anymore, and the way in front of us was dark. We went as fast as we dared, tripping into hidden holes and holding each other up as we ran up a hill clogged with grass and brush.

This should be easy for me, but my lungs were screaming like I'd been in a marathon for the past hour instead of just a few minutes. Something was wrong... I slowed involuntarily, trying to keep up with Lia who didn't normally have my running stamina. She looked back at me, concern in her eyes.

"I can't-" but I couldn't finish enough to say breathe. I fell to my hands and knees, trying to gasp with nothing coming out. My throat was closed up, nothing in or out, and panic surged through my system as it fought for air.

Lia grabbed my left wrist, said "Sorry," and sent something into me through her hand. A rush of orange flushed on her skin before entering me where she was holding me. A power was the only way I could describe it, and it seemed to pulse through me, pushing out whatever blocked my lungs.

I heaved, getting oxygen into my system while Lia pulled on me, still holding my wrist, which was beginning to burn.

"Come on, we have to run. They found you," she whispered, tugging on me. "You're not blocked like us. Maybe if we get far enough away..."

Still getting my breath back, I didn't question and ran with her. We zigged and ducked behind trees, bushes, whatever we could. Lia started to lag rather quickly, and once I got my breathing under control again, it became me pulling her along. We didn't speak for over twenty minutes, not even when we heard people yelling, or screaming in anger and pain. Whatever it was that had caused me to stop breathing didn't happen again. She never let go of me.

Thankfully, the Davis's land was massive and we didn't get anywhere near their homes or buildings. We were able to cut through one of their fenced in yards, but Lia pulled me along the edge and we crouch-ran the length of it.

After what seemed like an hour, we finally reached the distinct forest. Still, we kept on for another ten or so minutes.

When it felt safe, I looked at her hand where it still held my wrist. I wasn't imagining things, she was glowing orange under her skin, very lightly, like an ember in a dying out fire, and like a fire, my wrist was burning more and more painfully now that I had time to focus on it. Suddenly, I had to pull my hand out before the pain overcame me and I wrenched my wrist free with a hiss.

She looked down and winced. She got very close and whispered, "I'm sorry. I didn't mean to hurt you."

My wrist was discolored where she'd held me, and I was pretty sure there were blisters. I ran my left hand over the area as gently as I could, and bit my lip to keep from making noise when my finger pulled on the skin.

"Sorry," she said again.

"What happened?" I held up my wrist. "What is this?"

She grimaced. "Uhhh…" She was so articulate when she didn't know what to say.

"Lia, what is going on?" I tried again, taking time to say each question distinctly. "Who are those men? What's with the fire? Why are they after you and how did you do whatever it was you did to me?"

Her eyes shone extra in the moon light that filtered through the trees, a pale blue green. "I can't tell you."

"What do you mean you can't tell me? I deserve to know."

My wrist scorched in the chill night and I shivered, knowing we should keep moving, but needing some kind of answers. The fact that Lia was keeping things from me, well, I held the anger down until I could figure things out fully.

She nodded and I saw tears slip down her cheeks. "I know, I've always felt that way, but I was forbidden."

"By who? Westen?"

She shook her head. "No, my parents."

"Well," I scoffed, "I'm pretty sure they'll say it's ok since they're out fighting those guys, whoever they are, and your mom sent you off with me. That makes me in-the-know material."

"Dani... Janette and David... They're not my real parents."

The world shifted, and I wasn't fully aware of why. Lia just told me her parents, the Thompsons, who I've known my whole life, who had me over nearly every school day for the past umpteenth years, weren't really her parents. And she knew it. The whole time. She'd lied to me. The whole time. Why?

"So, are you adopted or are you a foster kid, like me? And *why would you have never told me!*" I kept my voice down as much as possible, but I'm sure it raised a few decibels in my anger.

"Dani, it's not like that."

"Well, how is it then? Because I apparently don't even know your real last name."

She looked like I'd slapped her, and I kind of felt like doing just that.

"It's Eir."

Before I could formulate my anger into more words we heard a noise coming toward us and Lia grabbed my arm, pulling me behind a clump of trees. Fuming, but not willing to risk our lives, I held still, feeling the pain pulse in my wrist in tune with my heartbeat. I felt a strong ache from my jaw and realized I was clenching it so tight I might pop something. Making a concentrated effort, I released it and kept an eye on where the footsteps were coming from, because it was plainly clear someone was running toward us.

I reached down, and as silently as I could picked up a softball sized rock. Lia looked at me and shook her head, but for what I wasn't sure. To keep quiet? Well, I was doing that already. To not attack? If it was one of those men and they found us, I definitely wasn't going to do nothing. I gripped the rock and shifted into a position I could spring from.

A dark figure broke through the bush and Lia let out a cry. Before I could figure out why she'd yelled, she ran to the figure and threw her arms around it. My chest sagged with relief and I dropped the rock.

"How did you find us so easily, Westen?" I asked, walking out from our hiding place. "And how did you know it was him, Lia? For all you knew, it was one of the attackers."

"I have really good eyesight," Lia answered quietly, and if I weren't mistaken, sheepishly. She was still clutching her brother, not that I blamed her. I was glaring daggers at her, still wanting answers from before we were interrupted.

"I followed the trail you made." He nodded back toward where he came, but we hadn't come from that direction.

I realized my mouth was gaping open and I shut it. "You two are so full of it! Fine! Don't tell me the truth. I'm leaving." I started walking off and dodged Lia's grab for my arm. "No! You've been lying to me, apparently, our whole lives, Lia, and now you're still doing it!"

Tears welled in her eyes. "I was forbidden to tell you or anyone about anything because they were afraid what's going on right now would happen. I *couldn't* tell you, Dani."

"You mean you wouldn't tell me."

"No, she couldn't," Westen answered, stepping in between us, which only made my anger arrow at him.

"That's bull."

"No, it's not. She, I, her wardens the Thompsons, we are all forbidden. Had Lia told you, she never would have been able to return. You never would have seen her again."

I shook my head, infuriated. What could I say to that?

"Dani, please," Lia sniffled, the sound making me stop my angry exit, but I was still mad as all get out.

"Here's what I know, the Thompson's aren't your parents." Westen gave Lia a look and she shrank a bit, but didn't leave his side. "You've got guys after you that can blow up a lake, and have flame throwers, make my car's engine blow up remotely, and stop me from breathing apparently. Oh, ya," I held up my wrist, "and Lia magically cured my not being able to breathe issue by burning my wrist just from holding it."

"Kalia!" Westen glared down at her.

Lia bristled. "She was going to die! They were suffocating her."

That was downright unsettling to hear out loud. I

mean, I knew I couldn't breathe, but... I looked at my wrist, seeing the raised blisters circling where Lia had held me. One was clearly a full finger print wide. I didn't know blisters could get that big. And it all burned from underneath. Vaguely I wondered if this was second degree or third degree.

Westen let Lia go and came over to me. I stepped back without thinking, as he seemed extra intense scary at the moment.

He held out a hand. "May I see your wrist, please?"

"Sure," I grumbled, holding it out. "Look at my wrist. Doesn't change what I-" I hissed involuntarily as he touched the more tender portions.

"Sorry," he muttered. Then his fingers fluttered over my blistered skin and I saw little tendrils of orange, yellow and red flicker up his finger tips from my skin.

I waited until he was done to say, "I didn't imagine that and don't you dare call me crazy. What did you just do?"

"I didn't heal it." He shrugged his shoulders back, standing up straighter as he did so. "I took the heat out of it, so it'll heal faster and hopefully not pain you as much while it does so."

I looked between the two. "So, you're witches and wizards or something. Like Harry Potter?"

"No," Westen spoke coldly and I took another step back, holding my still tender left wrist to my chest.

Lia leaned over, catching my eyes from behind her brother. "We're dragons."

CHAPTER

5

I snorted with laughter, I couldn't help it. "You're, sorry-" I was still laughing. Coughing, I got rid of the laugh but couldn't help the smile. "You guys... are dragons?" Lia nodded, though Westen just looked angry. "And you believe that?"

"Stop being a child," Westen growled.

"Stop treating me like one," I replied, just as snidely as I had the first time I'd said it to him tonight.

"This isn't a joke, Daniella!" Westen's lip curled up enough to show clenched teeth.

"I'm sorry." I wasn't. "But it's not exactly very believable."

Lia came over to me and took my hands in hers. She looked me straight in the eyes. "I swear on the Care Bears, Wish to Grumpy, that what we're saying is true."

Well, crap. I took a deep breath and nodded. "Okay."

Westen kept looking between the two of us before

blurting out, "Oh, come on!" He stomped away several feet before turning back sharply, pointing an accusing finger at me. "Me throwing fire, the warlocks choking out your breath, Kalia forcing their magic out, me taking the heat from your wound, none of that convinces you, but one word from Kalia about Care Bears, and you're all good?"

I looked at Lia. "I've never seen him lose it quite like this before. Is this as bad as it gets?"

"No way. He's way worse." She giggled.

I had received a lot of supernatural evidence the past hour or so that my mind had been going over and over as Lia and I ran in silence, and everything he mentioned in his little rant added up. Plus, Lia had just sworn on our sacred childhood bond, something we promised to never take in vain. We'd made that promise at nine years old, and to my knowledge, neither of us had ever broken it. Beyond everything that had happened, I believed her. I had to.

Lia sobered up real quick and looked at her brother. "Westen, what happened to Janette and David?"

Shrugging off his apparent anger at me, or at least putting it on a back burner, he walked back to us. "I don't know. I left David to take care of the rest when I came after you. I last saw Janette with you."

Lia looked out into the woods towards approximately where we abandoned my fireballed car. My insides twinged at the reminder of my now smoldering vehicle. It seemed silly, stupid even with all that had happened to feel a pang at its loss, but it was the biggest thing I'd owned, purchased and upkept all by myself. It had been my independence. Now it was a fire hazard.

"She covered us when the warlocks took out Dani's car." Lia sounded like she was going to cry, and I didn't blame her. Maybe they weren't her real parents, but they'd acted as her parents while she lived here, and I saw them interact on a nearly daily basis. They loved each other; I could tell.

"What are warlocks?" I asked. "Like, bad wizards or something?"

Westen gave me a considering look. "Basically, yes. They are the original oathbreakers, and our constant enemy."

Lia was nodding along as he spoke. "Ya, they're our bogeyman."

Westen scowled at her. "They are not. They are cowards who constantly scheme to take power which is not theirs."

"Why are they attacking? Like, what do they want?"

"To steal our magic," Lia said with wide eyes, as if it hadn't really been real to her before.

Westen nodded with a frown. "Warlocks have no real power on their own. They take it from innately magical creatures."

"And you're dragons, right?"

Westen arched an eyebrow, looking like he'd rather glare at me, which was his norm. He nodded.

"So..." I looked between them. "Can't you like, fly away from them?"

Lia sat down on a rock, looking crumpled. "I can't, yet."

Westen put a consoling hand on her shoulder. "Most dragons can't change until in their second decade of life. I can, but I'm not large enough to safely carry you both."

Lia sniffled. "Then we should start out. Do you know how far behind they are?"

I saw the look in his eyes. I knew what it meant.

"What are you waiting for?" I asked him.

Westen looked at me and we had an understanding go between us. He knew that I knew. I'd make it easy on him.

"Go, take her. I'll be fine."

Lia's head shot up. "No, we're not leaving without you."

Westen met her eyes. "Kalia..."

"No!" she rocked up, startling her brother into taking a step back. "Dani got us out of there. She saved my life. Twice, since she got me out of the lake. We are not going to just leave her behind to freeze in the forest until the warlocks find and kill her!"

I stepped in and hugged her, giving Westen a let-me-handle-it look. His face was sour, but he stayed back.

Kill me? Was that really a possibility?

I pulled back to look her in the eyes. "Think about it logically. I'm only human, right?"

"Dani-"

"No, let me finish. They'll think I either died, you guys took me with you, or you left me behind because I'm not important. No matter what, in their eyes, I don't matter." I didn't mention the fact that if they'd done any kind of research into us, they'd know we'd been best friends for over a decade. Hopefully, Lia wouldn't think of that, though I'm sure Westen had by the unhappy hunch to his shoulders.

Lia pulled out from the hug. "You do matter, and we're not leaving you."

I straightened out some of her hair that had gotten tangled. It would distract her mind a bit, and it made me feel better to do something, anything, that helped.

"I'll be fine; it's you they're after. They're going to follow you guys as soon as you head out, I'm sure. Besides, I'm the best runner in this crappy little town. They'll never catch me, if on the off chance they are looking for me." Not that I could do much running in the middle of the night in the forest without any light source. Again, I neglected to mention it.

Tears slid down Lia's face once again, and for a brief moment I envied her ability to shed emotions so easily.

"Westen..." she implored, giving him wet puppy dog eyes.

He was resolute. "She's right. They'll come after us. I'll make sure they see me flying. That's all they'll focus on."

"Where will you go?" I asked.

"I head south first, to try and throw them off a bit, but

our home is northwest from here. Here, Daniella, take this."

All of a sudden Westen unbuttoned his shirt and handed it to me. I'm fairly certain I blushed, and I'm glad of how dark it was to help hide that. Then again, they were dragons, maybe they could see it anyway.

"It's not much, but it'll help with the cold. Just keep moving until I can get back. Stick to the forest. I'll find you."

"Uh... thanks." There was no way I was putting on his shirt. At least not while they were here looking at me. And there was no way I was staring at his chest or abs glinting in the moonlight. Apparently being a dragon came with benefits.

"You promise?" Lia asked, looking up at her brother. "You promise you'll come back for her?"

He nodded and Lia grinned, nodding her assent. "Oh, thank you, Westen!" Then she turned and tumbled into my arms. "Stay safe! Just keep running, like you said. Don't get hurt, 'kay?"

I squeezed her with my good arm. "Of course. You stay safe." I swallowed the tears that threatened me, knowing full well that Westen may not be able to make it back to me. Lia was all that mattered, for both of us. I just got that. "Now you guys get out of here."

I looked at Westen while still hugging Lia. He nodded and said a quiet, "Thank you."

Then he started to blur and shimmer in a trippy, CG movie trick kind of way. Lia let go of me and turned to watch her brother. I'm pretty sure I gasped in there somewhere, because all of a sudden a ten foot dragon stood in the space Westen had just held.

I fell back on my butt when it, I mean, he, took a step toward us. My butt and mouth hurt, as my gaping jaw had shut hard on my tongue upon impact with the ground. Lia let out a giggle and I felt like pinching her in revenge when she gave me a hand to help stand up with. Ruefully I rubbed my aching hindquarters. The ground was cold and hard, and I'd hit it with a nice BAM.

"What?" I said sarcastically, which just made her laugh more. "Just because I said I believed you didn't mean I was ready for-" I waved my hand at the dragon, "all of that."

"All of that," she chortled, "is Westen."

"Gee, thanks, I got that."

A ten foot dragon didn't sound big, but damn if it didn't feel big staring it down. Imagine looking up at a ten foot tiger, that's what it felt like, and even though I knew it was Westen, my primal instincts were screaming at me to run from the predator or pee my pants. One of the two.

His coloring melded with the night and I had to squint to figure it out, which helped me calm my freaking mind out a bit. He was mostly grey, mixing from light to dark in various parts, and seeming silver in others. He stretched up his neck to take in the surroundings and I imagined him swallowing me whole, like a snake would. He was like a classic European dragon from the movies, minus the bulbous belly, kind of like Smaug in the Hobbit movies, except sleeker somehow with spiked horns making a line over the top of his skull. And his arms were regular arms, not attached to his wings like I'd seen some dragons in the movies have, so he could pick up Lia in them, which he did, but not before she gave me one last hug.

He held her with one hand supporting her legs and butt in a sitting position, and the other holding her back and neck in place. If he tried to hold us both it would be precarious at best, and would crush our backs in an attempt to keep us from falling at worst. For being a huge dragon, the arms seemed rather small; though, I suppose evolutionarily speaking, they weren't needed very much. Kind of like the T-Rex's little arms. I gave one chortle of stunted humor, imagining Westen with such tiny arms as those dinos had. It was a good thing his arms weren't *that* tiny.

Lia held out a hand toward me, as a final wave. I waved back, holding down my emotions as a burning ball in my throat.

Shaking his head like a cat, he bunched his lower legs and launched into the air, only to disappear right after takeoff. I blinked, wondering if I'd just lost sight of them in the dark, but I could hear his wings beating. I kept scanning the sky, and after a minute I saw them blink back into existence far to my left. Apparently invisibility was one of Westen's tricks. I wondered if all dragons could do it, or just a special few. Well, he had said he'd make sure they'd be seen flying. I guessed he didn't want them to see where they launched from. One more small layer of protection for me.

Shivering, I put on his shirt over my very inadequate tank top and buttoned it up. Too bad Westen wasn't into warm flannel button ups. This grey business type shirt wasn't much, but it had long sleeves and even though I wouldn't really notice the difference, it would probably still help. My nose wrinkled and I sniffed myself. Whew, Westen sure had sweat in this thing. Gross.

Ignoring it, I set out for the longest night of walking I would ever have to do. At least, I certainly hoped so, because I never wanted to do anything like this ever again.

I was picking my way through the forest with my eyes locked on the ground right in front of me. I still didn't see so many things – twigs, rocks, little indents that didn't show up in the shadows. I caught myself from falling multiple times, and I was worried I'd sprain my ankle in one of those holes and not be able to walk anymore. My arms were wrapped around me (my injured wrist on the outside, avoiding touching things as much as possible), trying to conserve my heat, when a bright light shone behind me.

It was bright like a cop search light, pointed straight out in a cone. I thought briefly of a D&D cone of light type spell, then I realized how stupid I was being. I spotted a small boulder a little to the left of me. I got on the other side of it to where that light was coming from, huddled myself up into a ball as much as possible, and waited.

In my mind, I imaged the warlock guys searching the place Westen had taken flight with Lia from. It was around where they were, barely a twenty minute walk to where I was. If they were looking for me, I just hoped that they couldn't see my tracks, and if they had infrared or something, that I would appear as a round unmoving blob that could be attributed to a sleeping... something. Large cat? Lost dog? Small bear? Whatever.

I kept my arms and legs tucked in, and my head hunched down so it wouldn't stand out. And I kept my eyes open and darting around. Mostly I saw my breath clouding in front of me and the light, too bright and unnatural to be anything but those guys. If it were police, there'd be a megaphone or red and blue lights, something. All there was, was that light, and it moved around. They were obviously looking for something.

While I waited I revisited the past few hours, everything that had happened. I was still hurt that Lia'd lied to me for so long, but, it was understandable. For a family secret, that had to be up there as one of the top reasons not to share. Still... I was glad Westen had gotten her out. She was the only person in my life that really mattered, and these jerk warlocks were trying to get her. Pretty good reason for being left behind, even if it did leave me with an ache in my chest.

Maybe Westen could come back, even if I didn't really think he could. To get Lia away they'd have to go pretty darn far. Regardless, I needed to stay away from these guys. Anyone wanting to hurt Lia wasn't worth dealing with.

I wiggled my toes to release some tension. My heartbeat was going far too strong for sitting here in the cold. Twice, I'd convinced myself the light was getting closer and I considered my options, either I sit here and hope they don't find me, or I pick a direction and run as fast as I could, praying I didn't trip and splat myself on some rock. Each time, just as I was panicking myself into running, it had turned and moved around back there some more, and I'd let go of the breath I'd been holding.

The cold was leaching into me more and more. My back against the rock and my butt on the ground were seeping with cold. It felt like ice shards were penetrating me deeper and deeper, moving in toward my core, and I knew it would be a struggle once I started moving again to get over the cold. I breathed on my hands cupped around my mouth and nose, trying to keep them and my face warm.

After another long stretch, ten? fifteen? twenty? more minutes had gone by and I was starting to think I'd have to run for it just so I didn't have to sit here anymore. It may have been warm enough today to visit the lake, but it would definitely get below freezing tonight, if it hadn't already, and I had terrible aches from the cold. I hadn't stopped shivering for at least the past five minutes. I'd been able to control it, turn it off before that, but not anymore.

That stupid light, and those stupid men, were still out there. They'd moved around, gone farther and closer, but they weren't leaving the area. How long had it been since Westen and Lia had taken off? Had it even been an hour? I thought so.

Not being able to take it anymore, I stretched out my legs in front of me, then stretched out my torso over it, keeping my ears focused on noticing if they'd heard me move. I didn't hear anything, and the light didn't suddenly focus on me, so I stretched and wiggled minutely for all that I was worth. It helped bring some feeling back, especially in my calves and lower back, but until I got up and moved, there wasn't much I could do for my thighs and bottom. I did small movements until I was sure getting up wouldn't put me into a seize of a dead leg "waking up" – it was about all I could do.

I took three steadying breaths, then stood up, looking back to see how they reacted. Nothing so far. I did a full body stretch, always keeping my eyes toward them. Once my body seemed good enough to go without risking a cramp, I turned my back on them and started out as fast as I dared. I silently cursed their light as it had tainted my eyes enough that I couldn't see nearly as well. I was tripping and slipping on things, trying to be as quiet as possible and failing miserably.

I caught myself against a tree trunk and I swear that darn light turned toward me. Not wanting to risk my night vision more, I pressed on. I scraped my hands on the ground catching myself and on trees when I misstepped. I tumbled on my knee, but I refused to make more noise or to stop.

I thought they were gaining on me, the light seemed to be coming, and I grimaced thinking of how it could be my light at the end of the tunnel. When it did sweep across me, I stepped behind a small tree. It didn't cover me fully, but hopefully it would be enough. My heart was pounding in my ears, but after a moment the light moved on, and I blew out the breath I'd been unconsciously holding.

I just couldn't see in front of me well enough to notice the drop until I stepped off the ground and found nothing under me. I immediately tipped so far forward that I fell. I slid and tumbled, hitting my head when I first went down and catching myself on a small tree before I would have started rolling head over heels down the hill. I took stock of myself, wiggling my limbs and finding everything intact. My head hurt, but it certainly wasn't the only thing hurting.

If nothing else, I hoped this would help throw those pursuers off. Their light was up and behind me a good deal, but I heard voices yelling in the distance. Looking down at as much of the hill as I could, I started a controlled slide down. I had to use all of my limbs to control my descent, and my blistered wrist hurt terribly every time it had pressure on it. If they did find where I went down, it'd be the easiest thing for them to see where I went as I was sure I was leaving a swath of mushed dirt and leaves in my wake.

Finally, I reached the bottom. Slowly, I stood up, leaning heavily against a young tree. Everything hurt. Everything was cold.

I glanced up, toward the top of the hill. I could still see the light, but it was far up and away now. That stupid hill had to have been at least twenty feet high, and my backside still felt every foot of it.

I gingerly touched the back of my head where it had hit on the initial fall. It was tender and had a bit of a lump, but seemed fine. When I pushed it, it just ached, it didn't squish or cause shooting pains or anything, so I was gonna call it good.

Turning away from the light above the hill, I once again started out.

I did my best to walk quietly, but I just couldn't see well enough to do so. Every sound I caused made me wince, and every sound I heard in the dark made me flinch. Besides the warlock guys I had to worry about (and really, weren't they enough?), my brain had to consider all the wildlife abundant throughout the Montana backwoods. It started going through the lists and all the stories I'd heard, like how a bear had killed a couple camping, or how wolves had gotten into one of the rancher's land and killed a bunch of their herd.

Black bears, cougars and wolves, oh my. Not to mention smaller things that could still mess you up, like coyotes, bobcats, or moose, should the moose be so inclined. Heck, the deer or raccoons could probably mess me up if they wanted. I was very low on the totem pole of predators out here with no weapons, tools or any kind of real defenses, and I was very, very aware of it.

So, every noise was suspect. I'd stare when I heard something, trying to see through the black and never making anything out besides typical foliage. I also kept glancing behind to see if the light was following me. At least when it was around, I hadn't heard any critter noises, but I still preferred it being far, far away.

After a while, it became a put-one-foot-in-front-of-the-other slog. I was terribly cold, aching all over, and shivering constantly. I was also hungry. That small meal I'd eaten at the Miller's before heading over to Lia's tree-house seemed so very, very long ago. I had no idea how long it had been since I started out from the bottom of that hill, or how long since Westen and Lia had lifted off. Or how long since this whole attack started. *No, don't think about all of that!* So, I didn't, and I kept going.

And I was so very tired despite the edge of fear constantly pinging my adrenaline meter. There was no friggin' way I was sleeping in these woods, though. If I was going to die, by warlock or beast, it sure as heck was going to be while I was awake.

Eventually the sun would come up, and then...? What? Could I even go to the Miller's? Surely these guys would know Lia and I were best friends and would be waiting for me.

Could I even go there if I wanted to? I had no idea where I was. I think I was heading north, or east, or northeast, something like that, but the forest out here was incomprehensibly vast and I had no idea where I was. The best I could hope for was figuring out which way was east when the sun rose and following that until I hit a road.

Why would that even matter? My feet slowed until I came to a swaying stop. If the warlock guys, and that just sounded stupid, but if the evil guys that attacked us were looking for me, specifically, where could I go? I didn't even have a car anymore.

Cursing myself as I started to cry, I gritted my teeth and shook my head, as if to tell my eyeballs "No."

"Stop it, stop it, stop it," I chanted to myself, forcing myself to march forward. Yes, Lia was gone and probably never coming back. Yes, my car had blown up and I didn't know if I'd be able to afford another one and still go to school. No, I didn't know if Westen was coming back for me. But crying about any of it wouldn't help, so I refused.

"Get a friggin' grip!" I wiped at my face angrily and got a spasm of pain from my injured wrist, which helped clear my urge to cry more than my pep talk did.

I didn't know why, but talking to myself out loud was helping. "Right, if Westen doesn't show up by daytime, I'll just... walk east 'til I find civilization and then figure it out from there."

There was a growling yip, off to my right, and I stopped cold. Before, all the potentially wildlife sounds had been far off and indistinct where I could ignore them for the most part, even while my blood pounded in my ears. This time, it seemed much too close. I strained my eyes, but saw nothing.

Wouldn't a wolf, or coyote, or whatever had made that yip just attack me if they wanted to eat me? Perhaps it was a warning, like a snake's rattler trying to get you to go the eff away. So, that was what I was going to do. Slowly.

I moved to my left, grimacing when I snapped something under my foot. But I didn't hear anything from my right. Should that make me feel better, or worse?

Light burst all around me and I was running by the time my brain realized it should panic. They'd caught up to me, or found me, or something, but I was running.

"I've got her!" someone yelled behind the light, encouraging me to sprint faster into the trees.

CHAPTER

6

My feet stumbled in the blind, and my body took punishment from branches I whipped by, but I was getting away.

Until my entire body seized up in place like a statue. My chest heaved with the need to breathe and with panic. I literally couldn't move any external muscle, my eyes open and staring at the forest in front of me, my arms frozen in motion with my legs, one firmly planted and the other coming forward for the next step that wouldn't happen.

By all laws of physics, I shouldn't be standing up. My inertia alone should have toppled me over onto my face.

Multiple people were walking up to me and my pulse beat against my skin.

"I'm glad to see your gamble paid off, Apprentice Moore," someone said to my left, but I couldn't turn my eyes to see. I hadn't heard him walk up to me though, which was freaking creepy beyond belief. My nostrils flared as I tried to panic breathe through it.

An old man stepped in front of me, but my eyes wouldn't focus, resolutely staring at what they'd been looking at when I'd been frozen.

He touched my forehead, I felt a zing down my spine and all my muscles noodled. I collapsed into a weak heap, coughing into the ground at the sudden release and feeling incredibly vulnerable.

I looked up, seeing the old man before me. There was also a younger guy behind me holding something. I squinted at it, making out the edges of a notebook. My notebook. It had my doodles all over the cover, pretty distinctive. Dread wound through me as I realized I hadn't even known it was missing. When had they gotten it? How long had they been watching us?

Someone moved closer and I saw a third person, a woman who looked youthful middle-aged and Japanese with draping black hair. She stood farther back than the others, staring intently at me.

"Don't try to run again." The old man spoke down to me with derision. "I won't be so gentle again."

He swished his cloak, a friggin' real deal cloak with full intent to swish it, before settling onto a log. While he did so, I adjusted myself on the forest ground to a neutral sitting position. I didn't think they'd let me be in an active stance, but this would let me react fairly quickly if the chance arose.

I just really didn't see how the chance could do so.

"So, ummm, are you guys waiting for me?" I looked between the three of them. "I've never been chased or interrogated or anything, so I'm not quite sure if I should go or if you go first…"

The woman took five brisk steps toward me and slapped me, hard. Like, nearly tipped me over hard, and it freaking hurt. She was so tiny to pack such a punch.

I glared up at her, refusing to rub my stinging cheek. "Really? A slap? Couldn't go for something with more oomph?"

Her teeth bared in a wicked smile. One slender finger touched my upraised arm and with a puff of red my body stopped breathing. My chest moved, I strained, but air refused to come. I tried not to show myself fighting it, I didn't want to give her the satisfaction, but my body started to refuse my commands. At first it was just my lungs heaving with no result, but soon the panic built within my muscles as they started bucking, spasming for want of oxygen.

I nearly seized, falling over when she finally stepped back, stopping it instantly. On a positive note, my face no longer hurt and I was no longer cold. Unfortunately, it was because breathing huge gulping breaths and burning muscles had taken over everything else.

Maybe I should stop being such a wiseass. Then again, she was looking so freaking smug.

I nodded like I approved. "Good, that had some more oomph. Maybe next time add some menacing dialogue to go with it."

"Stop," the old guy ordered before the witchy Japanese lady could do anything else to me.

She retreated back, giving the old guy a look, who I just realized was the old guy from the lake. I really should have gotten that immediately, but I gave myself a break on that considering the circumstances. The woman hadn't been there I knew, but the guy holding my notebook could have been the twenties-something I saw with the old man. Probably. Was that when he grabbed my notebook? Or maybe after the house fight? I shook my head, it didn't really matter anyway.

"Where is Kalia Eir?" the old warlock asked, going for intimidating and working it.

"Thompson," the young guy spoke for the first time. "She goes by Kalia Thompson here, or Lia Thompson, Adept Hodges."

I looked at him, evaluating, and ignoring the random spasms my muscles were tweaking out with randomly in pained remembrance. The guy hadn't sounded smug or arrogant or anything I expected, but he wasn't exactly simpering either. He still held my notebook. Why did he have it?

The old man, who must be Adept Hodges, whatever adept meant, let out a sigh. "I will not wait for long, and when my patience is out I'll let Adept Kiyama do what she wants before we take you prisoner. I'm offering you the chance to prove yourself cooperative and therefore of use to us. You want to be useful."

Trust me was implied. Or else, was also a heavy implication. I looked between them, gauging what I should do. Cooperation wasn't in me, but stalling? Giving false impressions? Sure, I could try to do that.

I looked between them, seeing if there was any distraction, anything I could take advantage of, but I was out of luck. The young guy nodded encouragingly at me. Ya, like I'm gonna trust you, buddy. Suuuuure. But I could try to play it.

I tried to do puppy dog eyes at the guy. "Why are you after Lia? What did she do to you?"

"She-" the guy with brown hair started answering before the man-in-charge cut him off.

"We ask the questions. Where is she?"

I raised my chin at him. "Why do you want her? I won't help if you just want to hurt her. She's my best friend." I figured they already knew that, and I hoped it would make me look like I was giving up info from stupidity.

His eyes narrowed at me. "Take her. We'll continue this at our base. She's of no use to us now, but we'll see what she's like under treatment."

That sounded legitimately ominous, which is what he was most likely going for. They didn't even try to play me into giving information. Ok, new tactic, born of actual dread. I kicked back a few feet, trying to keep out of reach of Kiyama who came at me fast. She'd touched me for the last spell, I didn't want her to again.

"No!" I screeched, not even caring my voice squeaked in actual fear. I didn't want that pain again.

"I warned you about my patience running out."

"Promise you won't hurt her!" I was breathing hard, running out of options. Westen had gotten her to safety, so they couldn't get to her no matter what I said. Right?

"Please," I let my voice break a little on that. "She's my best friend..."

Old man Hodges took two steps toward me, staring down menacingly. "*She* is a dragon, a primordial form of magic that will power our league for generations."

I felt like I was panting and I wanted to back up more, but I was against a tree. What could I do? Kiyama and Hodges were right there, and the young guy just behind them. Even if I got the jump on one of them, or two, the third could hit me and they had magic. Freaking magic. I just couldn't *do* anything. I tried to let that show in my face, let the realization of my utter powerlessness fill me. Sadly, it wasn't much of a stretch.

Kiyama reached out toward me, red swirling around her finger. I instinctively put my arm in front of me.

"Mexico!" I yelled, letting panic hitch my voice. "They went to Mexico."

Kiyama paused, inches from my skin, and looked at Hodges as he stared at me. I put my arm down and pushed back into the tree, the bark indenting into my skin. My eyes skittered between them, willing them to believe me. Westen had said he would fly south first to try to throw them off, and hopefully they'd noticed his direction when he'd taken off. At least I was ninety percent sure he'd said they'd fly south first.

Kiyama finally spoke, in a soft, light voice that seemed so out of place with how vicious she'd been to me so far. "That seems unlikely. The Waay Chivo still holds power there, and the Eir family is stationed in the north."

"They did initially fly south," the young guy spoke up from behind them. Though neither of the others looked at him or acknowledged him in any way, they weren't doing anything else either. Yes! Keep working, believe me...

"They-" I stuttered and coughed, playing it up, but not by much. "They said something about you not expecting them to go there, so it was the best bet. That they had a deal worked out to stay until it was clear." That sounded believable, right?

Hodges and Kiyama exchanged looks again, then Kiyama walked away waving her hands in front of her and looking really silly, but probably doing something magically complicated as swirls of red essences flittered around her hands.

Hodges pointed a finger at me and I flinched. I wish I could say I was playing that up.

"If you are lying, you will regret it."

"That's what I heard, I swear."

He finally turned from me, and I held back the relief that wanted to spill from me. It seemed like they were taking my bait, which meant Westen had more time to get Lia away. What did that mean for me when they found out the truth? I'd deal with that when it came.

The old man looked behind him. "Apprentice Moore, come get her restrained for transport."

Then Hodges walked over to Kiyama, and the young guy came up. He looked like he wasn't exactly sure what to do with me, like he went to hold out a hand, then turned it into a gesture of get up. I ignored it and listened in to Hodges and Kiyama.

"Join up with Novice Adept Davis and the others in the hunt for the wardens."

She nodded, never looking away from her red tendrils of magic. "We're not bothering with capture, are we?"

Hodges shook his head. "The loyal ones never turn, just kill them. We'll work on the friend; she knows more than she's saying."

"I agree."

Panic gripped me and I let out a small involuntary gasp.

Moore, already impatient with me ignoring him, grabbed my arm and pulled sharply. "Come on, or I'll fry you."

That sounded stupid, but he said it as a matter of fact, so I let him haul me up without resisting.

"Why do you have my notebook?"

He blinked and looked at it. "Tracking spell. You put a lot of yourself into this."

Well, that was just downright uncomfortable. "Shouldn't you need my blood or hair or something?"

Moore smiled and opened the front cover, showing a thin streak of blood at the top. A memory of me getting a papercut when I reached into my backpack right when I'd first gotten it, way back at the beginning of the school year, came to my mind. Wow. Like, what was I even to do with that?

Maybe I could grab the notebook and make another run for it. Could they freeze me like before without this? Hodges probably could. But, I had to try, didn't I? They said they were taking me to their place for treatment and to work on me, and I highly doubted it would be a spa day.

"Come on, get up," Moore said, then turned when a noise came from behind him.

A large ball of fire speared through the trees, aimed at Hodges and Kiyama. I watched as Hodges brought his hands up before it, sprouting a green bubble shield that surrounded him and Kiyama. The fire hit it, bursting into bright flames on the shield that shimmered, then bubbled under the heat.

Kiyama screamed even as the shield dissolved, a bolt of red formed in her hands. She was already moving, stabbing at a figure who ducked, turned, blocked, and backhanded her without getting touched by her magical weapon.

Taking my chance, I stood as fast as I could, ignoring my pained body and grabbing at my notebook while I did so. Moore, staring at the light, was taken by surprise enough that I was able to body check him into stumbling back. Not enough that I got more than a step away before I fell face first, barely catching myself with my arms. Moore had my foot, and his grip felt like solid stone around my ankle.

I looked at Moore and saw Hodges behind him with three spheres that coiled and left trails of green tendrils swirling around him. He also was chanting something and holding out a hand. The figure dodged nothing I could see and made an upward thrust with its arm. It didn't seem to connect with anything, but Hodges' hand flew back as if it'd been hit. Continuing from the thrust, the figure grabbed one of the tendrils and set it on fire so it hung sickly in the air.

The light from it burned too bright, so bright it hurt my eyes, but I could now see that it was Westen fighting them, two on one, looking like a trained martial fighter as he moved between them. I'd never seen anyone outside of a movie move like that. He threw fire from his hand at Hodges while pivoting a kick at Kiyama, knocking her weapon free where it dissipated with a fizzle when it left her hands. Before he was done, he grabbed another one of Hodges spheres and spun away, grimacing while closing his fist around the ball until it puffed out a second later with a sickly smoking goo residue that he threw at Kiyama's face.

Now when she screamed it was with a pitch of furious agony. She abandoned her latest attack at Westen to scrabble at her face which seemed to be melting under the goo.

Knowing I was wasting my chance to get away or help in any way, I stopped watching and tried to kick at Moore with my free foot. Before I could connect a shock ran up my leg from where he was holding me, so painful I cried out. It was like an electric channel was pushing up from his hand, burning me from the inside out.

I focused myself despite the pain and did a straight kick into his face. His head snapped back and red spouted from his nose, coating his chin and running down his neck, but he held on. Another electrical type surge spiked up my system, burning along my length and escaping out my mouth with an involuntary scream.

And then it stopped. I panted into the ground before trying to push myself up with wobbly arms when hands came around me. I bucked, trying to twist out of the grip.

"Daniella, it's me."

I nearly collapsed in relief at Westen's voice and let him help me up. It took my feet a few tries to get planted and hold me upright, even with Westen's arm to lean on. Once up, I saw why he was able to help me instead of fighting; there was no one left to fight.

Moore lay at my feet, face down in the dirt and un-moving, his hand reached out and limp. I edged away from him before looking for the other two. Hodges wasn't anywhere I could see, and Kiyama I could barely see her in the dark, except the stuff on her face gave off a pale glow. She was laying unmoving on her side, nox-ious smoke drifting up from her head.

I clutched at Westen, not caring how it made me look. Not even taking more than a momentary mental notice that he was still shirtless because I was wearing his button up and I was clinging to his bare torso.

"Lia's safe?" This was what was important. "You got her out?" I coughed, my voice feeling raw and rough.

Westen nodded and a knot of relief released. That much, at least, had gone right. I felt like laughing almost, but my eyes went back to the body next to us.

"Hodges? The old guy?" I clarified, looking around for him again.

"Teleported out."

"Right. Of course they can do that." Probably how they'd gotten to me in the middle of nowhere. And wasn't that just another thing to scare the jeebezurs out of me?

"He said, the old guy, that others were looking for the wardens to kill them."

Westen nodded. "I already have a dragon en route to pick them up once located. The Thompsons are trained for this. They know what to do."

"Trained..." I nodded, but it came out more as a head bobble. "Right, good."

My eyes drifted back and forth, and I couldn't help staring at the oozing surface of Kiyama's face and the motionless form of Moore, who couldn't have been more than five years older than me.

"Are they dead?" I asked quietly, staring at Moore's still hand that had been holding me moments ago. Holding, and hurting. My body shuddered at the remembered internal lightning bolt he'd sent through me. I don't know if that's what it had been, but that's what it had felt like.

Westen nodded very solemnly and my resolve crumpled. I turned into him and cried silently into his shoulder, his arms instantly coming around me.

I just didn't know what to think. Was I ok that they had died? With all they'd done, were trying to do to Lia and the Thompsons? Was I ok with that outcome? This was the first time I'd come face to face with it. Not heard about it, read it on social media, or in history books, but actually in person, in front of my eyes, death. Even when my mom had died, I'd only seen her in the coffin for the funeral days later. This was raw. I mean, he looked like he could stand up at any moment.

I forced my breathing to keep coming out as even as I could, though I felt suddenly very cold.

"I'm so sorry, Daniella," Westen spoke, his voice resonating through his chest and into me as I held on. "Are you ok?"

I shook my head, not knowing what I was shaking my head to, that he was sorry for saving me or that I was ok. I was already working to cut off the flow of liquid from my eyes. I *hated* crying in front of others. It almost never happened, not even with Lia, but tonight was apparently just too much for me. And to be crying while being held took it to a whole new level of things I wasn't comfortable with, even while I craved the comfort it gave me.

I took a few calming breaths and focused on the warmth he was giving off. My fingers were almost unchilled. At least I'd stopped crying. I pulled back from the hug, but not out of the embrace fully, and centered myself with one final breath. Finally, I looked at Westen.

"You came back for me." My voice almost tripped as I fully realized I hadn't thought he would.

"I said I would. I'm sorry I wasn't sooner."

"No." I tried to smile. "You came, and... You saved me. Thank you."

Westen's face seemed to lighten. It was something in his eyes, which were a cloudy blue grey right now. "You're welcome."

He looked around, scanning the area with an assessing eye and I noticed his right hand was scorched red and black. That was the hand he'd grabbed the warlock's magic with, and it didn't look happy for having done so.

"We have to get going. The elder warlock could be back with reinforcements."

"Right, of course." I stepped back, avoiding a smoldering spot in the ground I hadn't noticed before and ignoring the desire to hold on to him longer. I was putting that down to hysterics of the night. I hugged myself tightly.

Westen took a few steps to get more into a small clearing area and flickered in the dark. As he shifted, his face screwed up until he let out a wail that shortly became a roar I stepped back from involuntarily as it resonated through my body. His dragon self, sleek dark scales of black, grey and silver, all shook as he gathered himself. Then his wings shot out in a deep stretch, the moonlight lighting up the webbing of his wings like transparent skin before he snapped them shut again.

"Are you ok?" I asked, worried about him. That change to dragon hadn't been as smooth or fast as it had when he'd taken Lia away.

Westen shook himself and gave a distinct nod, his thick serpentine neck bobbing up and down. Which looked kinda eerie and kinda cool at the same time. Especially since he was towering over me.

He lowered himself down and held out his arms. I stared, hesitating because I wasn't sure how to get up and I didn't want to hurt his injured hand, but he'd need both of them to carry me. Also, it wasn't exactly like hopping on a horse saddle. Giving up, I just walked up to him and let him do most of it. He wrapped his arms around my back and legs, hefting me up against his, well, I guess his lower neck area where it joined his torso.

I thought he'd be cold, like a lizard would be at night, but he radiated warmth and I found myself leaning into him, trying to soak it in. It wasn't too comfortable, but it wasn't extremely uncomfortable either, that is, until he launched into the air.

I had warning as he bunched his legs under us, but I still whispered, "Oh no! Oh no! Oh no!" to myself as he lifted off and I was fairly certain I'd screeched a bit, but I couldn't hear it over the sound of his wings beating and our heartbeats. It felt like the worst, fastest elevator ride up I'd ever taken. My stomach, empty as it was, felt like

I'd dropped it as we lifted with ever rising crescendos of his wings beating.

I felt secure in his grip, but I still clung to him as much as I could, which wasn't much. His scales weren't exactly grip-worthy, but I held onto his arms, my right arm clutched around the one holding my back and my left gripping the one that went under my legs. I would have wrapped my arms around his neck, but I didn't want to let go to try. Besides, I wasn't sure my arms would reach all the way around.

Soon we were up enough to start moving away. I'd tried not looking at the bodies as we rose, and when I finally peeked down, I couldn't find them among the trees we were above. That was probably for the best.

I wasn't sure which way he was going, but he was going fast. So fast that the warmth he was giving off didn't seem to be enough to overcome the rushing cold of the night Montana air.

It was exhilarating, but frightening. Like being on a roller coaster with nothing but two arms holding you from falling. My breathing was shallow and I tucked into myself as much as I could, trying to give myself some room, but between Westen's own breathing, his arms holding me, and my unwillingness to let go of his arms, there wasn't much to be gained.

I had to just breathe and focus on holding on. Time lost all meaning. It became me living in the rush of the air, the beat of his wings moving up and down, me trying to even out my next breath while taking whatever warmth I could from Westen as the wind stole it away. I counted my breaths against his heartbeat, loud in my ear, but so much slower than my own. My mind could do nothing else, so it did nothing else.

CHAPTER

7

My face hurt. Something had hit it. I blinked my eyes open, not knowing where I was. "Ow," was all I managed, until I remembered that the last thing I knew was that I was flying through the air in the arms of a dragon and now I was laying on something.

I sat up quickly, thankful I already had a hand up and ready to hold my head. "Ow," I said again, this time as the blood rushed through my skull in pounding torment. Briefly, I held back the feeling of nausea. "What happened?"

I immediately noticed several things: we were on the ground, still in the forest, though if it was the same forest, I had no idea; the sky was getting light with false dawn; and Westen sat back from me in more of a falling than sitting manner, his chest heaving.

"Daniella, good," he breathed, obviously fatigued and struggling with the smallest of things, like sitting and talking. "I'm... you stopped. I mean, you went unconscious." He had to stop to catch up on his breath before continuing. Every few words he had to take a gulping breath. "While flying, you, you went unconscious and I didn't know if you were hurt or... I had to land to check on you. Had to change."

Change must have meant reverting to his human form, since that's what he was in. He didn't look too good. Exhausted would seem to be an understatement.

"Where are we?"

"Canada." Westen leaned back, looking over his shoulder and I noticed his arms were shaking from holding himself up, even though he was on the ground. "There's a town, with a hospital, just, just in case."

Wow, Canada. I'd never been outside of my state, much less my country. I don't think I'd even gone over 100 miles away from Janesville before, and here I was, in an unknown place with Westen of all people. I shook my head at the absurdity of it all, which was a mistake. My head was woozy and sent new waves of pain at the movement. Once they receded to a tolerable level, I took stock of myself and everything seemed to be functioning, besides being freezing and sore all over.

"I think I'm ok. Sorry, I don't know what happened."

"It's not your fault. Maybe too little air up there for you."

Huh, that never would have occurred to me. I figured my brain had just quit at some point, 'cause I darn well knew for sure that I hadn't fallen asleep up there.

He laid down on his back and I noticed tendrils of steam wisping off of his skin in the chilly air joining the healthy swath of steaming breath he was exhaling.

"Are you ok?" I asked quietly.

He nodded. "Tired. Need to rest."

His eyes were closed, but he was still breathing just as deeply. I didn't know much about flying things, birds and the like, but it didn't seem like they got so tired after just a few hours of flying. I opened my mouth to ask him about it, but shut it when I realized he didn't need to answer all my questions right now, not when he was barely functioning. I'd keep my questions and comments to the salient details.

"Are we safe to rest here?"

He reopened his eyes to look at me with a question in his eyes.

"I mean, is it safe for you to sleep? Warlocks can't find us, or humans for that matter?" I didn't want to explain a half-naked, barely conscious guy to any authorities.

Westen let his head fall back, eyes closed again. "We should be safe enough to stay for a few hours. We're far enough out no one should find us."

"Okay, let's sleep then. We could both use it." There was no way I was going to be able to sleep now that I was conscious – I was too cold and hungry, but I didn't want him to force himself to stay awake when he so obviously needed to pass out, and being the noble guy he was, if he knew I was staying awake he might just try to as well.

Suddenly, he looked up at me again, pointed at me,

and said, "Watch. Yes." Then he flumped back down again.

I swear I'd seen a flash of light off to my side, but when I looked, there was nothing there. Had he just put some kind of spell on me? Should I say, "Yes, Westen, I'll watch over you as you sleep, because that's not strange at all"? But he was already out, and whatever he meant would have to wait until he woke up and had more energy than a one percent cell phone battery.

I laid down where I was, a few feet away from him, and waited. I was cold, and very hungry, and even though I was tired, my brain was not. It kept reminding me of all the things that happened, and how hungry I was, and how cold it was, and that there was a town nearby. Stupid brain.

I thought of the warlocks who'd taken me and the fight they'd had. I peeked over at Westen's hand, but it seemed normal colored again. Maybe a tad pink, but nothing like the blistering red it had been. Healing seemed to be a bonus dragon attribute.

The forest was waking up around us. The birds became louder, and I noticed different types of calls around us. Occasionally I'd hear a squawk, or something moving far off, but nothing else. Nothing like the hidden terrors my brain had been imagining walking through the Montana forest at night. Daylight made everything better.

It didn't take long for his breathing to even out in deep sleep. As quietly as I could, I got up. He moved a bit, but nothing substantial. I found a small rock and scratched a message in the dirt, just in case he woke up to find me not here: went to get food in town brb.

It was getting brighter and brighter, but the warmth had yet to reach me. Figuring Westen was fine with his super-duper internal heater thing going on, I kept his shirt, but man did it feel odd leaving him lying there, on his own, in the middle of who-knows-where-Canada with no shirt on.

Knowing I would need to mark my way somehow, I searched nearby for something distinctive I could use. Thankfully, right outside our rest stop were some bright red berries I was pretty sure were bearberries, and I was pretty sure bearberries were edible, but not sure enough in my knowledge of either the berries' name or their edibility to try it out. I picked it clean and stored them in Westen's shirt, folded up from its bottom to make a kind of bowl.

Hoping animals wouldn't eat all my markers by the time I got back, I started out, dropping a berry and stepping it into the dirt every ten or so feet. Just in case the animals did get to them, stinking squirrels or something, I did my best to remember where I was going, but honestly a forest looks like a forest everywhere. There weren't a whole lot of distinctive markers around. Still, I took notice of the downed tree, and the two trees duking it out for sun by growing into each other.

I focused on my terrain as much as possible, to not think about all of last night and what had happened. To not think about the two dead people, or about how I had no idea where my life was going now that I was on the run with Westen of all people.

After a while, enough time for the sun to break over the mountain, I came upon a small stream and simultaneously thanked the forest gods for giving me a stream while worrying that the stream would lead me away from the town. I put a marker on each side then followed the stream down, hoping that it would go into, or at least near the town.

Ten or so minutes later relief rushed over me as I saw a break in the trees and buildings beyond. I used the last of my marker berries, seven in all, to verify where I'd come out from the forest and the stream I was to follow, but I didn't think there'd be a problem seeing as there was a warehouse type building directly across from me with the giant brown logo stating "Hooper's Discounts." Unless Hooper had multiple discount stores in one town, I felt secure in being able to find my way back to this spot.

On the other side of Hooper's I found a small road that went off toward what looked like the main part of town one way, the other toward a main roadway, where there was a fast food looking type building named Tim Horton's on the corner – I could see the bright sign from here proudly proclaiming its hours and being open to hungry travelers. I definitely qualified.

While making my way there, I thought about what I was going to say, like, "Hi, I'm a visiting American in desperate need of food because I'm running from evil warlock guys with a dragon, who's currently sleeping it off in the woods. Care to donate to a good cause?" Ya, didn't think so.

I went through all my pockets, just in case, and found a folded, washed and dried bill in my back pocket. I had no idea how it got there, but it wasn't the first time I'd washed money. At least it wasn't wadded up into a little crumple of a paper that I couldn't do anything with. With some fine finessing, I popped it back into shape and even smiled, before I remembered that I was in Canada and they had different money than us. Plus, five bucks wasn't exactly a whole lot.

Still not knowing exactly what to say, I went in and stopped just to soak in the warmth of the building and the smells. Coffee, doughnuts, breakfast sandwiches. They all smelled ambrosial and hit my nose with a force that made my stomach remind me just how empty it was. I took a moment to control myself, as my brain so helpfully reminded me that I might not get any of those delicious smells.

I reopened my eyes, which burned from lack of sleep, and checked out the place. It was a nice little breakfast coffee shop type place. Lots of clean red and tan surfaces. Right up front was a display case of their doughnutty goodness. Saliva filled my mouth to the point I had to swallow. Slightly embarrassed, I made my way up to the counter, thankful there was no line.

The cashier couldn't have been much older than me.

She was looking into the back area as I came up, so she said her welcoming line of "Welcome to Timmies!" rather cheerfully before seeing what I looked like. Her face froze, the smile working to stay, and I self-consciously tucked my hair behind an ear. Maybe I should have gone to the bathroom first to clean up.

"Uh, hi. I was wondering, if perhaps, I know it's a long shot, but I was wondering if you by chance took American money?"

"Eh?"

I think I short-circuited her brain.

I took out the five dollar bill and showed it to her. "It's all I have. It's ok if you don't. I totally understand. I mean, we are in Canada after all." That was so weird to say.

"What happened to you? You look like you've been through the woods in those runners."

I saw one of her coworkers in the back look over at us. I looked down at the counter, thinking furiously. What would be believable, but not so insane as for them to call the cops on me, either to take me in or to "help" if I was looking that bad?

"Well..." I figured, the truth. Or, kind of. "My boyfriend" hah! "and I are visiting his family. We went for a walk in the woods yesterday and got lost." She looked properly horrified and I worried about the whole cops option.

"It's ok, really, we just walked around a lot, got cold, but we're fine. We made it out about thirty minutes ago, but the car wouldn't start. The phone in the car still had some battery left, so we called his cousin. He's coming to get us now, so we're fine, but we haven't eaten since yesterday. I thought I'd see if there was anything we could get? All I have is this five dollars though. All our Canadian money is at his cousin's house. I was hoping for two sandwiches. One for me and one for him. If that's ok. If this is enough."

She seemed to be in awe, her mouth hanging open. "True. Wow, you give'er. You're lucky something didn't get you two. You go to the washroom and clean up while I talk to the manager. I'll see what I can do, ya?"

I smiled and followed her pointing finger to see the bathrooms. "Thanks, I really appreciate it."

Whew. At the very least, it didn't seem like she was going to call any cops on me.

Once in the bathroom, I used the toilet before anything, thankful to sit down and not have to worry about dripping on myself like I did in the woods. My feet ached at the relief, but I had to get up to get myself clean.

Standing in front of the mirror, I understood why she'd probably thought I was a crazy person at first. My hair was ratted and tangled, and yes, there were leaves, grass and twigs in it. I had smears of dirt all over – face, body, arms, knees. There were even dried tear stains on my cheeks through the mud smears. Wonderful, so everyone who saw me knew I'd cried. I mean, I knew some of what I looked like, but seeing the whole picture really put it in perspective. I looked like a vagabond run-away homeless kid.

Which, I kinda was, I guess.

Nope, don't think about those things. I shoved it all down. If some poor lady came in here, she'd see me cleaning up, not bawling to myself.

The faucet had a hot option that I cranked up while pulling bits of foliage from my hair. Once the water warmed up I thoroughly cleaned every bit of exposed skin I had, twice. I rubbed off the dirt from Westen's shirt and my jeans as much as I could.

Then I sat on the counter, which my butt did not appreciate after all the abuse it'd taken last night from the forest ground. However, that position let me put my feet in the hot water sink to warm them up while I picked through my hair one final time, until I could run my fingers through it without getting caught on knots.

Another positive, Westen's long sleeves covered my curiously burned wrist. This was the first time I was able to look at it in clear light because honestly, I hadn't thought about it much during my walk here. The blisters were circling my wrist like a giant bracer of puss from where Lia had burned me, and I was truly thankful Westen had sucked out the heat because that would have really, really hurt for a very long time.

As it was, my wrist only hurt when I stretched the skin, mostly where several of the blisters had popped during my escapades. I washed it all as gently as I could, pulling out the few pieces of grass and dirt debris that had stuck to my broken skin.

I had cleaned up as much as possible, and told myself firmly to ignore my scar. Really, it just didn't seem all that important, and I didn't think they'd make fun of me or ask me about it relentlessly like the school kids always did. Or stare at me either. So far they'd been too preoccupied with the whole mess of myself and my woods story. I made sure the sleeves were back down, covering my wrist again. If this didn't work out, maybe I could see about another diner in town or something.

Almost shyly, I exited and walked back up to the front counter. I looked outside, relieved to see no cops had been called – yay me and my convincing lies! The cashier was helping a guy ordering something called a double-double and a jelly filled dutchie, which turned out to be a coffee and doughnut.

She smiled brightly at me once the guy left and called "Mary!" into the back before talking to me. "You look a sight better! Feel better?"

I smiled back and nodded. "Yes, thank you. Did you have a chance to talk to your manager?"

"Oh, yes. She's a beauty. Coming now."

I assumed the manager's name was Mary, as a kindly middle-aged woman appeared from the back, carrying two heaping bags. She looked like a Native American, but since we were in Canada maybe she was a Native Canadian. She seemed to have something wrong with her knees as she kind of waddled, but it didn't seem to bother her as she had the brightest smile I've seen.

"Here, lovey," she said, plopping the two bags down. I blinked at her in confusion. "Jacie here told me all about your adventure." She pronounced about like 'a boot.' "This here, call it a charitable donation to the 'I survived a night romping around Harrison's Woods.'"

I stared at her, then at the two bags. "You mean, this is all for us?" I would not cry, I would not cry, I would not cry.

She nodded and pushed the bags toward me. "Now, some of the doughnuts might be a tad stale. They're from yesterday, but I figured you wouldn't mind, or at least your boy won't! I find boys don't care much about such things. You think you could carry coffee too?"

"Coffee would be great. No, of course we don't mind! The doughnuts. Of course." My brain was trying to process, and I wasn't sure if I was making sense. "Oh, thank you so, so much!" I grabbed the bags, feeling their weight and wondering how much they'd given me. I resisted the urge to open one and eat the first thing I could grab. "It's incredibly generous and kind of you. Truly."

The cashier was beaming at her boss, handed me a large to-go coffee. "Careful, it's hot."

I nodded, holding the bags in my left hand (mercifully they had handles) and the coffee in my right. I could feel the delicious warmth seeping into my hand through the cardboard sleeve.

Mary waved me off with a smile. "Go on, then. Get that to your boy. Be safe, you hear?"

"Yes, ma'am!" Trying to be as gracious as possible, while also trying to get going, I headed outside, back into the chill morning air while still trying to comprehend the amount of generosity just given to me. That never would have happened to me back in my town. I took a sip and scalded my tongue a bit, but it was delicious. It had a wonderful mixture of sugar and cream, and I felt the heat move down and settle in my stomach.

My breath clouded in front of me, and I missed the warmed building, but I was eager to get back to Westen. He'd been exhausted to the point of falling asleep within seconds on the cold ground, but that didn't mean he'd sleep forever. I must have been gone at least two hours, if not more by now.

I walked quickly, taking sips, but once I got behind the discount store I opened the bags. It was stuffed with breakfast sandwiches, wraps, muffins, doughnuts, even an oatmeal. I grabbed that and ate it down – delicious maple flavored oats. Then I ate a fried hashbrown, which reminded me of McDonald's, but better. Feeling I should let those settle a bit, I started out again, taking a long drag on my coffee. Sorry Westen, the coffee wasn't going to make it back to him.

I found my berry markers and kicked them out of the dirt and away as I walked by them. On the way I finished the coffee, a sausage wrap and a doughnut. By the time I returned, I was sure my belly would be sticking out from all the food I'd shoved down it. Even with everything I'd scarfed down, easily three-fourths were still waiting to be consumed. Mary had given me the ultimate hook-up.

I tried to be quiet, but I must have made noise walking because as I got back Westen was sitting up, looking straight at me, and he looked pissed.

CHAPTER

8

"Hey, that's totally not unsettling at all," I said as a greeting in response to his freakishly intense stare down. Was it strange that this was the first time I'd felt normal since the treehouse?

"Where were you, Daniella? What did she do?"

"Um, excuse me?" I managed to ask when a light blue little orb appeared, zipping in front of me. I very tactfully screeched and dropped the bags.

Westen was paying attention to the little hyper ball of light that mostly seemed to be hovering in front of me, but when he glanced at me, I swear he was smiling on the inside at my shriek.

"Not only did you go to town, but you went into a coffee shop? What did you tell them?"

Ungraciously, I picked up the bags and tossed them at Westen. "And hello to you too. Did you know that the myth about Canadians being super nice is actually true?"

As soon as I'd dropped the bag he looked in it and I swear I saw him salivate with hunger as he reached in. "That would be a legend, not a myth."

I ignored his correction. "And just what is that blue fluff that you apparently had follow me?"

He snatched a sandwich out of the bag and devoured it in three bites. The whole thing.

"Wow, man, you might want to slow down there."

"It's a sprite." He, in turn, ignored my food comment. "It agreed to watch over you, which I obviously was right to do." He grumbled about me walking off into town as he grabbed and inhaled a doughnut.

"A sprite?"

He nodded. I guess he wasn't going to explain further. Then he pointed a finger at me. "You shouldn't have gone. What if you'd been captured?"

I shrugged. "You were the one who said we were safe here."

"Should be safe to rest." He was already pulling out a muffin to eat.

"Look, you were sleeping, and I was hungry. No one saw me but some really nice ladies at the Tim Horton's place." He opened his mouth, but I pushed on before he could say something. "And, aren't you enjoying that food? It's pretty good, isn't it?"

I saw his nose twitch, but he didn't stop eating.

"Did the sprite say I got into any trouble?"

He glared at me, chewing. I took that as a no.

"See? So, it was a good thing I went. I may not be a dragon, but I'm not completely helpless."

I peeked in the other bag and grabbed out another doughnut despite not being hungry. It looked like one of those jelly-filled dutchies that guy at the store bought. I picked at it, sticking one tiny piece in my mouth at a time while watching Westen snarf down doughnuts and sandwiches at a rate I'm sure prisoners would find impressive.

The light blue ball came over to me, hovering just beyond my hands. I tried to see more definition, but it really just looked like a quivering ball of light. I held out a piece of doughnut. It and the ball disappeared in a blink causing me to jump.

Westen chuckled, probably at my reaction.

"What?" I asked with as much sarcasm as I could muster.

"Oh, nothing."

"Whatever," I grumbled, irritated at him, which apparently made him chuckle some more.

I gave him the side eye and got distracted. *Stop staring at his chest. And arms. And abs. Stop it!*

And with that reminder, I went to unbutton his shirt to give it back, but he waved me off before I'd started.

"Keep it. You'll need it when we fly again." Probably being able to create fire was a great internal warming mechanism, and it's not like he had a shirt when in dragon form.

Once he began slowing down, i.e. chewing more, I wanted to ask the questions I'd been keeping off my mind, but where to start? Warlocks? That still sounded stupid, even in my head. My life? Where we were going? Sprites?

I'd start with the most important thing. "Westen, where is Lia?"

He shook his head, as if clearing it of his previous thoughts. "I left her with an outpost we had at the border. They would have taken her the rest of the way home by now."

He'd left Lia with others to come back for me. Wow. I'm sure if I weren't in the picture he would have taken her all the way home, and not just leave her with others at the outpost.

"Is that where the Thompson's would go to meet up with the other dragon?"

"They might go there, but the dragon for them is coming from another outpost by the Great Lakes. Don't worry, the Thompsons have trained for this for decades. They know what to do, and when they make contact we'll get them immediately."

I was still going to worry about them. "Why didn't we go to the outpost thing where you dropped off Lia?"

"The two dragons stationed there escorted Lia for protection, so there'd be no point to go there now as it's empty, and with the attack the warlocks might know of it. I decided to head straight to our stronghold, but then..."

"I passed out."

"Here we are." Westen ate another doughnut, slowly this time. "Daniella, what happened to you last night after we left?"

Ah, great. I figured he would ask. That didn't make me want to talk about it though, so I'd be short and sweet.

"I hid for a while, then walked for a long time in the dark. Slid down a hill once." I waved a hand over the impressive mud skid marks on my pants. "Then they just found me. The young guy said he'd tracked me with my notebook, the blood in it. Oh crap, where did that go?"

Mild panic raced through me. I couldn't believe I'd completely forgotten about it! Could they find me again? How far did that spell or whatever work?

"It's ok. I burned it."

Ok, whew, but I didn't remember that. "When?"

"After I got you up."

Ahhh, probably when I was crying on his shoulder. Right. Great. Let's not revisit that particular point of the night.

"Well, I, uh, I tried running again, but the old guy froze me in place. They asked questions, threatened me. I lied." The end. I smirked at him with a bravado I didn't really feel, so it slipped away again.

He was eyeing me, obviously thinking things through. "What exactly did they ask you about? What did you say, specifically?"

Westen and his *specifics*. Sure, why not relive the

whole thing again? But he did save Lia, and me, so he deserved to have whatever questions he had answered.

"They asked where Lia was. I didn't tell them, and
they, uh, well, threatened me." I rubbed my arms absently. "The old guy, Hodges, said if I didn't give them
any info that they'd take me to their base or something
for a treatment, to work on me. But first he'd let the
crazy chick go at me again. I tried to play it up, you
know? Told you were going to Mexico. I think they
believed it, but that was before you showed up."

His eyes were hard. "Go at you again?"

I tried to shrug it off. "She hit me and then she suffo-
cated me with magic. It was different than when we were
running back at the house, like in one instant I couldn't
breathe at all. I was being a smartass. Guess she didn't
appreciate it." I gave a self-deprecating half-chortle. "But
she's dead now..."

There. I'd said it. The thing my brain had been danc-
ing around since it'd happened.

Westen sat very still, hands loose in his lap. "I'm sorry
you had to go through that."

"They said Lia would power them for generations.
What does that even mean?"

He got his holding-frowny face thing going, where it
looked like he wanted to frown, but wasn't. "Warlocks
don't naturally have magic so they have to siphon magic
from beings born with it. The more magical the creature,
the more they can steal. Dragons have a lot of magic and

dragons too young to tap into their powers, like Kalia, are one of the biggest sources on earth to tap from."

"And how do they steal her magic? Like, they take her prisoner or something, right? Does it hurt?" It had been nothing for them to hurt me, several times; I was betting the same would be true with Lia.

He seemed to get it. "We would never allow her to be so used, so yes, she would be a prisoner, and yes, it does hurt. Excruciatingly, from the accounts we've gathered. Eventually, they would kill her. We can't survive without our magic."

I clapped my hands on my knee. "Right, then I'm sorry, too."

His eyebrows scrunched together. "For what?"

"I'm sorry you had to do that, to rescue me and fight them. But you know, they were bad guys. Like, straight up villain, torture, murder, bad guys. Even the young guy, he..." fried me beyond comprehension. I shuddered at the memory and I swore my nerves tingled just re-membering it. I shook out my feet and looked back at him, meeting his eyes. "It was a fight to the death. I'm glad you won."

Westen looked like he wanted to smile. "Thank you."

We lapsed into silence. He went back to eating and I tugged the doughnut away from the sprite who'd tried to take it. The doughnut was bigger than it, so I didn't think it would be good to give it the whole thing.

I waited for him to elaborate his thoughts further, but he just ate in contemplative silence. I gave him a few minutes, then asked my next question while feeding another pinch of doughnut to the ball that was still hovering in front of me.

"Where's your stronghold thing? Here in Canada?"

"What? Oh, no, it's in Alaska. We're the bridge to North America for our people."

"Didn't want to be Canadian, eh?"

He looked at me with one of those classic Westen looks that said I was asking something stupid. Made me smile a bit more. "Our family settled there before there was a Canada or America."

And there, he'd proved I *was* stupid. "Ah," was my smart reply. "No Asian dragons? Like the cool flying serpents? You looked European, at least from like the classic lore and movies and such." I felt extra dumb suddenly, like hey, I can guess where you're from 'cause I saw something like that in a show once.

His mouth quirked up. "Yes, they exist as much as we do. At the time, North America wasn't important enough to bother with. Moving there was actually considered a pauper assignment. And my parents come from the British Isles and Greece, so I am technically of European descent. Their marriage, among others, helped unify the European factions, but we're at peace with the Eastern ones."

Wow, I never would have guessed. That explained Lia's deep tan skin and dark hair, she must have gotten those from the Greek side. Westen's nearly black hair was probably Greek too, come to think of it.

The sprite suddenly dipped down and I tensed up, not knowing what it would do, but it just settled on my knee, where it became a tiny blurry person type thing with overly large bright blue wings.

"Wow," I breathed, looking down at it. It was so delicate and beautiful with flyaway hair. I would have thought it would have blue hair and skin like its wings, but it had white hair that sprouted from its head and continued all the way down its backside, which looked good against its light green skin. I couldn't tell a gender, even without it wearing any type of clothing. It held out its teeny tiny hands with three delicate fingers each and I gave it some more doughnut.

"Daniella," he spoke with a cautionary tone, "you're going to make it pass out from eating too much sugar."

"But it's so cute!"

"Of course it is. It's a sprite."

Not wanting to stop looking at this cute new thing in front of me, but wanting to get some more answers, I looked up at him. He mumbled something about girls being obsessed with sprites. He seemed almost done with the rest of the food, so I probably didn't have a lot of time.

"Did you get enough rest? I mean, you pretty much passed out."

Westen raised an eyebrow. "I'm fine. I just overexerted myself last night. Changing takes a lot of energy, and to do it several times back to back after several fights, it all wore me out more than I expected. I'll be able to fly us the rest of the way easily enough."

"To your stronghold thing in Alaska?"

He nodded.

I wasn't sure I wanted to go, but it's not like I really had a choice, did I? At least Lia was there. I stared at the sprite again, which was still munching away.

"I can't go back, can I?" It came out rather pathetic sounding to me.

"No," he answered matter of factly, knowing what I meant.

I shrugged. "I wasn't planning on it, after going to college anyway. Guess, I can't do that either."

I clenched my jaw. This being exhausted and scared crapless for hours on end deal was really sapping my ability to control my emotions.

"Daniella, I'm not sure. At least, not in Flathead. Perhaps we can get you set up at another school?"

That seemed undoable. "I didn't apply anywhere else, and I, uh... don't have anything. I just, I guess..." I blew out a breath. "I just don't know what's happening."

Westen stood up and walked over to me, but not trusting my treacherous emotions, I kept staring at the sprite. Then Westen scooped up the sprite from me, leaving me with nothing to look at but dirt. Why was he always taking things from me?

"Thank you, little one," Westen spoke to the sprite, which was now a flying blur again. There was a flash of white and blue, then it zoomed away so fast I couldn't even see where it had gone.

Westen held out a hand for me to stand up with. I reluctantly took it.

"We'll get you to safety, then we'll figure out what we're doing from there. Right now, it's not safe for you in Janesville because of your friendship with Kalia. They will never leave you alone there, but that doesn't mean it's the end of your life."

Yes, Westen, it does. Because I literally have nothing anymore. Again.

I couldn't say that, so I just nodded. Besides, he was right. Knowing Hodges was out there and what he was willing to do me just last night, I could never go back.

"I'm going to fly lower and slower for you, but hopefully it being day will help you with the flight as well. Ready?"

I nodded again and sucked in a breath. "I'm ready."

He stepped back and did the transformation shimmer again. I blatantly watched. It looked even cooler in the daylight, the haziness of power that extended out as he filled the space with his dragon self like smoke filling a new shape. The scales glittered out into the sun like dark gems, and a shiver went down my spine when he shook his neck. As he finished settling down, I noticed there was still some food left in the bags.

"Uh, are we just gonna leave that?" I pointed.

He snaked his neck down and scooped them up, chomping them, bags, garbage and all.

"Gross! That can't be good for your digestive system, man."

He spit out a leftover foil packet at my feet, and snorted a puff of smoke out of his nose.

"I get it, you vape."

He was not amused at my joke. At least, he didn't seem amused. I thought I was hilarious and laughed.

Still laughing at myself, I picked up the foil packet and put it in my pocket because I detested littering, especially in nature. Then I stepped into his arms, and he shot us up into the sky.

CHAPTER

9

Flying during the daytime was exhilarating. At night, I'd just been struggling to stay warm and survive the freezing wind, but now I could really see everything. It was like the craziest ride ever. I was still cold, but not frigid like before, and I could make out rivers, lakes, freeways, and towns. Westen kept us fairly low, and I assumed he was using his invisibility trick because I never saw anyone freaking out at us, and no police helicopters came to intercept the unidentified flying object that we were.

As beautiful as it was, it did get a bit monotonous. Westen would occasionally settle down in some remote forest area for a break. It was pretty funny seeing him hold up one clawed finger in a "one-minute" gesture. He'd pop off to go wherever it was he was going, and I'd walk around in place, stretch my limbs, and go potty in the woods. He was never back in one minute, but he always came back shortly and we'd get going again.

I had nothing but time to think, but thinking did me no good. I was completely dependent on him until we got to wherever we got to, and then I'd have to see what happened. It was horrible.

I was wondering how much farther we'd have to go when Westen started descending again. It was afternoonish time, and I was getting fairly hungry. And if I was hungry from doing nothing all day, I was sure Westen was starving.

He swooped down to the trees, did a light lift and settled down with a soft plop. I disentangled from my hold and looked around. Whelp, it looked like all the other forest areas we'd been to recently, but this one had a little cabin off to our left.

I'd been expecting the "one-minute" figure again, so when I turned and saw Westen's human shape shifting into being I was momentarily startled. At least I didn't fall on my butt anymore.

"So, uh, where are we?" I asked as he finished. I looked over at the small, most likely one-room cabin. "I somehow don't think this is your family's stronghold."

He gave me a mildly amused glance. "No, it's not. It's a safe house of ours. Firehold is still several hours away with how I'm flying. While we could reach it tonight, I felt it safer to eat and rest, especially after last night."

My backside wasn't going to complain. At least not until it assessed the sleeping arrangements in the cabin.

If I had to sleep on dirt, I think it would complain heartily.

"What do you mean with how you're flying? That isn't your normal flying?"

"No." He started walked toward the cabin.

"Why aren't you flying normal? What is normal?"

He opened the front door and held it for me. "Normal is much higher and faster, and when I did that, you lost consciousness."

Oh ya, that.

I walked in and took in the accommodations. Not bad for a lone cabin way out in the middle of nowhere. Actually, it was down-right cozy. It had a little kitchen area, a fireplace, a loft I assumed was where the beds or cots or whatever were.

"So, all day we've just been lazily making our way to your place?"

He gave a small chuckle while working some kind of panel, which kicked in power. "In a way, yes. This is better," he said when some lights came on all around the place. They were the muted, not super bright kind, but it was still nice. "It has batteries stored, which get solar recharged. There's some dry foodstuffs in those cupboards if you'd like to find something. I need to check-in. They would have been expecting me much earlier today."

Westen was unpacking a solid looking storage box from the far corner, which looked to have some serious satellite phone hookup to it. Leaving him to figure that all out, I searched through the cupboards and found quite a lot of freeze dried and vacuum sealed stuff. It didn't look good, per say, but I started drooling anyway.

I ripped open some freeze dried apples, then put a pot on the propane stove as I munched on them. There was plenty of bottled water, so I filled the pot over half way then started throwing in stuff that sounded good enough to go into a soup/stew type thingy. Venison? Sure. Carrots and potatoes, check. White stuff that looked like some kind of vegetable? Absolutely. There was even some salt and pepper. I got out a bag to keep all the trash in, tossing in the piece of foil Westen had spit out in the forest.

Westen was still on the other side of the room, making the machine beep and click as he worked on it. I wanted to talk to him, ask him more questions, but really, what was there to ask right now? Plus, I was hangry and he was trying to contact his family.

And I totally eavesdropped when he finally got a call to go through.

"Eir Donem, selishuh pret timmen dee raklish. This is Westen, calling in, please respond."

Oooh, how fancy. He had to initiate the call in code. I snickered to myself, even while I ignored the all too good reasons he and his family had for doing that. Too bad it wasn't more like a walkie talkie or ham radio, or I would have been able to make out what the person on the other side was saying.

"Tell me everything you know so far."

"Yes, I understand." There was a long pause, until he finally said, "No, I did not follow as Kalia was priority. Yes. Kalia's wardens? I see. Yes, I have Kalia's human friend."

Haha, I didn't even get a name, just her human friend. How flattering.

Each sentence he spoke was punctuated by a pause as he listened before responding. I just kept stirring and eating my apple slices.

"It was necessary. She'd be captured for information."

Well, since they wanted Lia for her magic, that was probably about me. Wonderful...

"No. I'm currently at cabin seven on the Alaskan border. Because it was unsafe."

Hmm... he didn't seem happy, something in his tone. I glanced over, but his back was to me. His muscles were tense though. I belatedly realized that I should give him back his shirt since we weren't going to be doing anymore flying today.

"I do not think that is necessary. Yes, Faelen. Of course."

That didn't sound like an, "I'm happy to do this" of course, more like a "fine, if you're gonna make me" one.

"I will. We'll leave first thing in the morning. Yes."

Then he clicked off. No goodbye or anything. He just stood there and I debated whether or not to approach while he brooded. Finally, I walked over, but he didn't move.

"Uh, here's your shirt back. Sorry it got kind of trashed." I held it out to him. "Thanks. It helped."

He half-turned to take it from me. "Of course." See, that was an "I'm happy to have done this" of course.

"So, I probably can't talk to Lia on that thing, huh?"

He shook his head while putting his shirt on. "No, it's for emergency use check-ins only."

"It's ok. I figured. But she's for sure there, right?" Just in case I'd misunderstood or something.

"Yes, she made it home safely."

"Good." Something inside of me unclenched, something I hadn't even been aware of. All of a sudden, I felt relieved and lighter than I had since all this began. Probably since the lake. She was safe. We were safe, basically. Everything would be fine.

I went back to the kitchen. He seemed to need a moment more.

After a few more minutes of stirring I said, "Dinner, or whatever you want to call it, should be ready soon." I dipped in a spoon and tasted it, burning my tongue because I was too impatient to blow on it or wait. "It's weird, but doesn't taste too bad."

"Daniella, I must ask, were you aware of the warlocks' attack at the lake or house in any capacity or form?"

I gave him a look, but he sat there with that impassive blank look he liked to use when he was being a robot.

"You know I wasn't. I didn't even know they existed before last night."

"And you had no idea anyone was looking for her in town. No idea of anyone at all."

Now I was getting annoyed. "No."

Westen nodded. "I had to ask. Apologies."

I narrowed my eyes at him. "Why did you have to ask after what happened?"

"I just had to." He turned away slightly to fiddle with some of the satellite phone stuff, more to get away from my glare I suspected, than anything else.

Deciding the best course of action would be to ignore him, I got out some bowls and started serving the food.

"Here," I spoke curtly, shoving the bowl at him, just in case he thought I wasn't still mad.

"Thank you for making, what is this, soup?"

I clenched down on a smile. He would not make me laugh while I was mad at him. "Sure, we can call it that. It's got lots of dehydrated and vacuumed packed stuff in there, so it should be hearty, if nothing else."

There was a small counter that stuck out from the wall we both sat at in little camping chairs that fit under it. It was barely large enough for both of our bowls. Westen didn't seem to have that problem as he was already on his third or fourth spoonful. Apparently, it was good enough to shovel down.

I blew on my spoonful, and my mind popped back to the lake for whatever reason.

"Hey, what happened at the lake? What did the warlock guys do to her there?"

Westen raised his eyebrows in a way that reminded

me of our history teacher when asked a pertinent question. "They held her underwater with magic until she manifested her power."

"Why would they do that?"

"To test her. They weren't sure she was a dragon, but no matter how well we hide, if we're put in mortal danger our magic will manifest to protect us, especially in the young. When they held Kalia underwater, her power released to save her from drowning."

"The bomb in the water was her?"

"In a manner of fashion, yes. Her power escaped in a burst to break the spell, which caused the small tidal wave."

I realized I was tapping the bowl with my spoon in thought, and stopped. "So, they didn't know she was a dragon until the lake?"

"Most likely. Obviously they had their suspicions, which were confirmed."

"Why not take us there? Without you and the Thompson's there, they probably wouldn't have had much of a problem."

He pointed at me. "Many things seem off about how they carried out their attack. However, you were there, and so were a lot of other human children. Also, they probably wanted to recoup and make their plan of attack on our home. It only took them a few hours to get everything organized. They came at us with at least fifteen fully trained warlocks. I highly doubt they had that many in town when only doing reconnaissance."

Wow. I'd no idea how many there had been. I'd only seen shadowy flits of people fighting off in the distance as we ran. For a second, I wondered how many of them died in the initial attack. How many of them did Westen kill? They were deserved, but it was still there, in my brain.

"What things seemed off? Like, how they came at the house or their testing thing at the lake?"

He shrugged. "Yes, on both. I need to think on it more."

"Ok. But why were they able to find her in the first place? I mean, out of all the kids in our town, in Montana or the USA, or the whole world for that matter, how'd they pinpoint her in Janesville of all places?"

He shrugged, but I could tell by the bunching in his shoulders that he was bothered. "We're not sure how they track us, which is why we tend to move around frequently when not in our strongholds."

My stomach dropped as I realized what that meant.

"But Lia came back every school year." My voice sounded odd, drifty, but I didn't know what to do about it.

"Yes, she did. It was something she fought for every year."

"Because of me. She was found because of me."

"No," Westen spoke forcefully, startling me into looking up at him. He locked eyes with me, and I noticed they were a bright blue at the moment. "Because of you she had a real childhood. My kind, we're put into human life as we grow up so we can understand the world and the humans that run it, but we're constantly moved around. We don't get friends, and we don't get the experiences you do. That was something Kalia had and treasured. She loved it more than anything, so that is what you gave her."

Wow.

"Uh, ok. Thanks." Dumb, dumb, dumb, but I had no idea of what else to say.

What he just said really touched me, and even though I was still going to blame myself, because what else would I do, it still mattered that Westen thought I was such a good influence on Lia's life. Something he'd obviously never had.

I searched for a neutral topic to get us on.

"So, how are the Thompsons? Did they get rides back to the stronghold like Lia?"

"They are still unaccounted for."

Well, that bombed spectacularly.

"I hope they're ok." It seemed so lame of me to say, but it was true.

Westen nodded, I supposed in agreement with me.

Suddenly, he put his spoon down and looked at me with extreme intensity. Now his eyes were more grey than blue. How did he do that? It threw me off and I instinctively turned my face away from him, my scarred cheek side out so he couldn't see it. An old habit from years of children's cruel scrutiny throughout the school years, but this time it seemed silly, and I fought a blush of embarrassment. I realized I had barely even thought of it this whole trip, which was strange as it was typically on my mind when around other people besides Lia or the Thompsons, but it was also nice. No one, well, Westen and the people at the coffee shop anyway, had ever seemed to stare or make comments about it like I was used to happening in Janesville even though everyone probably knew how I'd gotten it as a kid. Stupid Billy Mason and his dumb idiot friends.

Westen was still staring at me, even if it wasn't at my scar, and he hadn't said anything yet.

"What?" I demanded more than asked when I couldn't take it anymore.

"Do you have anywhere to go? Anywhere at all? Some distant family, perhaps?"

I swallowed down the soup in my mouth, willing it to take the sudden lump in my throat with it. I blamed all of my reactions through this dinner on still being super tired from everything that had happened. I clenched my jaw to work it out before speaking. Looking down at my soup helped, but it made me feel even more stupid on top of everything. I did it anyway.

I answered in as neutral a tone as I could manage. "No, I don't. At least, none that I've ever known of. That's why I'm in foster care. If there was someone out there, they never found me."

"Of course. I'm sorry. That was mindless of me to ask."

I glanced up. Now he was the one looking at his bowl. "Then why did you?"

He shook his head, avoiding eye contact with me now. "I shouldn't have asked. Apologies."

Way to avoid my question, Westen. But, whatever. One bad question deserved another. I'd probably regret asking this, but I did it anyway.

"How many of the warlocks died? At the house, I mean."

Strangely, my heart was pounding. This conversation had been a rolling emotional coaster and it was in a loop right now.

He put his spoon down carefully. "I'm not sure, exactly. Do you mean how many died in total, or how many I killed personally?"

"Who else, oh! Mr. Thompson?" No way, that was too weird to think about kind, helpful Mr. Thompson. I'd been right. I was regretting asking. "I don't... Never mind, forget I asked."

I stared resolutely at the bowl in my hand, but didn't take a bite.

"Daniella... I fought and killed people that night at the house and in the woods with you, and I've done it before." He didn't ask if I was ok with that, or what I thought. He just stated it as a fact.

I looked up through my eyelashes at Westen. He sat so still, as if he were holding in his breath, but his knuckles were white around his spoon.

"Were they all in defense of yourself or others?"

He nodded and I trusted him. After a hesitation, I put my left hand over his. I believed him.

"Then they were justified. I'm sorry you had to go through that." I echoed the words he'd spoken to me this morning. I'd meant to pat his hand in reassurance, but I just let it lay there for a moment. He didn't move his hand away and I felt the tension relax out of it at my words.

His jaw flexed a few times before he said a simple, "Thank you."

I gave a squeeze, then took my hand back. At this point I felt I couldn't take any more deep conversation. I was too bruised inside and out, and suddenly, more than anything, I wanted to sleep.

"Bottoms up," I said lightly, to try and break the mood. Knowing I needed to eat as much as I could, I drank/ate the soup, pouring the bowl down my mouth and chewing as fast as possible. Westen didn't say anything, not even to point out the soup I'd spilled on my shirt. I also, valiantly, ignored it.

I washed out my bowl at the sink using the bottled water, since there was no tap or running water. At least they had a drain, though where it went I wasn't sure. Away, hopefully. I used a little extra to splash on my face. What I wouldn't do for a proper bathroom right now.

"I assume the loft is for sleeping?"

"Well, you can, but it'll be more comfortable down here once I start a fire. Mostly it's for storage. There should be four packs up there. I'll bring two down, then get the fire going."

I nodded, not having looked at him since I'd finished my soup. "I'll go outside for a short walk."

"Stay close."

I glanced over at him as I left. He was still at the counter/table thing, eating away. I'd easily made enough for four people, but I doubted there would be any left-overs.

The forest was just starting to darken, so I didn't go far, just enough to feel private while still being in view of the cabin. I just absorbed the sounds of vibrant stillness that was unique to a woodland forest just coming out of winter. When I felt the first shiver coming on, I took care of business and headed back.

By the time I got there a hearty fire was going and two cots were set up in the middle of the room with sleeping bags and pillow type things, one on the kitchen side, the other on the fireplace side. I felt better. Walking tended to let my body and mind relax.

"I know it's early," heck, it was still technically light out, "but I'm really tired. Do you mind if I lay down now?"

"Of course not. Yours is by the fire. Let me know if I keep you up."

I laid down, gingerly. I was feeling everything. My black and blue butt, my blistered wrist, my frayed nerves, and all the various scratches. I was amazed my whole body wasn't a giant throbbing pain, but laying down felt nice, and that fire felt amazing. When I settled down on my back, my head reminded me that I'd smacked it during my run. I felt it, but it was fairly mild as far as tenderness went, so I just laid on my side and ignored it.

As I was drifting off my mind circled things that had happened and we'd discussed. This was typical, but when it stuck on something in particular from the treehouse, I knew I had to have a real answer before I fell asleep.

"Hey, Westen." I looked over at him, pondering over something at the table.

"Yes?" He looked up suddenly. He'd probably thought I was asleep already.

"How old are you?"

It may have been the flickering firelight, but I swore he blushed. "I'm, uh, almost two hundred."

"Holy crap!" I couldn't help myself. No way would I have ever guessed he was that old. He just didn't act like it.

He sat up straight in his little camping chair, obviously trying to maintain some dignity. "I'm still considered a young adult to my people."

I cracked a smile, totally at his expense. "Sure, you are, grandpa." I settled back down into my sleeping bag, still smiling.

Then another thought came to me. "I knew you built that freaking treehouse," I muttered into my pillow.

"Go to sleep, Daniella." But I heard the laugh in his voice.

———————————————

I woke up sore, but fully rested. The sun was rising, its rays peeking through the door's cracks. Westen was still sleeping in the other cot, which he'd moved to the front door. Sitting up, I contemplated how to get outside without waking him, which seemed impossible given there were no windows. However, I needn't have worried because he opened his eyes as soon as my cot creaked.

"Hey. Uh, I need to go use the little outdoor ladies' room."

"Sure, right." He got up, shaking off his sudden awakening with obvious skill. Not only did he move the cot, but he folded it and placed it by the ladder to the loft, then started rolling his sleeping bag, all before I'd gotten out of mine properly.

It was exceptionally chilly outside. It didn't help that I was only wearing my jeans and a purple tank top, but I hadn't realized how warm the fire and sleeping bag had kept me until I had to pee on frozen dirt.

By the time I got back, all of our sleeping gear had been stored back up in the loft and Westen was munching on oatmeal, of all things, at the table. He held out an arm, indicating I should sit down.

"Yum. Plain oatmeal."

"It may not be Tim Horton's doughnuts and sandwiches, but it'll fill you up for the ride. You can add some dried fruit to it if you like."

"No, I'm fine." I started in on my very full bowl of thick oats. It was like chewing cut up cardboard, but if he could do it, then so could I. At least it put some warmth into me. "You're getting quite the little beard going on."

He ran a hand over his cheek. "Ah, yes. It grows rather quickly."

I smiled, enjoying the slightly awkward Westen, though why him growing a beard was a cause for embarrassment, I had no idea.

"It looks good. It would be nice if there was a bathroom in this thing." I could smell myself, and if I could, I was sure he could with his superior dragony senses, but there was no way I was going to mention anything remotely about it.

He nodded in agreement. "Necessities only, unfortunately."

I sighed. "Though why they couldn't store honey here is beyond me. It never goes bad, you know."

He plopped a little honey jar in front of me. I narrowed my eyes at him, but he stoically chewed, not acknowledging my glare.

"You had that the whole time." I eyed his oatmeal and saw it swirled into his goop. "Jerk."

Westen didn't laugh, but I could tell he wanted to. With as much dignity as possible, I poured honey onto my oats. It vastly improved it, but it was still oatmeal. Not exactly my favorite breakfast.

We ate in silence for a few minutes, until I couldn't take it anymore. If I was going to choke any more of this down, I needed distraction. The honey didn't help that much. "So, uh, how do you change shape with your clothes?"

He looked up from his bowl. "It only works with clothes that have been specifically enchanted to shift with our magic. All of my clothes can shift."

"Otherwise you'll be nekkie?"

I hid my laugh at his expression of annoyance/disgust with a big bite of oatmeal.

"Otherwise we'd shift in the nude, yes."

"And you used the invisibility thing on us while we flew like you did when you left with Lia, right?" He nodded. "So, how come I could see us?"

"Because it affects a marginal area around myself and outward, not inward. It would be difficult to do things not being able to see one's own body. That's very perceptive of you to notice."

"Gee, thanks, gramps."

He frowned, which made me smirk.

"I was being serious." He finished his bowl and went to cleaning the dishes made for our breakfast. "And I wish you wouldn't call me that."

I shoveled the last of my oatmeal and forced it down with drinking water. "And I wish you wouldn't call me Daniella, so I guess it's oh well on both our parts." I waited to wash my bowl, but he just took it from me and cleaned it himself.

"Thanks," I said, not wanting him to think me a thankless degenerate kid of the younger generations.

"Daniella is your name," he said matter of factly, like that was the only thing that mattered.

"And grandpa is your age. Actually, it'd probably be like great-great-great grandpa or something, but I figured that was just too long."

He gave a long suffering sigh that I thoroughly enjoyed.

I sat back at the table because I couldn't think of anything else to do to help. Everything had already been done. The fire had even been banked, and I could feel it. I rubbed my arms, noticing the blisters on my left wrist didn't seem as bad as before. At least, the ones that hadn't popped and scabbed over.

After a minute or so of me poking gently at my skin, not wanting to aggravate it, but not being able to resist, I spoke, quietly, trying for nonchalance.

"Daniella is my official name, but it's not who I am. I'm Dani."

He looked back at me, drying his hands on a small towel. "What do you mean?"

"It's just who I am."

Westen leaned against the counter's edge, giving me his full attention. "Please, explain."

"Ugh, there's nothing to explain. My name may be Daniella, but Dani is what I've always gone by my whole life. Daniella is for government forms and official titles, but it's not me."

He nodded. "I see."

Maybe he did. Maybe he got that my mother had always called me Dani before she'd died. That only foster workers, doctors and teachers had ever called me Daniella. And him, for some reason. Even Mr. and Mrs. Thompson called me Dani, but they also called Lia by her nickname.

"Here." He handed me an oversized coat. "It was in the loft. I've loaded the pockets with jerky, nuts and dried fruit. Plenty to last until we reach Firehold."

I put it on and it bagged down past my hips, but it was very, comfortably warm. I felt like a poofy green marshmallow. This would have been nice to have before breakfast, but I didn't want to sound ungrateful.

"Thanks, this is actually super nice. None for you?"

He shook his head. "I don't need it. Ready?"

I shrugged, making the poofy jacket bob up around my neck. "I guess so."

"It'll be several hours of flight, and... just prepare yourself. It won't be like anything you imagine."

I quirked an eyebrow. "It's not all magic and rain-bows?"

Westen seemed determined to return to his gloomy ways. He just minutely shook his head, he lips a thin line. "I mean it. Just be ready."

"What do you mean? Like, should I be worried?"

He looked off into the woods. "I can't say more."

I let out an exasperated sigh. "Then why say any-thing? Jeez." I knew he wasn't going to say more, the cryptic punk. Trying to change the subject to something he possibly, probably, could talk about, I said, "Where is this Firehold anyway? I know in Alaska, but like, where?"

"It's by a cluster of active and dormant volcanoes known as the Katmai group on the Alaskan Peninsula between the Gulf of Alaska and Bristol Bay. Do you know where any of that is?"

He held the door open for me while I answered, "No," and breezed on by. "What volcano are you closest to?"

"Mount Mageik."

I eyed him. "You're making that up."

He smiled at me. "Google it." Then he shifted.

I unconsciously stepped back as he did so, from his shifting body, but also his sudden shift in personality. I was going to get metaphysical whip lash from his change. One minute he was stern and unforthcoming, the same old grump I'd grown up with, the next moment he's teasing me. I just didn't get it. Why bother being nice and accommodating when he was just going to put a wall in my face on certain things.

However, I did think that was one of the few genuine smiles I'd ever seen him give, one that wasn't a smirk or half-hearted. I could remember a few from when we were kids, like when Lia and I had baked him a disastrous pink unicorn cake with help from her parents, but that was about it. He'd been a grump for at least the past five years.

Which, I guess, was like a weekend for him. I shook my head; I was never going to get used to him being *so old.*

Also, I was both annoyed that he'd trolled me, and impressed at how well he'd done it. And he could bet I would look it up, too, as soon as I had internet access again. Mount Mageik is where the dragons just happened to set up their stronghold, suuuuure.

He shook out his body and wings, snapping them in and out a few times and bringing me out of my brooding thoughts to stare at his serpentine form. It was ridiculously awesome looking. Beautiful and scary. His grey scales shimmered in the morning light, making them look more silver edged than I'd remembered, and I swear he was taller, or maybe he was just stretching out in the sunlight.

He settled down and held out his arms for me to step into. My butt already ached from the anticipation of sitting for who knows how long, but I was excited too. Flying was a rush. I stepped into his arms, getting secure before he launched up into the night, dropping my stomach once again.

It didn't take me long to get into the swing of things again. After a half-hour or so we started crossing lots of small islands, but it didn't take long to leave them behind. Then, all there was, was water. We must be over the ocean, or one of those bays Westen had mentioned bordered his family's land. I was starting to feel rather accomplished at flying, not that I was doing anything. It was totally all Westen, but still, no other human that I ever knew of could say they'd flown a dragon. Not even Lia, because she was a dragon herself and didn't count.

My brain wanted to whine about my lot in life. I felt the emotion start to bloom, but I tamped it down. No. Bad emotions. Stop. I didn't need to cry about Lia lying to me, because she had to, and when it really counted, she told me even though she probably still shouldn't have.

I didn't need to think about Westen's strange friendly to distant switcheroos. He'd come back when he didn't have to. He got hurt to save me, and pushed himself to exhaustion, so he could be moody if he wanted.

And no, I didn't need to think about the future. My life had always been a question mark. Yes, I'd made plans that had blown up literally, but now I'd make new ones. Brooding did nothing, and there was nothing to do until we got to the castle stronghold thingy, which should be later today.

I let those thoughts slip through me, then focused on the shine of the sun across the ever moving water. The heartbeat in my ear of this ginormous, incredible creature that not only was real, but was flying me across the country. The arms securing me. And the snacks I had.

I accidentally dropped a bag of something into the water, but after that I got the system down of slipping my hand into a pocket, gripping just what would go in my mouth, and bringing just that up, it went fairly smooth.

Eventually, we came to land, then more water, then land again. I could see various points of mountains, clouds and such. After a time, Westen squeezed me in the way he'd done to announce we were descending and I held on tighter, even though it probably did nothing but reassure myself.

He drifted down in a way I suppose could be seen as slow and easy, but was still a terrifying corkscrew dive to me. I don't think I'd ever get so used to flying that it would seem boring. I'd gone through it several times by now, and my heart still ticked up each time. Finally, he touched down on a mountainside. A completely clear mountainside. We had been going for awhile, maybe he thought I needed a potty break.

I slipped out of his carrying embrace and started stretching out my muscles when five guys wearing military type gear popped into existence right in front of me. They stepped forward, pointed things at me, and I meeped back to Westen's side, or as close to it as I could get since he was currently shifting forms.

"Put any weapons on the ground, raise your arms and step forward to be taken into Elbrel's custody," one of the guy's spoke. I suppose he was the leader. He was behind the other guys, the ones who were pointing things at me. They weren't guns or spears or anything, more like short staffs, but they looked serious and I took them as such.

"Who's Elbrel? Why do I have to go into custody? What did I do?"

Three of the guys advanced. I looked at Westen, who seemed almost done. He was still blurry around the... everywhere, but it was mostly human sized.

"You are entering secured lands of Eir without authorization. Submit, or we will take you by force."

I was starting to freak out. "Uh, Westen, are these your guys?" I figured he could hear me, even through his transformation. I kept my eyes on the squad of men, while still backing up in the general direction I knew Westen to be.

I nearly jumped a foot when he put his hand on my shoulder. He'd finished shifting.

"These are members of Firehold guard. You have to go with them."

"I... what?"

The forefront one of them nodded toward Westen and said, "Domen," like an acknowledgement of some kind. What did it mean?

Westen looked at me steadily, showing nothing. No emotion, just nothing. Dead grey eyes. "Just do what they say. Comply with everything."

"Westen?"

He put slight pressure on my back, obviously urging me to go forward. Outrage bubbled up within me. Why couldn't he warn me of this? Was this what he'd been telling me to prepare myself for? Capture? He couldn't have said, "Oh, by the way, when we get to my family's place they're going to arrest you. Be prepared for that." No, he had to be so cryptic I had no idea what was coming. So, I wasn't getting taken by the warlocks, but by the dragons instead?

I wanted to blow up at him, yelling out everything, but the five guys were advancing and now Westen was pushing me into them. Belatedly, I put up my hands, right before two of the guys grabbed them, twisting them behind my back, and leading me forward into an empty field.

If I thought that I'd wallowed in self-doubts along the way, boy was I wrong. Spending however many days in the equivalent of a prison cell, knowing that your life-long best friend and her brother, who you thought was on your side, left you there... Well, let's just say I gave in to my wallowing big time.

I didn't right away. For a long time, I rationalized things, about how they probably didn't have a choice, it was up to the Elbrel guys. How Lia may not even know I was even here, and Westen was working things out, explaining exactly what had happened the past few days. I pushed all the other thoughts away.

Instead, I went over my journey to this room, trying to remember all the details of the castle. How surprised I'd been when from one step to another an entire castle and grounds had appeared out of nowhere. I guess we'd walked through a magic invisible wall or something. The guards had to push me through my stumble of surprise, but they couldn't keep me from seeing the grandeur.

It reminded me of the Edinburgh Castle, but bigger. At least, I think I was thinking of the Edinburgh Castle... Our geography teacher showed us several famous castles around the world last year, like the swan something one Disney was based off of.

The wall was huge, and I wondered briefly how they were going to get through it until they led me to a small side door. Going through the wall took at least a full minute of walking. The grounds beyond were like stepping into a renaissance training ground mixed with a military compound: training, men, swords, bows, guns, and more things than I could take in. I saw pastures and huge garden plots. This place was a freaking town around a giant castle.

They took me straight to a side building, which led to a tunnel type of thing, and eventually wound up here. It was a good thirty to forty-five minutes from where I was now back to the outer wall. This place was massive, but I supposed it had to be to house dragons.

That occupied my mind until they started questioning me. It was one or two guys, occasionally a group, and they would come in asking me questions over and over, on everything from the lake to when Westen and I showed up. That was when my determination to see the brighter side, to give the benefit of the doubt, started waning.

Did I know the men at the lake? How did I get to Kalia

when no one else did? Why did I take her home? Why did I return to their house that night uninvited? Why was I the one to take Janette and Kalia away from the house? Why did Janette leave me alone with Kalia? How did I get Kalia to perform magic on me? On and on...

After going over all of that several times, they started asking the questions they really wanted to, the ones they thought I was hiding.

Why did I become friends with Kalia in the first place? Was the scar on my cheek really from that? Was the scar real? How did I get her to like me so much? How did I manipulate Westen to come back for me? What did I tell the warlocks before Westen had gotten me? How did I communicate with the warlocks once I was travelling with Westen on our own? What information did I gather before, during and after the attack for the warlocks? Who was my contact within the warlocks' organization? More and more.

I gave honest answers mostly, though I let them know when I thought their questions were really stupid, and when they repeated themselves I started giving snarky ones. They never changed, never reacted, just kept going at it.

And when they weren't asking me countless, pointless questions in their strange, unidentifiable accents that seemed to be slightly different from person to person, they left me alone in the little room with nothing to look at. I couldn't sleep though I tried, nor eat, since there was no food or water, unless you counted in the toilet.

At first I was starving, and my eyes burned with wanting sleep, just like they had in the forest. But it just sort of, went away. I wasn't sure if that was a good thing or not, and I tried not to think about the fact that I might be starving to death. Surely, I couldn't starve to death that quickly, but honestly, I had no idea how long I'd been locked in.

The room had a bench that I sat on most of the time, but there wasn't any padding and they took my poofy jacket. No sink, but there was a mirror. I guess so I could see how miserable I was. I used the mirror to trace my bruises and my cheek scar, because I had nothing else to do. My scar didn't bother me as much when I had such a plethora of other things to keep my attention. Plus my wrist was healing badly, maybe it would make a matching scar to my cheek, like a scar bracelet. Ick.

My bruises were very slowly healing. I took special scrutiny to see if they'd lessened in their color and shape, trying to gage the passing of time by their diminishing stature. Like, if it gets this faded, that has to be at least a day or two gone. I had some colorful yellows and browns, and a few stubborn black and blues, but those were mostly on my legs, and I checked those out while sitting on my bench thing. My head bump was just a tiny ache, and only when I pushed on it.

They'd put a cuff thing on my unburned wrist. It had weird symbols all over it and was super shiny, which I thought was strange, but I guess it had some kind of magic in it. Maybe that's why I couldn't sleep...

I guess it was after the second interrogation, when they started repeating themselves, that I really started to question Westen's motives in this and the phone call at the cabin. The way he'd acted in the morning, was he just setting me up? Making me feel amiable so that I'd fall for the trap easier? It's not like I could do anything else but go along with him, so why the big act? And with their questions, I knew he'd spoken to them. How else would they know Westen rescued me from three warlocks in the forest? He hadn't said that over the phone call.

But I never cried. They would not see me break, even if I did on the inside. And I didn't know if they were somehow watching me in this room, so I showed them nothing. I'd had years and years of practice, and they weren't going to see me weaken.

I did get one break in the monotony. It was sometime after the fourth or fifth interrogation, when I was being left alone for whoever knows how long. I'd been lying on my back, taking a break from my usual analyzing of everything that had happened by staring blankly up at the ceiling. My eyes moved from one spot of imperfection to another, when I noticed a green glow coming from behind the vent. It was a small grate type, put into the ceiling at least twelve feet above me, so there was no way I could even reach it, much less do anything with it. But there was definitely a green glow moving around back there.

I'd wanted to get up, get closer to try and see what it was, but I was worried if I moved, it would go away, or I'd alert someone to the fact that there was something there. So, I just kept laying there, watching it passively. It never came down to the grate itself, and I was convinced it was doing that so it wouldn't get caught. Briefly, I wondered if different colors denoted different genders, like blue and green were boys, then I wondered if that wasn't just my American color bias coming out. Maybe sprites didn't even have genders. It had left after a while, and though I occasionally kept glancing up at the vent, I never saw it again.

I was reminiscing over the green sprite visitor again, because what else did I have to do, when Jerk Interrogator Number Four came in my door (I'd started numbering them), and I rolled my head toward him.

He was looking well fed, well rested. He obviously didn't need to consider drinking toilet water. I had been sitting on the bench, head leaning against the wall, in yet another futile effort to rest when he came in. I didn't give any witty or sarcastic remarks anymore, I just waited. As he approached, I noticed several people just outside the door, but they didn't enter.

When he reached down and took hold of my shackled wrist, I didn't do anything. There was nothing to do. I wasn't James Bond or Lara Croft, and I had no real strength or power. I didn't even know how to fight. I could run, but out here it seemed rather useless. I was literally in the middle of nowhere Alaska. Where could I go to if I even did manage to get past all the guys surely surrounding me and the complex? Nowhere. I could do nothing.

I'd come to realize and accept this a long time ago, during one of my personal assessments of what the heck was going on. I wasn't sure how long ago I'd come to that conclusion, but long enough ago.

When he unhooked the cuff, I just wiggled my wrist a bit, enjoying the small feeling of freedom that patch of skin had gotten. Who knew how long it would last or what it would be replaced by.

"Come." Rather succinct, he was. I'd decided his strange accent sounded kind of Canadian mixed with a kind of Australian hint to it. I know it made no sense, but that's what it sounded like.

I debated asking "Where?" or saying something like, "We're going on a field trip?" but why bother. I just stood and wobbled forward. My legs weren't working too well.

He kept pace behind me, neither helping nor hindering my movements as I made it to the door. The guys outside were more guard types, like the ones that had brought me in here in the first place. No other interrogators that I could see.

One of them, the closest to the door, held out a pointed arm showing me to walk to the right, where there awaited, shocker of shockers, another closed in room. Once I got to the door, I saw it was a small bathroom with a standing shower in one corner. Not that the shower had walls or anything, the whole room was tiled with a drain, there just was a small bench by the door, a toilet on the right side and a shower head on the other with a soap dispenser thing under it.

The interrogator was at the door with the guards behind him. When I looked back at them, he started talking. "You will shower, and use that soap cleaning everything. Your clothes are to be left on this bench. You will be provided with new ones when you are finished."

I waited for them to back out and close the door, but that didn't happen.

"You gonna leave?"

His eyes narrowed. "You have no rights, prisoner. You will be monitored at all times, to ensure you do no more treachery to the Eir family."

"Yeah, no, I'm not going to do that." No way was I undressing and washing in front of a bunch of people, much less adult males. They could deal with my stinky butt, I didn't care.

"If you do not, we will be forced to do it for you." He said it matter of factly, but I could tell he was getting off on the power trip of it. Or on the thought of me getting naked, ew.

Something snapped in me, just a little. My nerves, my resolve, my emotions, they were all shot. I know, cliché and all that, but I just couldn't take anymore.

"I have done everything you've asked, answered all your dumb questions, even when you were just going over the same crap-o-la over and over again. You've kept me in a cell when it wasn't even my idea to be here. Westen brought me, not my choice by the way, how 'bout you question him for hours on end? Huh? Now, after days of you guys pestering me, starving me, keeping me locked up in a glorified toilet, you want me to strip down in front of you so you can get your rocks off? No way, pervert!"

Some guards shifted and I automatically stepped back. If they were going to make me, then they were sure as hell going to have to make me. I'd hit, kick, scratch, spit, whatever I could to whoever I could until they knocked me out. I was gonna fight as dirty as I could.

Jerk Interrogator Number Four turned to the guards. "Get her washed."

I was gearing to jump at the first one through the door, go for the eyes, but before he could come in someone yelled, "Halt!" from in the back, where I couldn't see.

"What are you doing here?" If sneers could talk, it would surely sound like that. "I'm in charge of bringing the prisoner on the Queen's orders, as I'm sure you are aware."

"And as I'm sure you know, Faela has personal interest in the prisoner and will take great exception to ill treatment." Not only did the new voice sound authoritative, assertive, and feminine, it too had a strange type of accent I'd never heard before.

Everyone here spoke differently; my brain was starting to get triggered by it. It made me feel incredibly ignorant and backwater. I mean, I knew I hadn't been exposed to much living in one small town in Montana my whole life, but goodness I felt stupid getting tripped up on accents and the like.

There was a pause, probably as they eyed each other. I could only see the interrogator, whose back was rigid.

Then the female voice continued. "Faela may be young, but she is still second in line. She ordered me here, and I will follow her orders."

The interrogator bristled. "Even against the Queen, Brielle?"

"I'm sure in your excitement to carry out the Queen's orders, you may have been overzealous in your execution of them; however, me being here is not contrary to her orders, but rather in parallel with them. You are to present the prisoner to a formal judgement, not terrorize her. She's just a human, after all, and you need, let's see... five guards to wash her? That seems excessive. I'll take over this part, to ensure it's done in line with both the Princess' and Queen's expectations."

I wasn't sure if I liked this Brielle or not. She was going against Jerk Interrogator Number Four, so that was awesome, but I just couldn't be sure.

"You will most certainly not!"

"Alright. Then I'll go report to Princess Kalia that you're having five guards, male guards at that, forcibly strip, wash and dress her friend."

My brain shorted. *Lia was a princess.* What was going

on? Oh, and not just a dragon, by the way, but a princess dragon. Couldn't have mentioned that, huh? I held my astonishment down, trying to focus on what was happening right now. I could go crazy over this later.

There wasn't too long of a pause before he caved. "I'll inform the Queen of this." Predictable, he got out-played and instead of conceding he was sulking in the most obvious and pathetic way.

"I would expect nothing less." And how did this Brielle lady manage to not sound smug saying that? Maybe it was her strange accent, hiding it from me.

"Come," he ordered the guards, I supposed to make himself feel in charge of something.

They filed out of the doorway and in came a formidable woman, dressed in similar clothing to the guards, but more fancy. I thought she looked Native Alaskan maybe.

She leaned against the doorframe and took in my appearance with a fair amount of nonchalance. "Hi, I'm Brielle. What's your name?"

I eyed her. "Don't you already know?"

"Yup." She smiled. "I was just trying to be polite."

"No need for politeness here."

She nodded ruefully and I fought some internal instinct to give her the benefit of the doubt. It was too easy to believe she was just being the "good cop" to the interrogator's "bad cop."

She seemed genuine, though. And nice. And strong. Like she could kill me without trying very hard. She just looked freaking powerful, like a firefighter or soldier.

The rather long sword at her waist told a story all on its own, and it wasn't just for show, I was sure. Her outfit was cool too, like modern military renaissance in red and black. I wondered if it was a standard uniform, or if she got to choose the side-split tunic type design. Normally, I would have just asked her, but these times weren't exactly normal anymore.

"Well, I'll just get to it. I can't explain a lot, because if it came out you knew certain things, I'd get in more trouble than it was worth. I can tell you, it'll all be clear soon, if that helps."

She paused, probably waiting for a response from me, which I didn't give. After a minute she shrugged and continued. "Right, to get to that point, we need to get through this. You have to be deemed presentable for your judgement, and that means washed and wearing appropriate clothing."

"Which is not this, I suppose?" I plucked at my many days old tank top, the dusky purple smeared with forest brown and green, spilled dried soup, and some good ol' B.O. stain from not being able to wash since before I went to the treehouse.

She couldn't quite hold back a snicker, but at least she tried. "No, they're not. While you're washing I'll get you the clothes and a towel."

"Is being starved and sleep deprived part of the appropriate presentation?"

"Are you though? Hungry? Sleepy?"

I took stock of myself instead of just flippantly saying "Yes! You've had me for days with nothing!" However, I couldn't actually say I was hungry or tired. I mean, I was, just not critically so. Maybe I hadn't been in there for days like I thought? Was I that off?

"I am," I said anyway.

"Hmmm... I wish you didn't feel so. However, we still must shower and change before anything else."

She gave very political answers for being a warrior type person.

"And if I don't?"

She shrugged. "I'll make you." I glared at her. "Hey, I'm the one who's trying to give you privacy and dignity. Like I said, it's required to move on to the next step in the process."

I crossed my arms, feeling very impotent. "Yay, to go to judgement. And doesn't that just sound so positive?"

"It can be. Judgement is not inherently negative."

"Not in my experience."

Another shrug. Awesome bedside manner.

"Well, I'm going to shut this door and go get your towel and clothes. Please put yours here on this bench, and I'll take them to get cleaned."

And she left, shutting and clicking the door behind her. Even though I knew that click meant she locked the door, I still went and tried the handle, just in case. Yup, locked. I eyed the room, but there just wasn't much to look at. Two small drains in the floor, a vent up top that was on, probably connected with the light.

I could sulk, sit down and do nothing, or turn the water on and sit in it with my clothes on, so when Brielle had to "make me" it'd be a pain in the butt getting my wet clothes off. I could try to fight, but with Brielle, I couldn't find the will. She'd diffused me, somehow.

So, I threw my clothes toward the bench and felt some defiance when I didn't pick up the ones that fell on the floor. I hated to admit it, but the water felt wonderful. It was nice and hot, and the soap didn't smell too chemically. I washed my hair three times.

During my slow wash I thought about Lia being a princess and the new guard Brielle, who was looked and seemed pretty awesome. I decided I couldn't figure out her accent and more than the interrogators'. Hers was like a mix of four or five different types, none of which meshed. What was up with this place?

Once done with my shower, I found there was indeed a giant fluffy looking towel and some folded off-white clothes that had replaced my old clothes. I hadn't even heard her open the door, but obviously she had. I thought about being creeped out, but eh. She hadn't stayed or stared or anything, which was as much as I could ask for in the situation realistically.

The clothes turned out to be a fairly simple cotton type of loose pants and tunic, all in the same off-white tone. No variations, no pockets. I guess it was so they could ensure I had nothing on me, like a weapon or something. I thought it would be scratchy, but it was actually soft. I guess that was to make up for the fact that they didn't give me any underwear, which was highly disconcerting. At least the clothes didn't show anything I would care about showing. Small favors, I supposed.

Brielle was waiting for me outside the room, sitting in one of the chairs off to the right side. She stood when I came out. I was slightly disappointed she didn't have a magazine or smart phone in her hand.

"Ready?"

"What? No styling? Is my makeup ok?" Not that I wore make up anyway, but that wasn't the point. Scar on my cheek, wet uncombed hair slobbering down my back, yellow and brown splotches of healing bruises dotting my jaw. I held up my head like it was on showcase, even though I knew I looked like a wet rag.

"Good enough. This way." Obviously, my sarcastic point didn't make much of an impact on her. She held out her arm to a stairwell next to her. I couldn't remember if it was the same one I'd come down, especially since there were three stairwells. I must be underground, because everything seemed to lead up. Not that I knew what was behind the eight or so other doors, but I figured more cells.

Apparently I was the only one in holding right now, or maybe they just didn't leave guards down here 24/7, because Brielle was the only one here and we were leaving.

"So," I asked with feigned nonchalance, "does that interrogator always make girls strip while he watches?"

Brielle glanced at her from the side. "Not that I am aware of. It will be addressed."

"I would hope so. None of those guys even spoke up against him."

"We follow orders."

"Following orders that are wrong is just as bad as ordering them done," I shot back.

She gave a conceding nod. "I understand your point. So far as I'm aware, this has never come up before. Believe me when I say it will be thoroughly taken care of."

It was probably more than I could have expected, and it did make me feel better.

"So," I changed the subject to lighten the mood and take my mind off the jitters that were starting to form in my belly, "do you have to wear your hair in that tight bun? Is it regulation or something?"

It was a shiny, thick black pulled back so severely the thought of it made my scalp tingle in sympathy pain.

"Hair is one of the easiest ways to force your opponent to move in a way they don't want to. Where the head goes, the body follows. Keep your hair minimized and you keep your vulnerabilities minimized as well."

"Why not just chop it off then?"

She looked back at me with amusement. "Because I like it long."

And I bet it looked great out of that bun. Ok, I got her to answer an easy question, how about a slightly harder one?

"So, who's going to be at this judgement thing? The interrogator guys?"

Brielle didn't answer, just kept walking up the steps.

So, I guess talking about anything else wasn't going to be happening. I didn't feel like empty chitchat, so I said nothing further, and Brielle didn't ask any questions as she led.

After the staircase that made my calves burn, we went down a long hall, turned to a short one, and ended at a door, which she opened to a small waiting type room. I didn't see anyone on the way, except for some people outside the windows just walking. The room she'd brought me to was nicely furnished and had a couple of chairs in it. No windows, of course.

"You're to wait here until they get you for your judgement."

"Yippy." I paused in the door, so she couldn't lock me in before I asked, "Did Lia really send you to help me?"

She smiled the type of smile that said, "I'm not going to answer you." Did she know Lia to me was Princess Kalia to her? Should I re-ask using her "real" name? Psh, never mind, she wasn't going to answer my questions.

I didn't watch her shut the door, but I felt it, and the lock sliding into place felt so very definitive.

I got over my anxiety by becoming rather bored. There was a clock, and I swear it was moving backwards at times. But the chairs were comfortable and I settled down into one, slouching back until my head was resting on the side, my legs over the other arm rest.

I must have fallen asleep because when the door opened I almost fell over, just catching myself with my foot slamming into the floor. I sat up, blinking rapidly to reorient myself.

"What?" I asked, taking a moment to rub my eye. I couldn't have been asleep too long, as my hair was still thoroughly wet. It'd left an impressive wet mark on the chair.

There were two guards, this time one was female, but not Brielle. She was the one to speak to me. "Follow us."

To my judgement. Oh, happy days.

CHAPTER

12

We left the room and took a moderate walk down yet another new way, turning a few times. I didn't bother trying to memorize the layout, because for one thing we kept passing windows where I could see their vast courtyard of grass filled with training soldiers who would all be happy to bring me back should I get anywhere I wasn't supposed to be.

I was taken to a narrow room fairly devoid of furniture and decorations. On one side were three very cushy looking chairs behind an ornate table, but other than that, I saw nothing of note. No windows here to distract my eye.

They led me to the far right, on the opposite side of the room from the chairs, where there was a circle design in the floor they put me in. Then they took up guard posts behind me. Very reassuring.

I was wondering how long they'd have me stand here

when five people entered in a second door on the opposite side of the room, hidden behind the chairs. The heartrate I'd been working on controlling spiked when the door opened, and I watched them file in. Two were obviously more guards, which took up stances like mine, but to the sides of the chairs where the three much more dignified and important looking people sat.

My blood was pounding in my ears and I had to focus on maintaining a normal posture and breathing. I didn't want them to know how scared I was; they didn't deserve to have that kind of satisfaction.

I recognized one of them, he was a regular interrogator, Jerk Interrogator Number Two. He wore the same interrogator robes he'd come in every time he'd questioned me, long red ones with interesting stitch work I'd taken time to follow during the long repetitive questioning. It reminded me of vines. He reminded me of a snake. He'd been in on the first round, and the most rounds thereafter. He sat in the smallest of the three chairs.

The other two were older, looking to be in their middle ages, and they clearly were the top dogs in the room. The woman had her hair pulled back in a severe bun that was ridiculously intricate with gems shining from hair crossing points. The man didn't have such decoration, but his face was covered with an impeccably groomed full beard that had lances of grey throughout the auburn color. They both wore similar styled robes in red and black, each with a large dragon crest on their chests, where their robes were clasped closed.

Once they were seated, the guy in charge turned to the interrogator. "Report."

"The prisoner gave inconsistent accounts of her relationship with Faela and the day of the attack, which –"

"I did not!" I yelled out before thinking. I could feel my cheeks flush.

"She also shows no respect for-"

A door banged open and I startled, stepping to the side. The circle around me glowed a bright yellow and I stepped back quickly, not wanting to find out what would happen if I tried to step out of it. It did nothing for my calm.

Neither did the person who entered – Westen.

He was looking fit and dignified, wearing some type of all black outfit that seemed formal, but not dress formal like the top dogs were wearing. Seeing him did help me clear my fear a bit, as anger crept into its place. Where had he been while I was sitting in that little cell? Getting well rested and fed, by the looks of things. I saw he'd gotten rid of the travel beard that had been growing in.

My jaw was clenched so hard I had to consciously unclench it. I wanted to yell at him, confront him, ask him what the hell? And I couldn't do *anything!* I couldn't even move, because who knew what that stupid circle could do. So, I just stood there, seething.

"Why are you present?" Top dog guy asked.

Westen gave a short bow toward them. "Faelen, Domett. I am here to advocate for the prisoner."

The prisoner. First "human friend" and now "the prisoner." My lip curled and I fought it down. I didn't care that I was being hasty in my judgement, that I wasn't giving Westen a fair shot (especially since he came here to advocate for me apparently). Right now, I was simply livid at him and everything was making it worse. From his ult suit to calling me "the prisoner" like I didn't have a name, like we hadn't talked about it the morning he brought me to this place, this interrogative prison.

At least I seemed to be in company. The top dogs didn't seem too happy with Westen either by the looks on their faces.

The woman leaned forward sporting a frown with eyebrows nearly touching each other. It reminded me of my third grade teacher when we wouldn't listen to her, but it was the guy who spoke first.

"We have not time for this, as you are aware."

He nodded at them. "Yes, I am aware of the plans currently underway, of which I am working toward in my capacity as Domen. However, this was the allotted time scheduled for the judgement, so I came to ensure the Orindrae was followed in regards to the prisoner."

The woman raised her narrow, pointy and rather straight nose in the air slightly. "An advocate is neither required of the Orindrae, nor desired with this hearing." Then she seemed to have lost some of her politic attitude with her exasperation. "What are you doing here, Westen?"

Westen kept his poise and his attention toward the

judgers. "While this prisoner does not require an advocate under the Orindrae for her race and status, she does receive exception for her recent actions regarding Faela."

So Faela had to be Lia. Why did she have so many different names? Wasn't her given name Kalia and her nickname Lia enough? Was Faela like her dragon name?

"It is those engagements which are in question," top guy responded seeming much more nonplussed than the woman, "and therefore cannot be grounds for exception until they are proven."

The lady raised her chin. "Agreed. How can she receive exception when she is the source of the situation?"

"Faelen, she did not cause the situation. Faela herself has told you so, and explained how the prisoner saved her from the attack, working with her and her warden, and following all directions."

So, top dog lady was called Faelen, which must mean the top dog guy was Domett. And the suspiciously close wording of Faelen to Faela, plus she certainly looked the age, and was haughty enough...

Suddenly, my mouth was dry and it felt like a rock had slid down my esophagus. If I was correct, then the top dogs were actually the queen and king of the dragons, Lia and Westen's parents. I felt dizzy, but had nowhere to sit. I was being judged, harshly and unjustly, by dragon royalty, and Westen was... standing up to them? I put a hand to my forehead, feeling nauseous.

Westen had his mother's dark brown, nearly black hair, but his father's blue eyes and lighter skin. Lia had the golden skin of her mother, the narrow nose and blue green hazel eyes, with the lighter auburn hair of her father. I remembered Westen saying his parents' marriage was between the British Isles and Greece. Well, it was clear to me his mother held the Greek blood.

They weren't waiting for my epiphanies or observations, and I scolded myself to attention. Whether I was right or not wouldn't change, but I needed to know what was happening in this judgement, that I may or may not be receiving from the King and Queen of the dragons themselves.

Faelen snorted, which was not something I was prepared for, especially since I just guessed she was the queen and all that. She leaned back into her seat and gave Westen (her son?) an impressive glare. "Kalia is an impressionable youngling with an unhealthy attachment to the human."

She said "human" the same way I might say "spider."

"Are you saying Faela misrepresented the events in order to show her lifelong friend in a more favorable light?" Westen asked, as if he was saying, "Oh, really? You really think that?" but in a much more political way.

Faelen shrugged. "Perchance."

"No," Domett interjected firmly. He was levelling the queen with an impressive glare of his own. "Kalia did not dissemble in any manner. She spoke honestly and in all conscience when recounting the events."

She eyed her husband for a moment, before nearly

hissing through her teeth, "We do not have time for this. The councilors will be assembling soon."

"Then we should quickly resolve this," he replied, speaking quietly in return, but giving nothing away in his voice or face as to which was he was leaning. Not that he could give much away with his face half covered in that impressive swath of beard. Was he helping or hurting my cause?

The king had an extraordinary impassive face. Westen had learned from him well, I assumed. The queen looked away from her hubby then back again before speaking, which I thought was rather telling.

This time she spoke loudly with a flourish of her hand. "Faela could have done it unintentionally. As I said, she is *very* young and attached to her *friend*, the young often change their mind without even being cognizant of it."

Nice emphasis, lady, very subtle.

I itched to say something, to defend Lia, to defend myself, but I knew, *knew* it was a dumb idea to speak up. I just felt so darn powerless! Like a fly stuck to a wall, unable to move as the swatter was held up.

"Are my explanations of the events under question as well?" Westen seemed to break the tension going between the king and queen by focusing it on himself.

The king answered after a pause, "No, naturally not."

The queen looked like she was clenching her jaw as much as I was. Westen obviously got his calm exterior from his father. The queen didn't look like she could hold back her scorn or anger from showing for anything.

"Since my account aligns with Faela's during the attack, and my report of what occurred after are not under question, are we in agreement that the prisoner's actions allow for exception under Orindrae?"

"No," the queen practically spat out. "We have not determined that she has not been working with the Warlocks this entire time, nor that she has not spied on, given information, or impacted the events that nearly led to Kalia's capture."

The seedy little interrogator chose now to pipe up, probably because he didn't want to get in the middle of a family pissing contest before. Honestly, I'd forgotten about him.

"Which is what my team was sent to determine, and-"

"And of which I have been tasked with keeping track of for nearly ten years in my capacity as Domen. Am I or my reports of such under suspicion, Faelen?" Westen totally cut the guy off, and he shrunk back in his chair, obviously deflated. I would have smiled if I wasn't so wound up from everything else going on. Take that Jerk Interrogator Number Two who was apparently in charge of all of it! That's what you get!

I wasn't sure if it was smart of Westen to push the queen mommy, but he seemed confident. Also, excuse me, but what? Keeping track of me for ten years?

The queen readjusted in her seat. "Your reports were ever taken in good faith."

"Is there any reason for Faelen or Domett to suspect I was incorrect or incomplete in my assessments of Faela or her various human acquaintances?"

The queen just glared. The king glanced at her, then said, "No."

"What of the warden's reports?"

"They were not pertinent to this investigation." The queen was practically spitting acid. Then briefly I wondered if dragons could have acid breath, or if they were all fire?

Westen nodded, ever calm. "Not specifically, but they back up my reports, as well as Faela's, do they not?"

The king sighed. "Yes, Domen, they do."

"So, unless a simple human," *hey!* "was able to conceal from me and the wardens, without any use of magic that could have been detected, a secret connection to warlocks, then there is no question that she has earned exception. She risked her life for Faela repeatedly, and never wavered in her loyalty."

"As you've said before." Man, the queen seemed livid.

"As I have." Westen nodded again, keeping that annoying calm neutral stance he always took. It seemed to irritate his parents as much as it did me. That was something, at least.

"You have, have you?" The king asked.

"Yes, Domett." Another bow, this time towards him.

Oh, snap! Westen had told all of this to his mom, who had decided not to share it with his dad, and his dad seemed none too pleased. I didn't know a lot about relationships having never been in one myself, but that didn't seem like a smart move. The king gave a look between Westen and the queen, who was now staring at a wall in what I assumed was defiance. How queenly of her.

"Domen's argument is accepted. The prisoner is hereby granted exception through Orindrea, and as such will be allowed an advocate."

"I wish to take on the role."

The king nodded. "As you wish, Domen."

I half-expected the queen to interrupt with something like "Absolutely not!" or "You're way too close to the case" or "Off with her head!" But she just sat there, holding in her rage from the looks of things.

"We will adjourn." I half expected the king to knock a gavel type item on the desk, but all he did was look to Westen. "Domen, speak with Jamison."

Westen nodded, then finally turned toward me. I instinctively stepped toward him, ready for him to get me out of here so I could question him about what just went down. A shockwave went up my system and I found myself locked in place like an electric current was freezing my muscles in place. I kind of squeaked, then all of a sudden I was released. I fell forward, landing on my knees. The guards helped me up. I let them because no one else was offering, and my limbs were still zinging. That was eerily similar to what the lady warlock had done to me in the forest.

Westen was still standing where he'd been, how nice

of him. He waited for me to stand, then directed me toward the door I'd come in. No words, no smile, nothing. Ugh, I was so done with this.

But, thank goodness, it seemed that I was. The king and queen were exiting through their back door, and Jerk Interrogator Number Two was already gone. That seemed to be it, but I was still cautious. I looked at Westen. He just went to the door I'd originally come through and opened it. I meekly followed. No matter how incredibly dismissive he was being of me as a person right now, he did just get me out of that judgement, which looked like it was totally railroaded against me, so I swallowed my feelings and went out the door.

Westen dismissed my two guards, who apparently were following us out, then told me to come with him. I looked around, found no one near us, and sped up so I was next to him.

"Westen, what is going on?"

He shook his head without looking at me. "No questions right now."

"But-"

He shot me a quick look that I would have to describe as a glower. "Not now."

I dropped back a step, so I didn't have walk beside him. I was so angry I could barely think. I felt like punching his stupid arm, or stalking away and slamming one of the doors we walked past, but some part of my brain knew both options were stupid. I'd wait until we got to wherever we were going, and then let him have it.

I stewed in my anger the entire walk, until we got to

the third staircase, and then my tired legs started taking over my attention. Not only had they been zapped by the circle thing, now they'd trekked through countless halls and up three staircases. He wasn't having any issues with the stairs, obviously. He had stupid freakishly strong calves, probably.

"Where are we going?" I asked out of desperate frustration or anger, I couldn't really tell which.

"To where you'll be staying for the time being. We're almost there." His tone was way softer than it had been. In fact, it reminded me of when we were at the cabin. It was throwing me off.

"And we couldn't talk on the way because?" I asked, not expecting him to really answer me.

"We're almost there." Hah, called it. Not an answer.

"Ya, you said that already," I grumbled, mostly toward my feet.

We came to yet another hallway, but only three or so doors down, Westen stopped and knocked. The door flew open almost before his knuckles left the wood and there was a loud shriek I knew all too well.

"Dani! Westen!" Lia swooped us both into her arms.

I ignored Westen trying to extricate himself and wrapped myself around the only family I'd ever really had.

"Dani, Dani, Dani!" Lia chanted in my ear.

"In the room, please," Westen spoke over us.

We ignored him, doing an exaggerated swaying hug that would have us tipping over if we didn't stop it. It was a competition almost, who would cave first to save their skin? Our shoulders would have bumped the door-frame on our next swing we were getting so exuberant, but before that could happen I got shoved from the back, which toppled me into Lia, making us fall into the room. She burst out laughing, not helping at all as I tried to get up from off of her.

"Thanks, Westen," she laughed sarcastically.

He closed the door and stepped around us. "I did ask you to come in the room first."

"Nice," I said, getting up from the floor, which was a hot pink color of carpet. "So you pushed us? That was your solution?"

"Apparently." That threw Lia into more laughter. "Besides, I didn't push. I nudged merely to get past you, as you were blocking the entrance."

"Suuuuuuure," I responded so he'd know that I knew he was full of it.

While Lia laughed it up at both of us, I took a glance around the room. Everything was in different shades of pink, it was so garish. Light pink walls, hot pink carpet, medium pink window curtains and bedspread. If this was Lia's room, I had some serious making-fun-of to do.

I held out a hand to her, and she took it to haul herself up. She went into a hug again, but more of a squeezing, happy one. "Oh, Dani, I'm so glad to see you!" She spoke to my shoulder, since she was still hugging me. "Were you totally crazy mad at us? I bet you were."

Because Lia didn't let me go, I couldn't look at her. So,

I looked over her shoulder at Westen, who raised an eyebrow at the question.

"Absolutely," I said truthfully, and a bit more bluntly than I probably should have considering they'd just gotten me out of it.

Lia pulled back to look at me, her dismayed emotions blatantly on display. Obviously she was torn up about what had happened to me, I just knew her, and I didn't want her to start crying, which she was pretty likely to do.

"Don't worry," I assured her, "I'm only mad at Westen right now."

"Of course you are." I swear Westen rolled his eyes, but he turned away as he did so, so it was hard to tell.

"Westen!" Lia chastised, "Don't be like that. And Dani, you don't know what's been going on."

Some of my built up anger and resentment pushed through the happiness this reunion had brought, and I forcibly pulled away from Lia's death hug of happiness.

"How could I?" I asked, through nearly gritted teeth. "I was kept in a room with nothing, only visited by those jerk-head interrogator guys. I had no idea where you two were or what was going to happen." I realized my voice was rising in slight panic at the thoughts I'd long held down, and I clenched them off, not wanting to lose control, and feeling like I might if I kept at it.

Lia's eyes started to fill up, her nose tickling with red as she fought her emotions down. "I know, it was horrid, but we didn't have a choice."

"A princess has no choice?" I asked more flippantly than I should have, still wrestling with myself. I felt the tiniest bit guilty when she cringed, but then all the emotions of everything threatened to overwhelm me and I turned away, towards the door to deal with them. I couldn't look at either of them, and I didn't want them to look at me. I was starting to tear up, and I hated, *hated* crying in front of others. Lia knew this.

"Ya," Lia said quietly. "I'm a princess. Wahoo," she spoke dejectedly. She put a hand on my back and I instinctively hunched up against it. "Sorry I forgot to mention that, but, you know, it's only a small addition to the whole dragon thing, isn't it?"

I let out a chuckle, mixed with a bit of a sob. "Ya, sure."

Westen cleared his throat. "I couldn't speak to you in the halls because there might have been others listening, even ones we couldn't see."

I nodded my head to let him know I heard him. I assumed he was trying to clear the air of anything he could, and really, I should have thought of that. Lia was rubbing my back as I worked to control myself. Even breaths, shallowed out so they weren't clearly audible, that was the way I did it. Nice and even. Woo-sah.

"We can't ever talk in the halls," Lia explained further while I gathered myself. I was betting just to fill the silence, or give me time. "It's so annoying. Only our rooms are really safe. This one is too, in case you were wondering."

I nodded again, and stared at the door in front of me. I would control myself. I took a quick wipe at my face to clear, hopefully, any tell-tale signs before turning around. "Why couldn't I have been warned beforehand what was going to happen?"

Lia looked chagrinned. Westen looked impassive. Of course he would.

"I couldn't," was all he said, and my anger flared, helping clear the rest of the pity party out of my system.

Before I knew it, I was yelling and pointing my finger at him. "I am so sick of that answer! Couldn't tell me, my butt. You sure could have! At the cabin, or on the trip. You could have visited me some time in my cell to let me know anything about what was going on!"

"No, he couldn't," Lia spoke quietly.

I swung my accusing eyes toward her. "To which part?"

"All of it." Lia was looking miserable, and she kept speaking in that quiet voice, so I knew she must be feeling hella guilty, but I wasn't ready to let her off the hook until I got some freaking answers out of it. She went and slumped onto the bed. Her soft white and yellow dress clashed horribly with the cover. It was also pink.

"If he had told you and they found out, or if he visited you without first establishing your right to such, it would have made you look even more guilty."

"What do you mean?"

"She means," Westen picked up the conversation, much to my surprise since I thought he'd remain silent in an effort to stay off my radar for the moment, "that our parents have never liked how Kalia always went back to Montana because of you, and since the attack, they were looking for a reason as to why it happened."

I realized my arm was still up and pointing, and I lowered it, trying to process things. "So...?"

"So," Lia answered, "you were the obvious suspect to them, Dani. If you were given more knowledge of us, or been warned, it would have been seen as more proof of your "power" over me." She even used air quotes for power. Then she glanced at Westen. "Or him, which would have been worse."

"What? Why?"

"Because he was the only reason I was ever allowed to come back. He vouched for my safety there, and had to do reports and everything all the time to let me stay. If they had anything they thought was proof of you or anyone in town influencing us for information you weren't supposed to have..." She petered out, which I supposed meant the worst thing I could imagine would have happened.

Lia was looking down at her feet which she was pushing into the fluffy hot pink carpet, something she did when she was avoiding things. Her little bronze toesies disappeared into the thickness.

I looked at Westen, but he was still doing his impassive thing.

"Oh," was all I managed. I didn't have it in me to apologize or give thanks quite yet, so I pounced on the next best thing. Distraction. "Ugh, Lia, is this your bedroom?"

She looked up, a hopeful smile playing at the edges of her mouth.

Westen snorted, getting my attention. "No, it's yours."

I was aghast, literally. "No!" I looked back at Lia, who I could tell was holding in a slight giggle. I'm sure she would have laughed if we hadn't just come off of some seriously downer topics. "How could you?" I played it up for her benefit. "Will the torture never end?"

My intended effect worked. Lia let out a light laugh and Westen's lip twitched, which was basically laughing for him, at least for the not-quite-so-carefree-Westen that I was used to. For a moment, I missed the Westen on the trip. We'd mostly been flying, but when we hadn't, it had been practically nice. Almost normal in our conversations. Oh well. Seemed like he was back to being a quiet stick in the mud. Well, mostly.

"Remember when I was, like, really into pink as a kid?" Lia asked.

"Hah, how could I forget? It lasted, what, three years? I thought middle school cured you of it, though." I did a circle, taking in all the other little pink nick knacks I hadn't noticed yet, like the small dresser with painted flowers, and a wall hanging of a pink unicorn. At least the small desk and chair under the window looked normal, except for being pink of course.

"I switched rooms and this one kind of just stayed stuck. It's my guest room now, so it's where you'll be staying. Ta-da!" She held up her arms like I'd won some kind of prize.

I scrunched my nose. "Sooooo much pink. And please tell me unicorns aren't real."

"Oh, they're real," Westen said rather ominously. "Mean, vicious things, and *not* pink."

"Yes, well," Lia spoke airily, "the picture is still cute."

"I highly disagree," I retorted immediately. "Guest room for who?"

Lia got a wicked grin. "For visiting dignitary daughters. You should see their faces," she let out a cackle I couldn't help but smile at. "Most of them get a room transfer. Oh, one time though, there was this cute little Tennyo who absolutely loved the room. She was just a tiny kid and it was so adorable."

Westen stepped into my space, distracting me from asking what a Tennyo was. I could tell by his face he was going to switch the subject to something serious again.

"I'm sorry, but I need to go. Before I do, I have to go over some rules."

I folded my arms. "Naturally."

"Don't be disdainful, they're to help you." Westen didn't wait for me to respond or reply, probably to stave off the mocking reply I had on the tip of my tongue for using the word disdainful. "Don't allow anyone into your room except for us or Brielle, you remember her? Good, she's Kalia's personal guard and is trustworthy. Other than us, don't ever go with anyone. If any person comes to ask questions or take you somewhere, no matter who they are, you have to say you will await your advocate as allowed under Orindrae. Do you understand?"

"I'll wait for my Westen advocate because of the Orindrae thingy, got it."

He seemed to wince, just a little. "Try to remember my wording, if you can. It'll make you sound like you know what you're talking about."

I glared at him. He was antagonizing me on purpose. "Yes, oh wise Domen. I shall indeed joyfully and faithfully await the appointed advocate, as granted to me by the honorable and wise Domett under Orindrae."

I meant to be sarcastic, but he looked mildly impressed. I had a good memory for names even under non-stressful situations. Stressful ones tended to stick in my memory even more.

"That will do nicely."

I stuck my tongue out at him.

Ignoring me, he turned toward Lia and held out an arm. She immediately slipped under it for a hug. He squeezed her for a moment and kissed the top of her head. I was flabberghasted; I'd never seen such familial affection from him before. I pushed away the small surge of jealousy that hit me square in the chest.

"See you tonight, minikin," he spoke to the top of her head. Then he released her and walked to the door, catching my eye before leaving. "Try not to break anything."

I would have stuck my tongue out at him, but I'd just

done that. I settled for giving him a snooty facial reply, but as he went to shut the door behind him, I called out.

"Westen, uh, thanks for everything."

He nodded, making it look like a formal bow, then shut the door.

I turned to Lia who was standing beside me and levelled her with my best I'm-super-serious face. "Ok, your dragony highness, you've got a lot of explaining to do, and you'd better not say can't tell me the answers or I will seriously lose it on you."

Lia rolled her eyes at me. Not unexpected, but unappreciated with my current mood.

"Dani, of course I'll tell you everything. First, let's get you out of those clothes."

"Yes, please," I whimpered half-mocking, half-serious.

She knew me so well, like knowing getting me into real clothes would put me in a better mood, and boy did it. Being in this tunic thing with no undies did nothing for my disposition or composure. It made me feel like they still controlled me, which they pretty much did, but I didn't want to *feel* like they did.

She was at the dresser, opening the drawers. "So, I brought in some of my clothes. Don't worry, I didn't include a bunch of dresses or flower prints, no matter how modern or cute." Lia gave me a side glance to let me know she thought I was dumb for not wearing them, but I didn't care how cute *she* looked in them, *I* didn't and I knew it. "But if none of them work, I can always see if Brielle can find something from someone. I'm sure there's athletic sticks around here that match your body type."

I silently mocked "athletic stick" behind her back as I came up to the dresser. "At least I'm not some voluptuous model type that has to laugh at all the guys' jokes and compliment all the other girls' hair because I'm like, so incredibly hot." I went into a valley girl accent for the end, making Lia smile in laughter even though she was mad at my words.

"Oh, shut up! I am not and do not. Here, try these on."

"Yay! Underwear." I was seriously happy. I quickly put on her clothes, a simple t-shirt (mercifully not pink, just black with a red sparkly heart in the middle) and jeans. They didn't fit me properly, because nothing of Lia's ever did, but they were good enough. Things that draped on her just drooped on me. These were a bit baggy in the areas where she had curves and I didn't.

Thinking on it, I was surprised at how normal her wardrobe seemed to be here, especially if she was a princess. Wouldn't they want her dressing in formal attire or something, like Westen was wearing? Instead of t-shirts, jeans and flowy summer dresses with yellow flowers on them? And seriously, a sundress? It was cold here, even inside, and she was strutting around in freaking summer wear.

Of course, I belatedly remembered it was probably

dragon warmth. That made her past clothing choices very understandable, and enviable. It must be nice to never be cold.

She took the tunic outfit from where I dropped it on the floor while I changed. "Here, let's just take care of those." And went to the window. She opened it enough to toss out the offending clothes. "There, that's better."

I grunted a laugh. "Well, that's one way I guess. Thanks, I feel better."

"Sure thing." She smiled, looking ridiculously pretty silhouetted against the setting sun through the window. Her dress soaked up the reds and oranges. She was just picking up something from the small table kept between the bed and the window. "Here, let's fix that hair, and I have some ointments for your wrist and bruises, if you want."

I took a quick look at the rest of the clothes in the drawers before shutting them. Lots of shirts, jeans and some sweats. Nice. Exactly what I liked to wear. Lia knew me so well.

"Oh, and there's shoes in the closet. I had Brielle find some running shoes in your size. And some jackets and stuff."

I was having a big awwww moment. I swallowed the quick surge of emotion. "Thanks. I'll try them on later."

"Come here, sit."

I obediently went to the bed and sat down in front of her, turning until my back mostly faced out.

"Here's the creams. That one is for burns, the others

help with bruises. Just rub it in lightly till it feels cool." She told me all this while brushing out my hair, pointing when necessary. It was really nice being taken care of and it almost never happened to me, so I took a moment to just sit in the feeling before taking out the burn cream. I'd do the bruise one when I had alone time in front of the mirror.

"Thanks, Lia." I tried to pour all my gratitude into it, even as I dabbed my wrist. It was healing fairly well, but the cream sure did feel nice.

"Of course. Now, to business. Sorry you were left in the dark. We just couldn't tell you anything before the whole trial thing, you know? Now that it's over-"

I cut her off, slightly turning my head and getting my hair pulled by the brush in the process. "Wait, it's over? Like, over over? I thought I had to go through another trial judgement thing, but with Westen acting as my lawyer advocate or something."

She waved her hand dismissively and went back to brushing. "Nah. Once he was appointed as your advocate, it's all on him now. He'll have to do a few things, but I bet it'll just disappear like most things, especially since there's something big going on. Westen won, and Mother knows it."

"What's going on?"

"No idea." Her voice sounded like she'd rolled her eyes while saying it.

She put down the brush, stating, "All done!" and promptly flopped down onto the bed, taking the pillow.

I scooted around until I leaned up against the wall. Pretty comfy bed, at least. "Ya... so, your mother..."

She propped her feet up on my lap once I'd settled. "Oh, don't I know it. Sorry about all that. We really were doing our best to get you out. Well, Westen was, when he was here. I wasn't allowed to do anything, same as always." She let out a dramatic sigh.

I frowned. "He left? Where'd he go?"

Lia focused on me with a look that seemed scared. No, not quite scared, but something close.

"He had to go get my warden dad, David, when he showed up in Washington. Westen's his commanding officer type person, so he had to go get him and check it out. It didn't take too long to get there and back, less than a day, but I haven't been able to see David yet. Faelen's orders. She doesn't like how close I am to them."

"That's stupid. And sucks. Sorry."

She went back to staring at things aimlessly. "Ya. No word on Jeanette yet, but it's been so long, she should have checked in by now. Westen keeps me updated."

I didn't know what to say. Obviously, it meant she was probably captured or dead, neither of which were happy scenarios. "I'm sorry," was all I could say. So lame, but I tried to make sound as honest as possible, since it was.

Her nose tinged pink and she sniffled. "Ya, it's ok. Just frustrating, you know? Anyway, I couldn't really do anything to help you but stay out of the way. Mother gets pissy when I push things, but she has to listen to Westen."

"Why's that?"

"Because he's an adult and third in control of our house, just behind dear old mummy and daddy. I'm always "too young to understand the implications" and dumb stuff like that."

"But, you're almost an adult."

Lia rolled her eyes. "For humans. I won't be an adult for like, a hundred and thirty more years. We are considered mature enough to start participating in things when we're about a hundred though, so just over eighty-two more years for me! Wahoo..."

It sure didn't sound like a happy wahoo and I was pretty sure my face showed how dumbstruck I was. Lia shoved me with one of her feet.

"Don't get like that. You're the only normal person I know, that can't change or I'll flip out on you."

I gave her smile. "And do what? Blow me up like at the lake?"

"Exactly. I could blow you through a wall. You don't know."

I patted her leg on my lap. "Don't worry. Westen will always creep me out more. He's ancient."

She sighed. "Ya, I wonder what he was like as a kid. I've only ever known him as an adult. He grew up in the eighteen-hundreds. Can you imagine?" Lia's eyes went wide, and she shook her head at nothing. "When he went to live in the human world, they used horses. They sent him to cities all over the country. He even stayed at a farm once."

I shook my head. "He doesn't sound like he's from then. I mean, he can be a bit stuffy at times. But, not like that."

Suddenly, I remembered a whole slew of times Lia and I teased him for saying outdated things. He always just shrugged it off, like my English teacher who didn't care about misspelling a word on the board, but we loved to pounce on the mistake anyway.

"It's amazing he keeps up with modern language the way he does. I think he does it for me, and he studies for it too. Reads my books, watches movies and shows and stuff. He takes notes." She gave me her I'm-dead-serious face. "Like, literally takes notes on how they're speaking. Words, tone, delivery style, everything. It's crazy."

My eyebrows were properly raised in appreciation. "That's quite the dedication."

She giggled. "Ya. I have to correct him on some things, but he's pretty good. It also helps he works with the human sqauds and guards and such. Helps him pick it up naturally, I suppose. My parents try somewhat, but they're not nearly as good at it."

"I noticed some really weird things. I just figured it was them using kingly and queenly speech."

"That's probably part of it. They do talk to modern people like Westen does a bit." She paused, then shook her head. "Man, my life is so weird and messed up."

I nodded emphatically. "Totally."

"Ha!"

"But mine is too, so that's cool."

"Ya, we're both messed up."

I thunked my head back on the wall with a sardonic smile on my lips. "Yay, us."

We went into contemplative silence for a moment, and my mind went back to where I'd been the past however many days. I traced the flower design on the cover, lightly distracting myself. "So, uh, how long was I down there?"

She sat up, looking horribly guilty again, and fiddled with her skirt. "Over two days."

"Huh, I was right. Mostly. How come I'm not dying of hunger or falling asleep standing? I mean, I got a nap in there, but..."

She shrugged. "I think it has something to do with the magic they use down there. I don't really know much about it, but I do know they don't have to use it, and Westen made them so you wouldn't feel it. Mother was so mad when he interfered, it was right after they brought you in. Oh, that reminds me, Brielle should be arriving with lunch any minute now. I sent her down as soon as I heard the trial was done."

"How did you hear that? We came right when it finished. Did we take the long way 'round or something?"

Lia laughed. "No, I used my sprites."

"You have pet sprites?"

"Kind of. They're more self-aware and intelligent then a dog or cat or something would be. Like, I can talk to them, but it has to be simple. If you get too complicated, they either don't understand or ignore you, sometimes it's hard to tell. Anyway, they choose where they want to be and they often choose to be with me because I'm so perfectly awesome." She smiled her sweet, cute, love-me smile and struck a pose. I laughed at her.

"And humble. Hey, did you send one to check on me in the cell thing?"

She gave me a sly look, which confirmed my suspicions. That warmed me a bit, that she hadn't totally left me alone.

"I could or would never send a sprite into a situation that would compromise Firehold's security."

"Ha! Right." I looked around the room, not seeing any. Well, unless they were pink and hiding among the various hues. "Where are they?"

"In the gardens mostly, they have a big tree they've infested, but they come visit my room all the time. Sometimes I call on them when I want some cute fuzzies. Most people around here find them annoying, so it helps keep visitors down, which is nice."

"Where is your room?" I was worried I'd be stuck in this pink monstrosity all by myself for who knows how long. Westen hadn't said "until I get things settled" or "figured out" or anything like that. I had to assume that while I was here, I was going to be under room arrest.

Lia sat up, pushing her feet into my legs to do so.

"Ow."

"Sorry, I forgot you don't know anything."

"Gee, thanks."

She swatted my arm. "You know what I mean. Ok."

She folded her legs into herself and sat up, like she does when about to do some serious gossiping. "So, this is my wing floor. Everything from the stairs on. My current room used to be my playroom, but when I outgrew needing a playroom I took it. It's at the end of the hall, and it's way awesome. You'll see. This room just kinda stayed the same." She shrugged. "But, Brielle is at the stairs, and there's a bathroom, a classroom," she made a yuck face, "and a mini-library that goes with it."

I nodded to let her know I got it.

"You should be fine as long as you're here, but if you see anyone, it'd be best if you came and got me or Brielle, or locked yourself in your room."

"Do you really think I'll need to?"

She made a sour face. "You can't really trust anyone, besides us, I mean. It's very political around here. We have people working here from all over the world, kind of like ambassadors, but not as official. Everyone knows they all spy on each other, but there's nothing we can do about it except be careful and try to outsmart them. That's most of what they make me learn in that stupid classroom. Ya, every summer you got to relax and do nothing, well I had to freaking go to dragon court school!"

I laughed. "Oh, no, not dragon court school. However did you manage?"

She shoved me, but I was pretty stable against the wall so I just slid back on it a bit.

"Some friend you are. And this time, you'd think

they'd let me recuperate after almost being abducted, but nooooooo, it's right back into lessons. I never get a vacation."

I exaggeratedly rolled my eyes. "Ya, 'cause staying with the Millers was a vacation."

"You didn't have to do lessons every summer, did you? And you got to vacation during your trip up at the cabin, didn't you? You got coffee and doughnuts and everything."

Ok, obviously Westen had told her what happened, and then Lia decided to fill in the blanks with a nice time.

"Ya, some vacation. Freezing, getting questioned by warlocks, passing out, so hungry I could gnaw on my arm, bruises up my backside from falling down a hill. Getting food from kind Canadians who thought I'd been lost in the woods all night." I closed my eyes, pretending to enjoy the memories, a grin on my face. "Ah, such a great vacation, running scared and not knowing what's become of my life."

"What were the warlocks like?" she asked, just above a whisper.

"Old white guy in charge, crazy torture lady, younger guy who shot electricity up my leg. The old guy got away." I picked at a spot in the blanket, pulling a thread until it broke.

Lia hugged me until I patted her off. I tried a smile, and gave up half-way through.

"It's ok," I sniffed. "Westen came and got me out."

"He promised he would."

I nodded. "Ya, but something could have happened. So, I think I've proved it was not, indeed, a vacation."

"Ok, fine," she drew out the word for exaggeration that made me chuckle. "But I still get squat. Anyway, as I was explaining to you, you pleb... Outside this hall I'd have to get you a map, because it all gets very complicated. Westen's quarters aren't too far, just a few stairs and halls away. My parents are up in the north wing. This fort holds everything, though. It's like a mini-city."

"Does it have Starbucks?" That made her snort, which made me point and laugh. "Hah! You snorted!"

Lia took on a dignified stance. "Did not. And no, no Starbucks, but the kitchen can make any kind of mocha or frap you want. They are the bomb. Just wait till lunch gets here." She sprouted a wicked looking grin. "I even go there sometimes to get out of meetings and things. There's a couple of workers who hide me and give me samples of whatever they're making. It's great. Don't you dare tell Brielle!"

I gave a prompt nod and made a cross over my heart with my finger. "Promise."

She looked at the door, as if Brielle would be magically summoned by her speaking of how great the food was and how she ditched her responsibilities there.

"Hey, Lia, what is the Orindrae and Feela-"

"Ugh, Faela. That's me. It basically translates to Lady Daughter, or Ruler Daughter, something like that. Orindrae is our sacred dragon law we have to follow or risk punishment by the big bad dragon ruler guys out in Europe known as the Dreki Order. They enforce the Orindrae for dragons all over the world. Well, except in Asia. They have their own thing going on."

I was betting the big bad dragon ruler guys, multiple ones, were a lot more scary than she was making them out to be. In fact, just knowing there dragons her parents had to follow made them seem even more big bad.

I shook my head lightly, admonishing myself. It's not like I'd ever have a reason to go to Europe to meet them, and I doubted they'd come out here for me, or even knew I existed. Probably. So, I made myself stop getting anxious about things that weren't even an issue, and stay focused on the ones already here, like Lia's mother.

"If Faela is Lady Daughter, is Faelen just your mom? Like Lady Mother or something?"

"It's closer to Lady Ruler. Domett is my dad, Lord Ruler, and Domen is Westen, Lord Son. They're our fancy titles." She pretended to fan her face and I was half-expecting her to end it with a "dahling" at the end.

I pulled up my knees and put my head on them. "Huh, they seemed so much more grand when they kept calling each other that in the trial. I thought it was some kind of special title."

"It kind of is, though. Whenever we're in our official capacities we *have* to use our titles." She gave a deprecating look. "Half the time I don't even think of my parents as Mother or Father, but Faelen and Domett. I'm pathetic."

"Hey, you're not pathetic. You're not!" I re-empha-sized due to her reply mocking face.

Lia started fiddling with her skirt in her lap, twisting it up and letting it fall back. "I'm, umm, sorry I didn't tell you about any of this before, you know..."

"Ya, I know."

I tried to put sincerity in my voice, because I really did get it, even if it still hurt. But she still looked depressed, so I moved over and hugged her. She hugged me back and I smiled.

"I do get it, you know. Probably some giant Orindrae law about not spilling dragon secrets."

She chuckled, but it wasn't happy sounding. "Exactly."

"I just need some time to adjust to everything. It's a lot, you know?"

"Ya..."

There, she looked sad again. *Great job, Dani,* I thought sarcastically. I knew what she needed. Some good ol' silly diversion. I pulled back and eyed her critically up and down, until she said, "What?"

"Am I crazy, or is your skin more glowy than usual? I mean, I know you have the golden skin of a goddess, but this seems a bit much."

She held up her arm in one of the last rays of sun coming in from the window before it set and I swear her skin nearly shimmered.

"I think it has to do with me being home, like in the family's power or something. It makes my power kind of manifest, but I can't do anything with it, so I just kind of glimmer sometimes."

"How come Westen doesn't glimmer?" I smirked at the thought of him being sparkly like some kind of new agey vampire.

"'Cause he can control and use his power." She sounded mockingly resentful. "He doesn't have to deal with flares and stupid stuff like that."

"Flares?"

"Ya, kind of like at the lake, but on a much smaller scale."

A knock sounded at the door and Lia popped up. "The food!" Sure enough, she opened the door to Brielle, carrying a tray with two people following, one carrying two trays and the second carrying what turned out to be a fancy looking folding type of table.

One of the guys looked white as could be, and the other seemed to be Latino. The nationalities were a question I'd have to remember to ask Lia about, in a more appropriate time. I'd seen various people, on the grounds, the interrogators, the guards, etc., that seemed to come from all over. Why and how did they get workers from all over the world to come to their fort in Alaska, of all places? She said they had ambassador types, did she just mean a common worker? Like, would they really send a food server?

"Faela," Brielle spoke seriously, and nodded to her as she entered.

The others kept quiet and set up with efficiency. I expected Lia to start prattling about things to me or Brielle, but she just stood demurely by, watching our lunch being set up.

"Thank you, Stephan, Brent," Lia spoke very formally, giving a head nod to the helpers. "Brielle, please remain."

"Of course, my Lady." Brielle went and shut the door behind the two after they left.

Then Lia returned to normal. She hopped up to the table and removed the tray lids. "Oh, yummy! Yes! Dessert!"

Brielle smiled. "I told them it was for you and a friend."

Lia clapped like a little kid. "And they totally gave me the hookup! Here, Dani, you've got to try this chocolate cake ball thingy. It's sooooo delicious."

She practically shoved it in my mouth, but darn was she right.

"Wow," I finally managed to say, after chewing and swallowing some of it.

"I told you, our cooks are *amazing!* Here, have one of the sandwiches. They put magic in it, I swear."

I sniffed at the one she handed me. It seemed like some kind of chicken or tuna salad mix, but when I bit it, it had some crunchy yummy nutty things, and some sweet type of fruit, and it all totally worked. I made yum noises and nodded my approval so I didn't have to speak since Lia was obviously waiting for my response.

Lia's smile widened. "Told you. Hey, Brielle, eat."

Brielle took a sandwich and obediently bit into it. "Any new information from the hive?"

Brielle shook her head. "No, everyone's still talking about the human girl Westen brought and trying to figure out who she is. No one really knows anything."

Lia saw my face as I took in that I was castle gossip.

"Don't worry, like she said, no one knows anything." I know Lia was trying to comfort me, but it didn't.

Brielle continued, "You should hear some of the conspiracy theories."

Lia gave an appropriate, "Oooh!"

"Like how Westen kidnapped her, or that she's a warlock, or a witch, or that the she's a plant from one of the Eastern factions."

They both laughed, but for some reason, I didn't feel like laughing along with them. I wasn't comfortable being what everyone was talking about, much less having people think I was an evil guy or a plant. I hadn't liked being the gossip in our small town where everyone knew everyone, much less being talked about here where I didn't know anyone and couldn't tell my side of it or confront people. I couldn't even leave this hallway. I had no way of knowing what some random castle person would do when they saw me, so even if I wanted to sneak around the castle or take a tour, I couldn't.

And just like that, I felt trapped. Again.

CHAPTER

15

Feeling trapped didn't stop me from eating, though.

We had some nice, mindless chit chat after that, which helped settle me down a bit, and Brielle actually answered my questions, but I did keep them pretty light in content. I found out that she was twenty-six years old and had been raised at Firehold; her father worked with the horses and her mother was in the guard too, though much higher up. She'd been in training for her job since she was a child, and had been assigned to Lia for five years. She seemed really chill, and Lia obviously liked and trusted her.

"It's late, Princess, you should get going." Lia groaned loudly, but Brielle continued her point. "You have lessons early in the morning that you won't be excused from, no matter how much you whine about being tired."

Brielle came over and pulled on Lia's arm, who was

doing a deadweight resistance, so Brielle pulled her arm, making her slide on the bed, rumpling up the blankets as she went.

"I don't wanna!"

Brielle dropped her arm, letting it thump on the bed. "Fine, you deal with Instructor Wilson. Seven am, don't be late or he'll make you copy the dictionary again. I'll send someone up to collect our dishes. Bye Dani, it was nice meeting you."

"Same." I was a little astonished to find I meant it. She was growing on me.

She paused at the door, then looked at me, all seriousness. "Stay in this hall. Don't go with anyone. I'm the door right at the stairs if you need anything."

I felt suddenly somber. "Right. Thanks."

"Spoil sport," Lia snarked as the door closed. As soon as it was closed she sat up on the bed and popped a chocolate ball in her mouth. "She's right. I do need to get going to bed."

I tried to swallow, but my mouth had gone dry, so I nodded. "No worries."

"Did you, uh... want to have a sleep over in my room?"

I eyed her. Was this pity? "You sure?"

She threw the pillow at me, which I neatly caught and put it into my lap, giving me something to fidget with.

"Of course I'm sure. These past few days have really sucked. Besides, it'd be like we were back home. I've got this couch in there, it's small but cushy. I mean, if you want to. I totally get it if you'd rather sleep in the bed or be by yourself."

She was giving me an easy out, but I could tell she was being genuine. I just had to figure out if I wanted to be alone or not. I mean, it seemed obvious I shouldn't want to be alone after all the isolation I'd just gone through, but a small part of me wanted to push her out and curl up on the bed. That was a small part though.

"No, I'd really like the sleepover. If it's cool."

"Duh, that's why I offered. Come on." Lia grinned and hopped off the bed, grabbing my arm to pull me along. "Just leave the door open so the servants don't have to worry about knocking or whatever to get the trays. Oh, this door is the classroom, boo. And here's my room."

It was the end room of the hall, the door opening to the hallway itself, and it was a really big room. Easily as big as the Miller's living room. No wonder she had a couch in there.

I gave an appreciative whistle as she pulled me in.

"Remember I said it used to be the play room? Anyway, welcome to my abode." She walked over to her bed, which was a canopy bed, but not the cheesy, over-the-top type. It looked quaint, especially in the cool blue tones. She did presentation arms, like Vanna White. "And here's my illustrious bed. There's the closet wall, and yes, it's full of my junk. My personal bookcase, not full of stupid school books, you'll notice." I figured it had novels, but it also had some pictures, one I could see of us as kids, and a Wish Bear I'd given her for one of her birthdays.

"Hey, get out of there! You better not be nesting in my books again!" She was making shooing motions at the bookcase and I saw three fuzzballs zoom out: orange, green and grey. I heard high pitched twittering, which I assumed was laughter. They flitted around her head as she play batted at them, then they sped out the open window.

She followed them, kneeling on the couch just under the window to look out at their departing forms. I joined her. Their colors dropped out of sight around one of the castles edges. "They're probably going to their tree for the night. It's over there and sprites don't usually do anything once it gets fully dark. Here's your "bed" by the way." She air-quoted, shut the window, then spun around and plopped down in the couch we'd been kneeling on. "See, isn't it totally comfy?"

I followed suit. It was a nice sinking kind of cushion. "Mmhmm."

"Oh, I'll get you some blankets and a pillow." She popped right back up again. The girl had boundless energy.

"It's nice to see you didn't make your new bedroom all one color," I joked as she threw a blanket out of her closet to land behind her as she continued to scrounge around. The room had neutral blue and grey tones throughout, with pops of turquoise, like the inner window lining and the couch pillow I was sitting on. It actually looked pretty sophisticated overall, like something you'd see on one of those home makeover shows.

"Ya, I got to do what I wanted, which never happens outside of my rooms." Her voice was muffled into the closet. "Here! A real pillow." She grabbed up her stuff and hauled it all over, throwing it on top of my face.

"Gee, thanks," I said monotone, dragging them off as she closed the window curtains behind me. There were two blankets and one pillow, all super soft and very inviting feeling. Living in a castle apparently had some perks. "What time is it, anyway?" I asked as we made spread out the blanket over the cushions.

She glanced back toward her bed, where I supposed her clock was kept, not that I saw it, but I hadn't been particularly looking for it.

"Uhhh, almost ten."

"No way! Really?" I looked at the window, seeing the last of the sunlight fading.

"Ya, the sun sets late up here. That's why Brielle was telling me to go to bed. It's so not fair that I still have to go to lessons!" She melodramatically collapsed onto the couch once we'd finished. She even had an arm over her eyes.

I sat down next to her and took the opportunity to poke her armpit, making her jump and exclaim, "Hey!"

"You are super cranky if you don't get your full night's beauty sleep, and if your lessons are at seven, how early do you have to wake up for it? Six? Five thirty?

You barely have enough time to get your rest in if you passed out right now."

She grinned. "I know, right? I get up at six, by the way. Have fun with that." She slapped my knee as she got up.

"Oh, I will," I called to her retreating back. "I'll just go back to sleep while you're in school."

Lia turned her head around to stick out her tongue as she got to her dresser. "Here, meany-head." She tossed me some sweats that were probably a bit oversized on her, but would fit me nicely for bedtime.

We changed and I got settled into the couch as Lia turned off the lights. There was enough ambient light coming through the window I could still see everything. The suffocating fears I'd been working against were creeping their way back into me without talking and moving around to distract me from them.

"Hey, Lia?"

"Ya."

I fiddled with my top blanket, adjusted it to settle over my shoulder. "What's going to happen?"

She shifted in her bed. "I don't know."

Well, that was comforting, I thought sarcastically, then admonished myself because she was just being honest.

"I mean," she continued, sounding thoughtful, "Westen will get you out of trouble, and then, I don't know. I guess you'll go off to college. For me, this has always been it. You were the only one that ever gave me anything different to look forward to, and now that I can't go to Flathead Valley... I guess, I'll just have to do dragon duty full time."

"That sucks," I commiserated. "Can't you go to college somewhere else? Somewhere you've never been?"

"Maybe... I doubt it though. After they came after me, I don't think dear old mummy or daddy will let me go anywhere."

"You can always ask. Make up some kind of presentation on the benefits of attending a human college." Her parents seemed like people who loved logical reasons over emotional ones, so I figured that was her best bet.

Her eyes seemed to agree as they lit up just a bit. "Ya, that could work. They could get me into anywhere they wanted, so I can point that out. I'd even let them pick. Then you can come and join me wherever it is!"

She made it sound like a given that Westen would get me off the hook and I'd go on with my life, but honestly, what college? Where? I hadn't applied anywhere else, and if they knew she and I were friends, wouldn't the warlock people just find me no matter where I went?

"We'd probably have to change our last names. How do I even do that? Would your parents pay to have my identity changed?" That was an interesting thought, not necessarily bad, but daunting.

"I honestly don't know, Dani. Look, we'll talk to Westen about it tomorrow and get some kind of plans set up, and some back up plans and all that." She settled back into her bed, then spoke quietly. "If I'm not allowed to go to college, maybe you could stay here, you know, if you wanted. Get a job working with us?"

She made me smile at the quiet earnestness I could hear.

"I bet your mother would just *loooove* that."

Lia laughed. "Wouldn't she?"

"I'd take any job I could."

"Poop scooper?"

"Ew."

Lia's laugh lifted my mood.

"Ok, your highness, we'll talk about it tomorrow. Now go to sleep."

"Alright, fine." But I could tell she said it with a smile. "Night, Dani."

"Good night."

Like every sleepover we'd ever had growing up, Lia fell asleep rather quickly and I sat there, rotating myself every ten to fifteen minutes or so until I could drift off.

I woke up suddenly, startled as the door opened. I bolted up, trying to orient my sleepy brain on what was going on. There was a dark figure standing in Lia's bedroom door.

The figure stepped into the room, going toward Lia's bed and my heart rate shot up until I could feel it pulsing in my neck. What should I do? Jump up and try to scare them? Keep quiet because I had no idea who it was or what they wanted and this could be a perfectly normal thing Lia has happen? In her room... at night...

"Kalia, get up," the figure said, and I immediately

calmed down. I knew who it was just before he switched on the light.

I scowled, at him and the light. "Jeez, Westen, what are you doing here at... what time is it?" I looked at the window and light was barely creeping in. It was before sunrise.

He turned, obviously startled by my outburst as Lia made waking-up protest noises.

"Daniella, I wish you weren't here."

I felt slapped almost, and didn't know how to take it, so it took me a moment to formulate my response. Should I say, "Same to you," "Gee, thanks," or just a good old "Screw you"?

I settled with sneering, "Nice to see you, too, Westen." He did save me yesterday, after all. I felt very gracious for my sleep interrupted response, no matter it being snide.

Lia was sitting up. "Whaaaaat? I don't have to get up for over a half-hour."

Westen turned away from me and enveloped Lia in a hug before I could blink. "Janette's dead."

She let out a sob and I saw her clutch at him. Tears sprang to my eyes and I automatically went to get up, but Westen turned and held a hand out, pointing me back to the couch. I still wanted to get up and my muscles strained holding me in an awkward half up position.

"No, you need to stay there. You'll be seen by the guards if you go to your room, so you might as well stay, but it'll be better if you're over there. With no reactions, if you can."

I slowly sat back down, wanting desperately to console my best friend, even if I didn't know what was going on outside of Lia losing her caretaker mother.

Mrs. Thompson, you were so kind to me... I clenched my feelings down and wiped at my eyes.

"Westen," I spoke quietly, "what's going on?"

He pulled back from the hug and made Lia look at him. "They're coming. You know what that means. Are you ready?"

I heard Lia's quiet sobs stall as she slowly stood up, Westen moving with her. He helped her stand, then wiped her face.

"Control it," he spoke quietly, but in a command sort of way. Lia nodded and I saw her shudder then stiffen, raising her head. "Good."

Then he took off his tear stained over shirt leaving a thin undershirt on and threw it in the open closet. They both walked forward toward the door, like moving statues. Lia had a few more shudders, but she visibly stopped them while walking barefoot forward.

He took a quick look at me. "Don't say anything, please."

I had no freaking idea what was going on, but I wasn't going to do anything to mess whatever this was up. I could tell it was serious, not just by the fact that Janette had died, but because Lia, who I knew loved that woman, was doing her best to act like an emotionless drone, something she'd never done before that I'd seen. I didn't know she could hold back her feelings, she usually let them all hang out. I'd teased her about it, but she'd always say something like, "Why hide who you are? If people don't like it, screw 'em." But here she was, holding it all in as much as she could, and doing a fairly decent job of it.

Actually, she was acting like Westen did a lot. All shut in. Nothing showing.

We heard footsteps a few moments later, coming from all the way down the hall. They seemed to take forever. I slunk into my blankets on the couch, lying down to try and be as unobservable as possible without covering my head to make it obvious I was trying not to be seen. Westen dropped Lia's hand just before the footsteps reached the room. They stood nearly a foot apart then, both placidly facing their parents as they entered.

"Father, Mother." Westen gave a short bow. "I woke Kalia for your arrival."

"As I can see." Their mother really was a negative, mean lady. She sounded irritated.

Her father stepped forward, toward Lia. "Kalia, daughter, your warden Janette Thompson's body was finally found. She died not far from the home, in the woods surrounding the property."

Lia still had a small reaction, but it was small. It took a couple of tries for her to work her mouth properly. "I see. That is unfortunate. She was excellent as a warden." Lia was doing her best to be unemotional, but I could see her shoulders shake occasionally and her nose had turned bright red. "Did the warlocks kill her?"

A curt nod from her mother, while her father said a simple, "Yes."

They'd killed Mrs. Thompson... I thought of the still forms lying in the forest, one reaching out an arm, the other with acid smoke drifting from her head, and I was suddenly glad. I was glad Westen killed them when they'd killed Mrs. Thompson, one of the few people in my life I cared about, who was kind and generous and didn't deserve to die.

Lia's mother and father seemed to be studying her a bit much, and they gave no move to comfort her. And I thought my relationship with my foster parents was strained, but this was ridiculously unreal. No wonder Westen was so closed off all the time. He had to be with parents like this, bosses he had to constantly report to and apparently never show any emotion towards. Why? Did they find it a weakness? That's what I was betting.

I felt a huge wave of pity toward Lia and Westen, something I haven't really felt for them before, because they'd always had it all in my eyes. But now...

"Yes, she will be missed," her mother said, not sounding the least bit truthful. "We knew how much you regarded her, so we thought we would tell you personally straight away."

Lia gave a head bow. "Thank you, Mother. Father. Is there anything else?"

"Yes." Her mother shot a glance at me. Busted. "What is she doing here? Why is she not in the south wing?"

The king swung around to look at me. Apparently, he

hadn't noticed me at all. Not that it made him happy or anything. He was frowning slightly, looking in thought. Go look somewhere else with your thoughts creepy, powerful old man who could kill me whenever he chose to.

Westen spoke up before Lia could. "Since we established at the judgement that Kalia and my accounts held, I saw no need as her advocate to isolate her further. Kalia and she have had a friendship spanning nearly a decade. I felt it would ease the transition and aid in cooperation if she stayed in Kalia's empty guestroom."

The queen pointed at me and I felt the weight of it. I shrunk back in the couch cushion a bit, not at all comfortable being under her scrutiny.

"She is *staying* right there, as you can see."

"I asked her to sleep on my couch as a gesture of kindness, towards her continued cooperation." Lia impressed me with her political lie of an answer. They must teach it to everyone here. Her voice, however, sounded very small and she looked to her father even though she had been talking to her mother. "Was that wrong?"

"Not wrong, little one, but..." Her father seemed to want to admonish her, but couldn't bring himself to.

Her mother did not have the same compunctions. "But it is inappropriate and unorthodox. It will not happen again."

Lia bowed her head again. "Yes, Mother."

"Elbrel, Westen, come. We will call the counselors to meet early today." She turned to Lia sharply. "Do not be late for your lessons."

"Yes, Mother."

The queen swept out, the king following in her wake. Westen hung behind long enough to squeeze Lia's hand when they couldn't see, but I noticed. He nodded at me as he left, and I just didn't know how to take it. Seeing them interact with their parents, it was really informative. Terribly sad on so many levels, but enlightening.

Once the door was shut, I shot up and ran over to her. She hugged me so tight I thought I'd get new bruises, but I didn't care. Not making hardly any noise, she cried into my shoulder and I did my best to comfort her as the sun started to rise.

After ten or so minutes, she started to pull back. Her cheeks and nose were red, but the kind of crying red that made her look pretty and innocent, like a Disney princess. I smiled at her, fixing her hair as I reminded myself that she was indeed a princess, so her looking like one made sense.

"Sorry," she hiccupped, running the back of her hand over her nose, which was not so princess like. I dutifully ignored the light slime trail she'd made and kept rubbing her upper arm, trying to give what little comfort I could.

"Don't," I said softly, but firmly. "There's no reason to be sorry. Mrs. Thompson was amazing, and I know she loved you."

This made Lia cry some more, but she stood there, wiping at the tears instead of diving into my shoulder again. She tried to talk a few times, and didn't make it, so I hugged her close again until she got over it.

The next time she pulled back, she seemed more determined. "I'm ok." I gave her a sympathetic look. "I'll be ok," she amended. "I'm just going to go shower."

"Are you sure? Couldn't you take a few days..."

Lia was already shaking her head, so I drifted off.

"My parents would never allow it," she explained. "That's why Westen came in to warn me, so I could prepare myself. They would have been upset if I'd reacted too much to her..."

Death, I thought, finishing her sentence without giving voice to it. She suddenly stepped away, going to her closet.

"I'm sorry, Lia." I tried to keep my voice soft, but I couldn't fully. "That's beyond stupid. Mrs. Thompson was amazing, and she took really good care of you."

I saw her shrug as she pulled out some clothes, but I could hear her quietly sobbing as she did so.

When she spoke, her voice was thick and warbled at points. "They don't like us getting close to humans. I wasn't supposed to stay with them for so long, but I kept going back there and they couldn't change my fake parents every year when I was living in the same place, so I got to stay with them. I think it made Mother jealous."

No wonder her mother hated me. Not only was I her daughter's friend and the reason she kept going back to Janesville, but apparently the reason her daughter got a pair of human parents that actually seemed to care about her.

Lia was staring at the clothes in her hands. I walked

over and gave her a side hug, rubbing her back as I did. She leaned into me for a moment.

"Thanks." Suddenly, her head popped up. "Oh, no! David." She took a step toward the door, then stopped, looking conflicted.

"What?"

"He must be devastated. They were really married." Tears ran freely down her cheeks to drip beneath her chin. "They got married when I was eleven. I think it was because they were together so much watching me, you know? And they fit so well together acting as my parents. They loved each other so much…"

And the hits keep coming. Ouch.

"I could tell they loved each other, Lia, and you. The real kind of love that stays strong." Not like my foster parents who were basically roommates at this point, but she didn't need the comparison, so I left it out.

She grimaced and angrily wiped at her face. "I want to see him, but I bet my parents are watching for that. It'll just get him in trouble."

"Hey, hey, hey," I soothed, trying to help. "We'll talk to Westen, okay? Maybe he can get you in to visit, or maybe make up an official meeting somehow. I'm sure he would." And for some reason, despite the past few days, or because of it, I knew he would.

Her eyes were staring off, but she nodded. "Ya, that could work. I'll send Brielle before Instructor Wilson shows up."

"Are you sure you have to go to class?"

She gave a curt nod, and I dropped it. She was steeling herself up again, and I didn't want to bring her back to tears by questioning the cruelty of making one go to something as trivial as lessons when you found out a person you loved had died. I guess her parents would get mad if she skipped for being sad over a mere human they didn't want her to be close to in the first place. Man, the more I learned about them, the more sucky they were.

Lia straightened her shoulders, clenched her jaw, and went to the bathroom. I walked her there, then took hold of the door behind her.

"I'll be just in my room if you need."

She nodded, clutching at the clothes she'd change into. "Thanks, Dani. I know everything is all sorts of messed up, but I'm glad you're here."

"I am, too. Now, go soak in that hot water and feel better."

Lia gave a small, but genuine smile.

I shut the door for her, stayed a second longer feeling bad, then turned and went to my room, the pink monstrosity. I had a small gift of my old clothes being folded and placed on top of my dresser. Brielle had said she'd have them washed for me. I put them away slowly. I wasn't sure what I should do, or even what I could do, so I just went and rifled through things while my brain wandered.

I liked the Thompsons a lot, and I felt very bad that the mother had died, but I wasn't devastated. I had a hard time imagining that. My own mother had died when I was so young, it didn't really register as a pain, more as a sad regretful memory. I'd never known my dad, and never had any siblings. If one or both of my foster parents died, I'd feel sorry, but it would be more of a "Gee, that sucks" than anything else. I just wasn't attached to them, nor them to me. I bet if I died, they'd be more sad about the foster money going away.

I paused as I looked through the small assortment of jackets and two pretty dresses (Lia probably couldn't help herself giving me at least a couple of girly to wear) in the closet. I'd been gone for going on a week now. Had they missed me? Did they call the cops or family services about my absence? Had they even tried to call my phone, which was in the treehouse, if the treehouse was even still there? Or, did they assume I went up in flames with Lia's house. Probably that one. I wondered if they felt bad at all. I doubted they cried, which didn't bother me, I was more curious than anything.

The only person who would truly shatter me if they died was Lia. But, even with her being the only person I truly cared about, I was used to her leaving, and I'd been preparing myself for our adult parting of ways for over a year, assuming she wouldn't be going to college with me. I was pathetic. The only person I really loved and cared about, the only one I'd truly mourn, and here I was, logically figuring that I'd be completely fine after getting over the initial shock and sadness.

I laid down on the bed and stared at the ceiling, wondering if anyone I knew would truly be broken over my death. Lia would be sad, absolutely, but I'd just seen her react to her "mother's" death (and Mrs. Thompson was more of a mother than the queen was to her, I was sure of it). She'd taken that pain and swallowed it to do her duty, something I didn't know she was capable of. It was so at odds with how she acted when we were in school together. She'd always shown her feelings to anything we were doing. What else didn't I know about her?

I sort of hated myself for all these thoughts. I knew Lia was in pain, and that she'd be grieving for a long time, and she might get to express those feelings at a later time, but in my quiet pink solitude, I couldn't help but think these things, no matter how horrible they were.

I blew out a breath. It wouldn't really matter if I died. Lia would swallow it and get on with her princessy dragony life, and no one else would care. So, what did my life matter at all? College, degrees, jobs, any of it?

Vaguely I wondered why I wasn't breaking down right now, bawling into my borrowed pillow, but I think my mind and body had just gone through so much recently it kind of shut down a little bit.

A knock at the door startled me so badly I felt my blood race for a moment. Then I hopped up and went to answer, not wanting to call out so early in the morning. Plus, who would I be calling out to? Surely not Lia. Thoughts of requesting my advocate rang in my ears as I opened the door, but it was just a serving type guy holding a tray, one of the same ones who'd brought our food previously. What was his name? Brant? Brent? Brett? Something like that.

I said, "May I help you?" anyway, out of politeness.

He held out the tray. "Breakfast."

"Ah, thank you." I took it from him and he was off before I could do anything else.

Vaguely I wondered if there was something in my food. I hadn't worried last night because all of it had been prepared for Lia and I highly doubted anyone would poison their own princess, but this was made just for me. Considering the royal parents seemed to hate me, I wondered why I was being catered, but then I thought, maybe they just wanted to keep me confined and that meant sending the food to me. Probably that. Plus, they could have killed me plenty of times before now if they'd really wanted to.

I put the tray on the desk under the window and opened it up. Pretty simple fare of scrambled eggs, toast and a bottle of juice. After I'd eaten the breakfast, and selected my clothes for the day (more jeans and a teal colored long-sleeved plain shirt) and went to the bathroom. Lia was long gone. There was a guard at the stairs who watched my every move, but he didn't do anything else, so after a moment I decided to ignore him unless he spoke to me.

I looked toward Lia's room, but couldn't tell if the light was on. The classroom one was, and I went up to the door, but couldn't hear anything through it. Had

Lia's lessons already started? Should I leave her alone if they hadn't and she was in her room?

I decided that yes, I should leave her alone. If she'd wanted to see me, she knew where I was, I didn't want to push her if she wasn't ready.

The bathroom was nice, and I could easily see Lia's mark all over the vanity to the left. Make-up strewn over the counter, hairbrush full of hair, tampons rolled out of the box. It wasn't dirty or anything, she just filled all available space, like she'd done with her bathroom in Janesville. There was a sparse and clean sink, toilet, and a really nice shower/bath combo. I decided that I didn't care who wanted to come into the bathroom, I was using that tub for forty-five minutes at minimum.

As the water filled the tub, I took stock of myself in the large mirror. My bruises were starting to clear away, except for a really nice one on my back right hip. I hadn't been able to get a good view of it in my cell, but man was it a beauty of a shiner. It'd probably linger for another couple of weeks. My wrist looked decidedly better as well. I held it up to my cheek, to see which one looked more obvious. It was a toss-up.

When I got back to my room, I was going to have to use those lotions Lia got me. I brushed my hair out using one of Lia's brushes because I knew she wouldn't mind and I didn't have one, then climbed into a blissfully hot tub.

I soaked, I played with the water and tried to think of things to help Lia. Maybe I could go on a long walk or hike with her sometime, once everything was all settled. She always liked hiking in Montana.

After however long I took, I rinsed off and got dressed, then back to my room. I applied the lotions, taking my time rubbing them in, then looked around my room, seeing nothing new. Closet along the wall with the door, bed to the left next to window with a small desk, dresser to the right. Pink everywhere. Nothing to do.

I rifled through all the drawers and nooks and crannies. No books, or computers, and I didn't even have a phone. I worked out for a while to fill the time, pushups and sit-ups mostly, there wasn't really anything else I could do in the small space. I checked the hall a couple of times, but couldn't tell if Lia was in class or her room.

I really, really wanted to check out the classroom, but figured that would just get her or me in trouble. I thought about slipping into her room and borrowing some books to read. I knew she wouldn't mind, but it seemed rude, and if she was in there I didn't want to disturb her.

Eventually, I just laid down and rested. I was worried I might break down and cry if I thought about everything, but my body didn't seem to need that. Mostly, I was still tired, not having gotten enough sleep last night to make up for all the previous ones, and sleep was welcome.

There was a knock at the door some time later and I blinked my eyes awake. Gah, my cheek was cold where my drool had reached it in the pillow. Gross. I flipped the pillow over and went to the door, figuring it was lunch or something.

It was not.

CHAPTER

17

"Oh, uh, hi Westen. What's up?"

He was peering behind me at the empty room. "Is Kalia here?"

"No."

He looked agitated, which was a look on him that I knew fairly well. He had on the same black semi-formal type of outfit again. Did he only ever wear that one thing while he was here?

"Are you sure?"

I raised an eyebrow and stepped back, holding out my arm in silent invitation for him to check it out himself. Which he did, of course. All he had to do was take one big step inside to see the whole room, including the closet I'd left open.

"What's going on?" I was suddenly worried. "Is she missing?"

"In a manner of speaking. Her lessons ended hours

ago, and she typically visits me during training before she has to go to her afternoon duties. Also, she had Brielle ask me about setting up a meeting with David Thompson. Normally when she requests something of me she comes to follow up as soon as she can. Today, she did neither. I thought perhaps she was with you."

I hugged my arms to myself. I wanted to be sad she hadn't visited, but I mentally chided myself for being a child before that thought completed itself. She was grieving for goodness' sake. Worry swirled through my brain and I just hoped she was ok.

"Well, that's not good," I finally said, since he was just standing there. He frowned, which I suppose was his way of agreeing with me. I tried again. "Do you know where she could have gone? Like, maybe to talk to someone?"

"I'm was just thinking of that. She has several places she likes to go, but no people I know of beyond myself and Brielle."

"Makes sense. You should go find her, and, uh, let me know if she's ok, ya?"

"Domen," someone from the hallway said, very formally.

Westen turned his back to me to look at whoever had spoken. I moved over and peeked around his shoulder, seeing a fit little guy standing very rigidly. I waited for him to say something else, but he simply held out an envelope. And not the kind we plebeian humans would buy at the store, but one that seemed handcrafted down to the paper making itself. It even had a wax seal on it, but I couldn't make out the design from this far out. I was guessing a dragon.

Westen took the envelope and nodded at him, which apparently dismissed the deliverer, because he promptly left. I could hear his feet drumming down the stairs while I waited for Westen to read the letter and then do something, like leave and go look for Lia. Instead, he just stood there, staring at it.

I couldn't take it anymore. "So... good news? Bad news? Anything to do with Lia?"

He shook his head sharply, almost like a spasm. It was then I noticed how tense he was, muscle wise. He might rip the paper just by holding it, he was clutching so tightly on it.

"Hey, whoa, everything ok?" I edged around him and shut my door, staying between him and my door in the fairly small space. "What's going on?"

He looked up at me and I noticed his eyes were much more grey than blue, which was not a good sign in my experience. Neither was the intensity of his gaze or the grinding jaw. If it had been anyone else, I would have shrunk back against the door, but I knew him and I knew he wouldn't hurt me.

I'd known that since I'd been a highly bratty teen and in one fit of anger I'd cut his car's tires when he'd come to get Lia one summer. Not my finest hour. He'd been mad as I'd ever seen him get, and knew it was me, even then he didn't do anything but lecture me. Which worked, by the way. He'd made me feel so darn remorseful I'd never even considered doing something so rude or outright mean ever again to anyone.

Westen took a breath, obviously gathering himself. "It's nothing. Sorry if I bothered you."

Gee, thanks Mr. Robot, but I'm not buying.

"Come on, tell me. I promise I won't tell anyone." I did a mock X over my heart. "Not that I have anyone to tell, but I still promise that I won't."

He folded the letter precisely, taking time to crimp it, then tucked it into his front jacket shirt thing. What was it exactly? It was split up the middle, but with no discernable buttons or zipper, and the back blended in seamlessly with the front so you could barely tell there was an opening there to begin with. It looked ridiculously cool. I forced myself to ignore it, and focus on Westen. His taut face seemed to ease a bit, though I doubted he was even remotely close to cracking a smile.

"It's just new reporting orders, is all."

"Reporting for what?"

"As Domen, I'm in charge of overseeing the training and security at Firehold. These were orders from the Domett about changes needed for the upcoming days."

He was doing his upmost to play it off like it was nothing, but he wasn't fooling me. Like I didn't know it was direct orders from his dad about something he was internally furious about. I crossed my arms over my chest, giving him a stern look.

"And?"

"And nothing, Dani. That's all it is, new orders. I should go find Kalia."

I blinked. Was that the first time he'd used Dani while talking to me? And he was doing it to throw me off-balance, the jerk. Time for my own jaw to be clenched. I pushed past him, back into my pink realm.

"Fine, don't tell me. Keep everything bottled up like you always do. And don't!" I turned, jabbing my finger at him so he'd know how incredibly angry I was. "Don't use my name against me."

My eyes and throat felt tight. Stupid emotional self. This should not cause me to fight back tears, but with everything that had happened, it was just one more thing I couldn't quite seem to handle as well as I should. However, I would not let myself cry in front of Westen, so I clenched down, forcing myself to deal with it.

He gave me a nearly blank look, but he was turned toward me and not leaving. Last week, I was betting he would have just left.

"I was not using your name against you," he finally said after a few moments of me fuming.

"Ya right." I didn't feel I needed to explain further, and I kept glaring him down. We could have a glare off if he wanted. He may be two hundred years old, but I was a stubborn American seventeen year old.

Westen looked like he was winding himself up to argue with me, then he let out a sigh.

"You're infuriating."

"Thank you." And I meant it.

He stepped into my room a bit, just a few small steps, but it brought him into the space while he gathered himself.

"It is orders from my father about what I'm to do while he and the other draeden go after three of the warlocks' bases." He paused and I was about to ask him was a draeden was, but he just started rambling it all out on his own. Clearly, a dam had burst inside of him.

"It doesn't make logistical sense for them to go after these bases, as they're not even the headquarters of the warlocks, if they even have one. It's just three bases we happen to know about and taking them all out won't do anything substantial except show as a power move. I bet this was Garrin's idea. He's all about showing power regardless of the consequences, like chasing after minor warlocks and leaving Firehold with only two dragons and the human guard, which won't do much if a serious threat approaches while they're gone."

"Is that likely to happen?"

"No, but that doesn't mean it should be ignored."

I bobbed my head in acknowledgement as he was already pushing on.

"This whole affair has been off from the beginning, and this retaliation isn't any different. And as Domen, I should be leading this fight. It's my job. I'm the one in charge of Firehold's defenses, yes, but I am also the one in charge of the draeden, and have been for over half a century. The king and queen hold the stronghold while the fighters go out and deal with threats. That's how it's always done. And I know the warlocks. I've been fighting them for nearly a hundred years, and Father hasn't engaged in combat for almost that long. I should be the one leading a charge if there's to be one."

I gave Westen a moment to see if he'd start up again, but he just stared angrily out the window.

"So, he's punishing you for helping me, right?"

He whipped his head around toward me. I half-expected him to make an excuse of some kind, but he simply said, "Yes."

"Sorry." I was saying that a lot lately, and I meant every one.

"No, this is not your fault."

"Oh, I'm not taking fault, 'cause that's all on your parents, but I do sympathize. He shouldn't be punishing you like this, especially if you're the best person for the job. That's just cutting off your nose to spite your face."

I saw the corner of his mouth twitch.

"That's an old saying I haven't heard in quite a while."

I gave an obviously overdone nonchalant shrug. "I'm very well educated. The finest Montana public schooling has to offer."

"We shall have to write them a congratulatory letter."

I smiled. He was playing along to relieve the tension. I felt bad for him, but I couldn't help but feel relieved too. Not only would the king and queen be gone for however long this would take, but Westen would be here, and that was a positive.

"At least you'll be here for Lia. It probably won't make

up for being put in timeout, but I know she'll appreciate you being home. Especially after everything that's happened."

"Yes, that's true."

He seemed to be taking my words in seriously, which I appreciated. And then I remembered a crappy thing that could be an issue with the whole raid they were going on.

"So, Westen, with your father leaving and all, what does that do to my trial thing?"

"It's been postponed until he returns, but I don't want you to worry about that. We have truth on our side, and it will win out over fear and prejudice."

Hah, cause that's how the real world works.

He started turning toward the door and I remembered something else that I needed to know, and since I wasn't sure when I would see him again, even though this wasn't the best time, I needed to ask.

"Oh, just a quick question," I blurted out, not the smoothest transition I'd ever made. I took a breath and plunged on before I chickened out. "Back in Montana, what do the Miller's think happened? I mean, if you know?"

His demeanor seemed to sag a bit, even though he hadn't really moved, but I could tell and my emotions flip-flopped within me.

"I'm sorry, I thought Kalia had told you."

"It... We didn't talk about, I mean, it didn't really come up. Are they dead?"

I wasn't sure how I would actually react to that, but he was already shaking his head.

"No, they're fine. Nothing like that. It's just, they thought you were at the Thompson's house, and since it was destroyed in the fire along with your car-"

"They think I'm dead," I finished for him. I felt strangely calm, and empty somehow.

He nodded and I just stood there, trying to figure out how it made me feel. My body and mind didn't seem to know what to do. I was short-circuited.

"We had a team down there early the next morning. They put your car in the garage to solidify the story and got the official record to read it was a gas leak."

I heard him explaining the details, but they seemed to kind of drift by without actually settling in at all.

Finally, my brain clicked. "Did they... have funerals? I mean, if they figured we were dead?"

Westen made a movement like he might step over, but stopped and brushed his hand through his hair instead.

"So far as the town knows, the Thompson's remains were shipped out to be buried by family in another state. You, being a ward of the state, and without a body, well..."

I unclenched my jaw. "What did they do?"

"They offered a place marker to the Millers. There was no funeral, though the school did hold a memorial for you and Kalia."

I nodded, roughly brushing at my face with my hand

and baring my teeth in annoyance at myself. What had I really expected? This really, if I was honest. Sure, there was a buried hope that the Millers would be sad at my leaving (originally thought for when I went to college, but this didn't seem too far off the mark), however, that was why I had kept it buried. They hadn't even bothered to give me a funeral even though I'd been living with them for over ten years.

Had they even gone to the memorial? I doubted Westen would know, and I didn't want to ask really. At least the school had acknowledged us. I'm sure some of them included me in their thoughts as they mourned Lia, who was much more outgoing and friendly to pretty much everyone. She would be the real one they cried for.

Westen looked uncomfortable, and I was sure he didn't have a clue as to what to do for me, but I wasn't blubbering or anything, so I gave him a thin smile. I'd process later.

"No, it's fine. I'm fine. Thanks for telling me." I blew out a breath, calming and centering myself at the same time. "See? Totally good. You should go find Lia."

"Are you sure?"

I smiled, more at thinking what he would try to do to cheer me up than to prove to him I was fine.

"Absolutely. Oh, hey, Lia will get to see Mr. Thompson, right? It was really important to her. I'm sure it would help her a lot."

Westen nodded. "I've arranged it." He started to turn

toward the door, then stopped, catching my eyes with his. "Thank you, Dani."

His genuineness was obvious, and his intensity threw me off a bit. Also, his eyes were shining extra blue, and I found myself staring at them. I had to make myself look at something else before he thought I was staring him down or something. Ah, the ugly unicorn poster would do. I took in its bright rainbowy hair and sparkly gold swirly horn all encompassed by bright pink, and was able to get out, "Of course," in a mostly normal tone.

But Westen didn't leave. He just stood there, probably still looking at me. I did a quick glance. Yup, still looking at me with a curious type of look on his face. I focused back on the ugly unicorn pony.

"And are you doing alright? Being here?"

I gave a half-hearted laugh and turned back to him, feeling if I kept staring at the poster, I'd give myself away. I had to blink a lot. Smooth operator, that was me.

"Better than the cell."

His brows knitted, and figuring he was going to worry about me when he should be focused on Lia and all the stronghold's defenses and such, I knew I should let it go.

So, I tried for a very sincere voice when I said, "It's nice being here. Really. Lia's here, and I have food and a room. I mean, the color is ridiculous, but what are ya gonna do?"

Westen walked up to me and put his hand on my shoulder, making me meet his eyes again. Guess I wasn't a good actress.

His hand was warm, and the heat melted through my shirt. It made me realize I was chilly, and it made me want to surround myself in that warmth. Like with a hug, but that was not going to happen. I doubted either of us would be comfortable with that.

It also made me feel tiny. I felt like he was hulking over me, even though I knew he was only half a foot taller than me.

"I know how difficult this must all be, but it will get straightened out soon enough and know that you are safe here. If you ever feel that isn't the case, just remember to ask for me, as your advocate."

And there, he made my traitorous emotions surge up again, trying to get me to react. I swallowed the little ball of pain that sprouted in my throat. I tried to smile, but it wasn't very convincing, even to me.

"I know. Thank you." My voice even sounded off. Traitor.

He gave my shoulder a squeeze, then pulled back, going to the door and opening it. He looked back at me to say, "I'll find Kalia."

I believed him and gave him a small goodbye wave. "Good luck. Be careful with her."

"I will."

He shut the door behind him. What a roller coaster of a conversation. Thinking on it even gave me vertigo. And now I was alone once more, wondering where my best friend was, if she was ok, and when I'd see her again.

CHAPTER

18

I was getting a rumbly tummy again, and considered going down the hall to ask the guard about lunch when another knock came to the door. This time, I didn't automatically expect it to be food, however, so I didn't open the door with nearly as much enthusiasm as I probably should have.

It was Brielle, carrying a box. I gave her the "I wasn't expecting you, and what is that" look. It was all in the eyebrows.

"Come on in," I said, backing into the room so she didn't have to squeeze around me.

"Thanks." She came in and plopped the box on top of the bed. "Here are some things for you. To make your stay in the little girl's pink room more bearable, I imagine."

I opened the lid and looked in to find quite the small

collection of books, a drawing pad, some colored pencils and gel pens, some puzzle books and the like.

"I don't know whether it's a little kid's greeting box fit for the room or for me," I joked. "No, it's awesome though. Oh, nice, I love the Chaos books. Did Lia send these?"

Maybe I could get some kind of history books on dragons to read as well? Surely they had something like that for Lia to study during her lessons.

"No, Westen did."

I looked at her in surprise, which she apparently thought was funny.

"When did he do that?"

Brielle sat on the bed and absentmindedly pulled out a book, looked at the cover, tossed it on the bed, repeated. She sure was comfortable and relaxed for being a guard, but it didn't bother me. Actually, I kind of liked it. Made me feel a bit more normal to have one person besides Lia and Westen treat me like I wasn't an outsider.

"Not too long ago. Probably when he went looking for Princess Kalia."

"Don't you know where she is? I mean, you're her bodyguard type person thingy, right?"

She gave me a raised eyebrow look. "Yes, I am, but only during official meetings, outings and the like. I do stay here as her main guard, and to be an extra precaution through the night, so I'm close at hand in case anything happens." She pointed at me sternly. "But, I am not her babysitter."

Point taken. "Right. Sorry."

Brielle waved a negating hand. "I get it. You're trying to understand how things work around here, and there are some that would call me a glorified babysitter..." she glowered and I could imagine who would do that. All of the interrogators and their guards came to mind as suspects.

"But, that is not my job. During the day, while Princess Kalia has her regularly scheduled duties, I go to training with the rest of the guard. When she slipped out, I was with them. This isn't the first time Princess Kalia's disappeared though. She has her favorite hiding spots, though usually they're reserved for official meetings she's trying to get out of. I'm sure Prince Westen will find her in short order."

I sat down, putting the small stuffed toy dog in my lap. Why had Westen, or Brielle, or whoever put the box together, decided to put in a small brown puppy was beyond me, but I liked him. I would call him Puppy. Original, I know, but I had always been practical when it came to naming stuffed animals. Not that I would let anyone else know he had an official name. Especially not Lia or Westen, who would make fun of me in different ways for the same thing.

I looked over at my kind-of guest. "Can I ask you something?"

"Sure." She tossed another book. I'd have to clear off the bed when she left.

"I know you grew up here and all that. Was it ever

weird being around dragons when the rest of the world thinks they're made up?"

"No, not really. I learned all about the outside world and their perceptions of us at a very young age, so it was pretty normal. They like to keep their stronghold help in family lines, so they don't have to worry about outsiders. I think it makes training and keeping people easier as well."

"Is that why you all have weird accents? I mean, not weird, uhh," I blushed, feeling very foolish and rude. "Sorry. I've just never been around people from so many places before. I feel so dumb."

"Don't feel dumb." She laughed good-naturedly, putting me at ease. "To me, you're the one with the accent."

I gave a grudging nod. "True. But, it's like you're all really close to the American accent I'm used to, but not. You know? Like you're all slightly off in different ways. I feel so stupid. I don't want to assume or label people..."

She waved a negating hand. "You're not stupid, you just don't know. Be respectful of differences, that's all anyone can ask, and you're fine." She patted my hand. My embarrassment must have still showed.

"I suppose that comes from where we live and who our people were," she continued. "I bet if you went to Anchorage, Alaska, you'd find their accents the same. More of a Canadian slant than you're used to, even from Montana. You'd probably find other places in America strange, as well, like New York. Plus, we have people constantly coming from around the world. Accents tend to get blended. For instance, my mother is Aleut and my father is Japanese."

Wow, I never would have guessed, and just knowing that made me feel so culturally deficient.

"Aleut is a Native Alaskan tribe, right? If you don't mind my asking." I didn't want to assume, and doubted my own knowledge on the subject.

"Nah, I don't mind. They occupied the end of the peninsula we're on. There's quite a lot of Ogulmiuts, Kaniagmiuts and other tribes still around still as well. They were heavily recruited back when this place was first settled. Some of them are the only ones left of their tribes. The world thinks them extinct."

"When did they recruit your families?"

"Oh, over five hundred years ago, at least. I don't quite recall, but I do know that it was King Elbrel's and Queen Nephele's first independent assignment from the Dreki Order, and that they were so successful they were allowed to settle permanently and have heirs."

Jeez. That meant they had to be way older than five hundred, to be given such an important position, and if dragons didn't even get to adulthood until one hundred and fifty, they had to be well over six hundred and fifty. Maybe even a thousand, who knows? I must be a snotty little speck of dust to them, no more important than a fly that would die in a few days.

"So, is Brielle a family name? I've never heard it before. Or, what was your tribe again?"

She laughed, and it involved her whole face. Her eyes crinkled and her cheeks popped out with the mirth. It felt very genuine.

"No, not a family name. Or Aleut. My parents just like unique names. And Disney. They deny it, but I'm pretty sure Mother got the end of my name from a certain little mermaid." She leaned in and whispered, "And trust me, she looooooves that movie."

I smiled at her infectious enjoyment. "At least it's a cool name."

"Yes, though it's not completely unique. I've heard of others with my name, on the internet at such."

"Well, I've never heard it before and I like it. Oh! The internet. Can I use it? I need to find out the closest mountain to here."

She looked at me quizzically. "Why do you need to look up Mount Mageik?"

"Never mind, you just confirmed it. Hey, I really appreciate you talking to me about everything. I don't want to offend or anything, so thanks."

She gave me a warm smile. "You bet. You never know where someone in the castle may be from, so just be mindful. Be respectful. Be polite."

"I absolutely will. Is it rude to say you're totally gorgeous and I'm envious of you and your parents?"

She stared for half a second then let out a loud laugh. "Rude, no. Too much, probably?"

"Right, don't go telling random castle people how good looking they are." I was making a joke, but I did mean it. Brielle was very attractive, and I wished I had her striking looks instead of my plain ones.

"Oh, I have one last question if that's ok. Are there any kind of history books I could read on the stronghold or dragon history in general? I'd like to know more about this place, and dragons obviously."

"I'll see what I can do." She stood up, obviously done flipping books onto my bed. "I have to get going, but I'm sure Princess Kalia will be back soon enough."

"Of course. Thanks for coming and bringing me stuff, and talking to me. It was really nice."

"No problem." She glanced around a moment after getting up. "Did the staff already get your lunch tray?"

"No, I didn't get anything. I thought maybe I was supposed to go somewhere?"

Brielle frowned. "No, don't go anywhere, remember?" She waited to continue until I gave her a nod of acknowledgement. "Brent should have brought lunch up an hour or so ago. I'll check in on it on my way down."

"Thanks," I called to her as she left with a wave back at me before she shut my door.

The box was a very nice surprise, and I took my time going through it. I think the most surprising thing was that Westen had it made for me. Lia I would totally understand getting me some of my favorite things, or at least things that used to be my favorite (I was heavily into drawing my freshmen and sophomore year, before I phased it out for more running and training). And these things had to have come from him specifically. No way was Brielle or some servant able to guess my favorite authors on a whim.

While I was rearranging space to accommodate the new items, lunch came. Pretty tasty for a simple sandwich, but I enjoyed it, and started reading one of the books I hadn't read before.

I nearly jumped out of bed when my door opened suddenly several hours later. Lia came in, walking slowly.

"Oh, sorry." Belatedly she gave a small knock on my already open door.

"No, it's fine." I sat up and dropped the book on the desk. "Come in. Are those sprites?"

She nodded, and several of the bright balls of fluff attached to her hair bobbed with her. I could see six distinct forms around her, four of them seemed to be riding her hair in various places, the others on each of her shoulders. Two of them were purple, but of slightly different shades, and I wondered if they were siblings of some kind.

"Sorry I didn't come earlier. After lessons..." She just shrugged to finish her sentence.

"Don't worry about it, Lia." I wanted to say something like I was just glad she was ok, but she didn't exactly seem ok, so I opted for something else. "Do you want to talk about it?"

She shook her head, but started speaking anyway. "Wilson just went on and on, and got mad at me when I wasn't reading what he told me to, but I just couldn't focus. It seemed so pointless and dumb."

"Makes sense." I stood next to her, waiting for her to give me a clue as to what would help. One of the sprites, a bright orange one, jumped onto my arm for a moment, but hopped back to her after just a second.

"After, I don't know, I just needed some quiet." She held out her hand in front of her face and a yellow fluffball landed in it, seeming to snuggle her nose. "I went to the sprite's garden. There's a kind of off the path area I go to when I want some solitude sometimes." She kissed the little sprite. "It's nice. They knew I was sad…"

"That's why they're still following you, right?" She nodded, confirming my guess. "They love you, and want to comfort you." I knew I was just stating the obvious, but sometimes that's what people needed to hear.

Lia sniffled, and her eyes started pooling. I knew what was coming and pulled her into a hug as she started crying. The sprites got energized by her reaction, moving around her, flitting in to touch her face or arm before moving on. I let her take her time, just trying my best to be calming while letting her vent some of her grief. After a long time, she began to settle down, but we stayed where we were, holding on to each other.

Eventually she said, "Thanks."

"Of course. Whatever you need. You know I'm here for you."

Lia squeezed my middle tight for a moment. "Always."

She moved to sit up. "Ugh, my face is a total mess."

"It is not and you know it. You're a beautiful crier. Poopy-head."

She gave a small chuckle. "Don't be jealous. Just because you get all splotchy and puffy doesn't mean we all have to."

I stuck my tongue out at her before getting up and going to the dresser. I grabbed one of the plain shirts to hand to her. "Here."

"What, am I supposed to change into this?" She gave it a mock-horrified look. "That would totally ruin my outfit." Which was true. She was wearing a matching short and shirt combo that sported pretty curls and butterflies in pink and purple tones, and my shirt was all brown with nothing else on it.

"No, silly. Use it like a tissue. I don't want to walk to the bathroom, so this is what I've got."

She smiled lightly, and used the shirt daintily, dabbing at her eyes and cheeks. "When did you get those?" she asked, nodding toward the box on my floor and the books now on top of my dresser.

"Brielle brought them earlier. Westen sent for them, I guess."

"I should have thought of that." Lia got a fragile look in her eyes I didn't like.

"Hey, you thought of a lot. All the clothes, that awesome dinner last night, letting me sleep on your couch. I think this was a spur of the moment thing." Though for being spur of the moment, he did hit on quite a few things I actually enjoyed.

"He came and got me in the sprite circle. He... He's a good brother." She rubbed at her nose again, staving off more gooby runners.

"He certainly seems to be. Not at all the Westen I'm used to dealing with. It's weird."

And unsettling. And enlightening. And kind of scary, in a goodish way. I felt like I was finally getting to see the rest of the real him, the parts I'd only been able to glimpse before. Like when he took Lia and me to the zoo before they left for the summer, or when he bought me new shoes because my old ones were holey and my foster parents wouldn't. He didn't know I knew about that last one. Lia had ratted him out.

Her chest bobbed up and down with her slight laugh, which I was sure was being held down by the heavy emotions still going through her. Still, it was a move in the right direction.

She smiled lightly at me. "Hah, ya. He's always so reserved and formal and follows *all* the rules. I guess you know why now."

"I certainly do." I didn't want to start ragging on her parents, which in my opinion were the absolute worst. I didn't want to risk setting off Lia's tender emotions again by even mentioning them in any way, not when she was still so raw. So, I held out a hand toward the shirt. "Want me to throw that out the window for you?"

She face lightened. "Why would you do that?"

"Well, I figured that's what we did with dirty clothes around here, since you threw mine out that way yesterday and all." I got a real chuckle out of her then. "Besides," I continued, "it's not like I know all the proper etiquette for doing things in a dragon castle, after all."

She got up, still laughing, and went to the closet. The sprites bobbed and zoomed around her as she moved.

"You know why I did that. And you know there's a perfectly good hamper right here." She was right, I did. She dumped the shirt into it, then spun around with some light in her eyes. "Hey, you wanna go to my room, watch movies, and order outrageous things from the kitchen?"

I grinned. "Absolutely."

The food we got was delicious, and indeed outrageous, including a brownie sundae nearly as large as my pillow that we barely got a decent dent into after the fried chicken, veggies and cheese we'd just eaten before it. Brielle said she was disgusted with our choices when she came to check in on us, which only made us laugh.

About half-way through the first movie something crept in the window like a spider, but was easily the size of a bobcat.

"What is that?" I screeched, having seen it slither in out of the corner of my eye.

Lia smiled and went over to the thing, holding out her arms. It leapt and curled into her. "This is a gargoyle. He likes to stay near my room, yes he does," she cooed, scratching under his chin.

I could tell, once she'd told me what it was. He had a squished face and little horns circled his head. Stone grey skin, wings, buff little arms, and a winding tail wrapped around her arm.

"Wow, what's his name?"

He snorted at me with a puff of dust.

Lia giggled. "They don't like names. Families tend to look similar, but you can always tell them apart by their cracks. No two gargoyles have the same crack lines. See?" She traced one on his ear that traveled a jagged path down his neck while he chirped happily.

I nodded. "Can I pet him?"

"Ask him."

I held up my hand like I would a dog. I mean, he kinda seemed like a dog, I half expected his tongue to loll out. "Can I pet you?"

The gargoyle leaned out and shoved his head into my hand. It nearly knocked me back with its power, but my hand slid over the rough, pebbled skin that felt just like rock that moved, like flexible stone. And he was cold, as cold as the castle floor beneath us.

"Wow, you're amazing," I spoke to him.

He preened, pushing into me and chirping something that sounded like a mix between a falcon call and a lion chuff. Suddenly, he took a swipe and dived, Lia barely able to hold onto him as I took a big step back, worried I did something wrong.

"No! No chasing the sprites!" Lia struggled to keep a hold on him. "Sorry, he loves to try to eat them. Hey, get the ice cream."

I grabbed it and joined her at the window, where she'd walked to while holding tight to the little gargoyle.

"Alright," she said sternly, "do you want to have ice cream or go after sprites?"

His neck swiveled between random puffs of colors around the room and the giant, mostly uneaten brownie sundae. I have expected to hear stone on stone grating as he moved. He snatched the container and hopped out the window in one smooth movement.

"And no sprites!" Lia yelled at his back as he flew away.

"Wow…" What else did I not know about Firehold and its inhabitants? "What about the bowl?"

"He'll eat it." Lia laughed at the shocked look on my face.

The sprites fluttered around energetically, seemingly spurred by the gargoyle's visit. At one point it seemed like they were playing tag around the room. The orange one hid between my folded legs for a while, until being spotted by a pink one who dive bombed into me, sending me falling backwards trying to avoid being hit and squishing any of them at the same time. Some more came in the window to join the festivities before they all had to go away for the night.

Lia left some cookies out for them, letting me know Westen would be irritated if he knew because, "It's not good for them, Kalia, and you know better," she said in her best impression of him.

It was a great distraction, and during the third movie

she fell asleep. I moved around as quietly as I could, getting the plates and food off her bed, putting them outside the door, and turning off the TV (and why couldn't my room have a TV?). I flipped over the blanket from the other side of the bed, laying it over her like a big blanket taco. She was so out of it, she didn't even budge.

I debated between going back to my room or sleeping on her couch again, which still had the sheets, blankets and pillow from last night. I didn't think she'd mind if I stayed, but I remembered her mother proclaiming I was never to sleep in her room again. It would be best if I didn't push things.

I made my way back to my room, even though I didn't want to be alone yet. I settled down into the bed, wondering what was coming in the next few days. Lia would probably have to continue lessons and endure her clueless and relentless instructor. I would probably have to stick to my room. But I hoped Lia would start to really heal, and get to see David. Hadn't Westen said he'd gotten her the meeting when he came looking for her? I couldn't recall. Hopefully that would happen soon, for both their sakes.

And of course, there was still my judgement trial conclusion thingy. Regardless of Lia's and Westen's assurances, I just couldn't shake the ill feeling of impending doom.

Even though I was barred from having sleep-overs with Lia in her much more awesome room than mine, at least her parents weren't outright barring us from hanging out when she wasn't scheduled. Except, that time seemed to be getting less and less with each day.

The next several days settled into a semi-regular routine. Lia had lessons throughout the morning, during which I would take extended baths and read, do mini-exercises in my room, and generally fill the time with whatever I could. Afterwards, she would go to alternating afternoon activities, usually popping in to bug me during lunch. Sometimes she had training, sometimes meetings, it all varied. Then, we'd hang every evening, work on her college proposal, and try to forget where we were.

And I hadn't talked to Lia about our "funerals" and memorial at the school yet. Or even about the fact that we'd missed our graduation at this point. She was doing a great job of holding it together and working through her feelings, but I could tell she was still very raw. Sometimes she'd just cry, or need to be alone. The day Westen had gotten her in to see David had been particularly hard for her. I gave her whatever she needed, just trying to help. Having her work all day every day probably didn't help, stupid parents.

All of my bruises, bumps and scrapes had mostly faded to nothing, except the spectacular bruise I'd had on my back right hip, but even it was nearly faded out. The creams and such that Lia had given me must have magic in them for how fast everything seemed to clear up. And my wrist was nearly clear, just a few stubborn patches of scab from where blisters had popped during my night-scapade. I was poking at one when Lia burst into my room.

I had stopped getting super startled when people unabashedly came into my space, especially since my foster parents had never done that growing up (something I was appreciating about them now), but it still made me jump, if only on the inside.

"Guess what!"

I didn't even try to get out an answer.

"Dad and the dreaden have all left!" Lia flopped onto the end of my bed, happier than I'd seen her in a while.

"Ok, so what does that mean? And what are dreaden?"

"Dreaden are the fighting dragons. And it means that

we get a break! With him gone Firehold keeps running, but it's more on low-key mode."

"How many dreadon dragon dudes live here? Are there other dragons here that don't fight?" I'd only known about her family.

Lia laughed, her voice nearly tinkling. "They're boys and girls. Usually we have ten to twelve stationed here from various European allies, but we're the only other dragons here. Westen doesn't have to go on rotation because he's being groomed to take over here, but I'll have to eventually."

She rolled onto her stomach and put her head in her hand, a perturbed look coming over her face. "Of course, Mother is still here... She'll probably make me keep up with all the lessons and such. Oh, never mind, this is lame. Why couldn't she have gone too?" She ended it with a nice long whine noise.

Because she wants to make our lives miserable? I didn't say that though, for obvious reasons. Instead, I patted her shoulder.

"Thought you'd get to skip all your meetings?"

She let her face fall onto the bed where she groaned into my blanket. She mumbled something I thought was along the lines of "This sucks."

"Ya," I commiserated. "It really does. And you're sure that you can't ask Westen for any help?"

Lia just rolled her head back and forth a few times slowly. We'd talked about it before, but with him already fighting for me, and how the parents typically were, Lia hadn't wanted to risk it. So, she suffered it in silence. Mostly.

And occasionally she went AWOL and they had to send people out to find her and drag her to whatever she was skipping. That girl had a lot of great hiding places. Just yesterday she told me they'd found her in a broken down furnace room. It had malfunctioned last week and they hadn't gotten around to fixing it yet, so they turned it off and locked it up until they got to it, but Lia had gotten in first. How had she even known about it? I guessed it was her sprites. She read most of one of my books while there. I hadn't even known she'd "borrowed" it that morning.

"Well, at least he's here." I tried to think of something, *anything*, positive. "And with your dad and the other dragons gone, surely he'll have more time, right? Maybe he can't help you get out of your lessons, but maybe you could spend more time with him?"

Her head popped back up. "Ya, that might work. They've been having me train with the draeden, but with them all gone, I bet I could get training with him instead. That would be cool."

"Maybe I could join you guys? It'd be nice to get out of this hallway."

Her face lit up. "That would be so incredibly awesome. I'm sure Westen could swing it. Like, he's testing you about the warlocks or something."

Ugh, that wasn't quite what I was thinking, but an excuse was an excuse, and I wouldn't turn it down. "Do you know how long they'll be gone?"

Lia shrugged, which was awkward looking considering she was holding her upper torso up with both elbows being planted on my bed, so mostly she just wiggled a bit.

"At least a few days. I know there's no warlocks anywhere near us. They all got wiped out ages ago and they do regular patrol type thingies to make sure it stays that way. I think they like to stick to big cities anyway. So, it'll probably take them at least a day to reach anything. Westen would know where they're going, but I don't think he'll tell us."

"Ya, probably not."

"He takes his security job pretty serious. Which he totally should, being in line to run this whole place and such, but it'd be nice if he didn't keep us in the dark about *everything*."

I nodded, knowing exactly how she felt.

"Hey, maybe you can talk to him about the college stuff we've been working on. I bet he'll give you some great tips about how to best present it to your parents."

"Yes!" She yelled so suddenly I leaned back from the sound. "I'll go get the notebook. Wait here."

"How about we plan in your room?"

She smiled with a laugh. "What? Don't want to spend *all* of your time in here? Is my old room not good enough for you?"

I rolled my eyes. "Lia, I'm freaking dreaming in pink."

She let out a genuine, full laugh and grabbed my hand, leading me out to her room. And that was the next hour or so, until lunch came and then Lia got pulled, literally, by Brielle to go to a meeting with her mother. I heard her whining all the way down the stairs as I made my way back to my room.

Evidently her mother kept her late today, as I didn't see Lia until after dinner time. I was brushing my hair out from the shower when I heard them coming up the stairs. She came trudging up with Brielle dutifully behind her. I expect it was to either stop her from running away and hiding again, or to catch her if she fell back. The girl looked exhausted.

I gave a low whistle. "Dang girl, you looked bushed."

She gave a half-hearted wave. "Stupid political stuff. She says we're going to host some of the other high dragon families over the next few years, and that requires a lot of planning to be done now. I mean, come on, the first one isn't even for something like six more months! How much planning do you need?"

She threw her arms out to illustrate, then nodded at Brielle who slipped into her room with a wave after the hall guard retreated down the stairs to leave us alone in the hall.

"But noooo," Lia kept right on with her rant. "I have to help decide on room selections and decorations and daily activities to keep them properly entertained and make our family look good, and not at all like the backwoods cousins we seem to be because we live in the "new" frontier of Alaska."

"That really sucks."

"Ya, it does. And most of the time Mother doesn't even listen to me. She just does what she wants no matter what I say or suggest, so I don't know why she makes me be there!" She leaned against the doorframe, obviously dejected.

"She thinks it's time I start stepping into the Faela duties more, which apparently means I have to just sit there and nod at her. Oh, but she's making me choose the food." She gave a sarcastic thumbs up. "That's my big contribution. They all still consider me a kid, but they're going to make me choose meal plans for basically, the equivalent of foreign dignitaries who won't like the food I like. If you're going to make me do that, at least let me out of history lessons."

"I completely agree." This seemed like a big I-need-to-get-it-all-out rant. I had lots of those, so I totally got it.

Lia sighed. "I'm just gonna wash off and fall in bed. Can you believe she's still having me go to lessons tomorrow, after she sucked up all of my day?"

I gave her a one armed hug, the other holding my hair brush and old clothes. "Go straight to bed. No requesting decadent desserts just because you want to wallow in your misery."

She stuck her tongue out at me, so I smiled serenely at her before heading out. I was worried about her, but nothing I could do more tonight, so I went to bed.

It still amazed me at how late the sun went down here. It wasn't too much later than Montana, I supposed, but it just seemed so much later. And colder. I wore warm, long pajamas to make up for the lack of heating in this place. I mean, I got it that the dragons didn't need heat seeing as they produced whatever heat they needed, and I guessed the humans were just used to it. I wasn't. Even though Montana has some wicked cold weather, I was always just a little bit chilly. I put my things away and read a book while my hair dried out enough that I could sleep on it without waking up to a wet pillow.

I did like how it was quiet, at least once the sun went down. Made it easy to drift off to sleep not having someone watching TV too loud in the other room, or coming home late at night and turning on lights while getting a midnight snack from the fridge. Just distant noises from far outside that lulled me to sleep.

Someone was shaking my shoulder, waking me up. I tried to ask "What?" but it came out as more of a weird mutter. My fuzzy brain noted that it was dark out, and that when I got woken up in the middle of the night around here it was never good news.

"Get up," Brielle whispered urgently. "Get shoes. Keep your light off. Understand?"

"Yes."

"Hurry. I'll be back."

Then she was gone and I fumbled around in the dark, my feet freezing on the floor, trying to get socks and shoes, waiting for her to get back, and wondering what was going on.

My thoughts got interrupted when a jet of fire streamed across my window.

I ran to the window and saw the fire blink out, leaving a glow on the ground where it had struck. I couldn't really tell because it was so far away, but I thought there was movement. Blackness on blackness.

The fire had originated from the sky, so naturally I assumed dragon, but there were only two here, Westen and the queen. Which one was up there shooting flame, and why?

Belatedly, I remembered Brielle's orders, which now had way more urgency to them, and I jammed my shoes on. I went to my door and opened it as quietly as I could before peeking into the hallway. Everything was dark. I kept looking back and forth, trying to see *anything* in the hall. When Brielle and Lia emerged from her bedroom's side of the hall it nearly gave me a heart attack they melted out of the darkness so quickly.

Of course, that might have to do with Lia's skin giving

off a faint, pulsating light. They'd probably popped up in my sight when they came around her bedroom door. She was wearing long sleeves and full length pants, but her hands and face were still lit up slightly, and it showed me how worried she was.

"Control it," Brielle spoke quietly into Lia's ear; they were close enough now I could hear them.

"I'm trying. It's harder when I'm stressed, sorry."

"Don't be sorry, be careful. This is the real thing."

She rubbed her arms self-consciously. "I know."

Brielle motioned me to join them and we made our way toward the stairs where two guards were standing, watching downward, though they both glanced at us as we came up to them. One of them seemed to stare at me a moment before turning back.

"What's the real thing?" I whispered. "What's going on? I saw fire."

"It was Westen," Lia spoke just as quietly, looking anxious. "I saw it too. Mother's is more of a blue tinged color."

Brielle went to the two guards, speaking quietly to them. One kept glancing back at us. I moved closer, wanting to hear, and caught Brielle saying, "Domen. Do your duty."

He nodded and turned back to the stairs, but he didn't seem happy about it.

Brielle moved to the head of the stairs next to him, motioning us to wait as she checked it out. I wondered if she could see better in the dark than I could, because I doubted I'd be able to see very far down those steps with all the lights out, which was weird, because usually there were little night-light type lights in the hall when I went to the bathroom after dark, but they were all gone now.

She waved us forward. "Firehold is under attack. I don't know by whom or how many, but I suspect it's the warlocks. Our priority is to get you to a safe location and wait it out. Follow me. Be quiet."

I had a ton of questions. How did the warlocks get past the no-see-me barrier thing I'd had to go through? Westen was in the sky fighting them, but where were the tons of human guards I saw when I first got here? Were they out fighting as well? Why was everything so darned dark? How far was the safe location and how safe was it?

But I knew I couldn't ask any of them. Brielle was already on the move, stepping down into the dark with her sword held out in front of her in her right hand, and the weird short staff stick thing in her left. Lia and I kept a few steps behind her. One guard was on our left side, blocking the other side of the stairs as we descended, and the other, the one who'd exchanged words with Brielle, waited until we passed to take up position behind us.

Everything was incredibly nerve-wracking. Even though we'd just come from a closed hall and had a guy protecting our rear, I kept glancing behind to make sure we weren't being followed. My eyes were straining, trying to see more than they were physically capable of doing.

It didn't help that I had a bobbing light walking next

to me, constantly catching my attention while simultaneously draining any night vision I might have had. I knew Lia couldn't help it, so I didn't say anything, but it did make me feel like we were even more of a target. She had tucked her hands away and tried keeping her face down, so I was sure she was thinking the same thing I was.

There was a loud bang somewhere and Lia let out a small yelp, jumping into me and grabbing my arm. I held onto her tight, wildly looking around and not seeing anything but the small section of hall we were in.

Brielle pushed us on, moving at a near jogging pace at times. If I wasn't so scared, I'd be much more interested in how she guided us, moving from place to place and pausing to take stock of the situation. The guards moved with us, following her movements with no spoken word. It was like in the movies when elite military teams infiltrated places.

Noises were becoming louder the further into the castle we moved. Lia kept jolting against me at each new shout, crash or cry, and I gave her my hand to squeeze into oblivion as we made our way.

Brielle suddenly stopped and crowded us against the wall, pushing Lia down behind a chair. Someone was running our way. More than someone, and they were approaching fast. One guard stayed in front of us, Brielle and the other disappeared into the room. My hand was cramping where Lia strangled it, but I didn't let go.

The steps were almost on us when I heard a rushing noise and a clank. Something heavy dropped.

"Stop," Brielle barked in a hushed yell. They were too far away for me to make anything out except shuffling, but Lia's gaze was fixated to the left and she relaxed against me.

I heard Brielle whispering, but couldn't make it out. There was some return whispering. Someone said "home" I think, then two figures, a limping older man and a younger woman holding onto him went hurrying past us without pausing. I don't even think they noticed we were there. They looked like castle workers of some kind.

Suddenly, I found it disconcerting that we hadn't seen other people in a castle this big besides just those two. I mean, it was a relief, too, to be sure, but where did everyone go? Surely they weren't all sleeping through this? Hopefully they had their own safe place to go to when things like this happened.

The guard in front of us motioned us up, and we moved to join Brielle and the other at the far side of the room. Another boom sounded, this time I felt the ground shake a bit beneath us. The outside noises were getting louder, and I could feel my adrenaline amping up with each new sound. Brielle opened a door to the side. I could distinctly hear men shouting, giving orders, chanting, and one was screaming. She slowly led us in, moving us around debris that littered the floor from the blown in windows and scattered furniture.

After getting into the room, I couldn't keep my eyes from what was happening just outside of the used-to-be-windows. There were flashes of lights, shadows of men running, and a giant orb of red far out with a figure inside of it.

Streaks of something wizzed around, and I saw one hit a guard, who went down and didn't move. One of his companions knelt down next to him for a moment, then got up and continued on, the three other guys following. They were moving like a hit team, and they quickly became moving blobs among many moving things. I didn't know if the guy hit with the grey bolt was dead or not, but I assumed he was and I was glad Lia hadn't seen.

A huge jet of fire speared through the sky and I let out a small cry as I flinched away from its light piercing my eyes. I kept walking a few steps with Lia as my guide until my eyes adjusted to the new brightness. The fire was still going.

Blinking and looking out the side of my eyes, I saw a humongous red dragon in the sky, sending a steady stream of fire so hot it ran blue through most of its length at the red orb I'd previously seen on the grounds. The smudge of a figure inside of it became clearer with the fire and I saw a man holding up his hands inside of it. Flicks of darkness pelted against the dragon, but it steadily blew flame until the orb simply collapsed from one instant to the next, the fire washing against the ground in a small explosion.

The fire suddenly ceased completely, dropping the

sky into darkness again, and an awesome, fierce roar split the air. The strength of that dragon's cry, the absolute power, made me shiver. No wonder the queen was such an arrogant being, because that red dragon, at least ten times larger than Westen's mixed grey form, could only be her.

Lia seemed to be shining brighter, and I thought it might have to do with her fear. I wrapped her hands up in mine and tried to stay between her and the outside wall, hoping to obscure her light from any warlocks who might look our way.

Something crashed into the room and I knocked into Lia, sending us into the wall. A guard grabbed my outward arm, and pulled us forward so that I nearly stumbled to keep up. We reached the far side of the room shortly after and went through another door, the guard closing it behind us as soon as we were through.

We passed through twisting halls, heard people close and far, but we didn't have to go through another blasted out section again. We were in a room with a broken window that showed nothing but empty grass when Brielle motioned for us to stop.

"Here." Brielle moved a drapery hiding small door that blended in with the background. I never would have noticed it, even if I were looking for it. "In, and stay quiet."

The guard next to Brielle whispered something about "the other," before she cut him off, hissing, "All three of you in, now!"

Giving a curt nod to Brielle, he led us in. We had to

crouch a bit just to get through the door, but the space opened up soon enough. The guard turned on a pale light just as I heard the door close and lock behind us.

"Isn't Brielle and the other guy coming?" I whispered.

The guard shook his head, then went and pushed some buttons in a panel before unrolling a heavy drape I hadn't seen secured above the door's entrance. While he tucked it in, probably to make sure no light shone through, Lia pulled me over to a padded bench built into the wall and sat down heavily upon it. She wasn't letting me go, though, so I got pulled down with her.

Objectively, I knew that it had probably taken us less than ten minutes to get to this room from Lia's hall, and a bunch of that had been brief pauses by Brielle taking assessments. It must be the closest safe room, but I wondered how many there were in this castle. It didn't seem like everyone got to go to a shelter, like the two workers who'd run by us. That seemed unfair, but I got it. Protect the royalty at all costs, and hope the others stay out of harm's way.

"I didn't see Westen out there, when we went through that room." Lia sounded timid and her voice warbled a bit.

I squeezed her hand. "I didn't either, but we saw him before we left our rooms, so he's out there. Probably just at some place we couldn't see. And your mom, wow."

She gave a half-hearted tense giggle. "Crazy, huh? Westen said the older you get, the hotter your fire becomes, and that mom and dad could melt the stone in the castle if they wanted to because they're so old. I've only seen her and dad in dragon form a few times, but never in an actual fight before..."

Sheesh, if they could melt stone, it was a wonder the warlock in the bubble survived as long as he did. He must have been powerful before the queen had ended him. I blinked a few times, trying to take stock of myself. I'd just seen people *killed*, and just because I had the week before didn't make it normal or easy. It was a fight to the death in Montana and it was a fight to the death here. I shuddered and felt a drop of ice slide down my center. Was this regular life around here? Kill or be killed?

The guard took up stance on the right side of the door entrance, but he looked back at us when we talked, clearly annoyed.

"You shouldn't be talking."

That only got Lia's attention on him. "Why couldn't Brielle come in, too?" she asked, immediately followed by, "How many warlocks are out there and how did they get in?"

He looked like he wanted to shush her, but she was the princess, so he probably couldn't. When he spoke, it was almost as if he'd just bitten into a lemon with the face he was making.

"Protocol is we all come in, but with the outside room being breached, Brielle ordered herself and Adin out, to provide as much defense as possible." He paused to lean into the curtain as some small rumbles and pops came from somewhere out there. After a moment, he turned back to us. "I don't know how many of them there are. I was awoken and told with Adin to get Brielle and protect you, Princess."

He spared me a cutting glance before turning back toward the curtain and I just knew he thought I was superfluous. I must have been "the other" he'd tried to speak to Brielle about. I'd originally thought maybe it had been his guard buddy, but it was obvious he didn't want me along, which made me wonder exactly what he'd questioned Brielle about back by our bedrooms. I bet it was about bringing me along at all.

Well, I guess I didn't blame him. I was just *the prisoner* to the castle, but that didn't stop me from flushing in anger and wanting to verbally slap his stupid face.

Thankfully, Brielle seemed to be higher ranking than him and she'd gotten me. I was going to have to get her an enormous thank you gift for everything she'd done since I arrived, especially since she'd only just met me.

After a few moments of silence, Lia leaned into me and whispered. "I hope the sprites and gargoyles are ok."

"I'm sure they're fine. They know how to hide, right?"

She nodded, but a tear slid down her right cheek, quickly followed by the left. I knew she wasn't only thinking about them, but probably about everyone. Westen, her mother, Brielle, David and others I didn't even know about. I pulled her into a bear hug and rubbed her back, making soft shhh noises into her hair as she shook.

"It's... it's all because of me, isn't it? I should be out there, helping. Somehow..."

"Hey, we don't know that. Stop it." I pulled back and made her face me, ignoring the guard who was glaring at us even though we were whispering. "I know you're stronger than this. Remember how cool you were when your house got attacked? You didn't break down then, you did what you needed to do to. And that's what they need right now. They need you to stay strong and safe, so that's what we're going to do."

She sniffled, but gave me an affirmative nod. "But I can't just sit here quietly or I'm gonna go crazy thinking about it."

I rubbed her hands. Going on a trek through the woods like we did last time wasn't going to work here. We had to stick to this room. And despite Mr. Grumpy Guard, we were whispering and no one could possibly hear us outside of the room. Unless they had superhuman hearing, which, I conceded, was a possibility. Still, Lia needed something to distract herself from her thoughts, and I couldn't think of anything else.

"Ok, tell me about warlocks. How many of them are there? In the world, I mean. What are their powers?"

She nibbled at the bottom of her lip, thinking. "Ummm... I don't know how many there are. I don't think anyone really knows. They have all these little camps all over the place, but they're not like *everywhere*, ya know? I think I heard Westen say we knew about 35 of their places in North America, but they could have more we don't know about."

"What about their powers?"

"Their powers are different from ours because ours come from within ourselves, like other magical creatures. Some humans have it too, natural born witches and wizards. Warlocks though, they get theirs from stealing, which is why they want anything born with magic. All magical beings are targets to them."

Westen had said young ones had the most potential for warlocks to take from, young like Lia. They were specifically targeting Lia because she could power them for generations, I remembered Hodges saying way back when this whole thing started. Vaguely I wondered if Hodges was out there.

Lia tucked her hair behind her ears, and I knew she was feeling a bit more normal. When she really got stressed out, she didn't care about her appearance at all, so this distraction seemed to be working.

"What do they do with the magic once they take it? I mean, dragons breathe fire, but I didn't see any of those guys spouting flame."

"They can use fire, I think, they just don't. Umm... Westen told me once..." She closed her eyes, obviously in an effort to remember. "I think they just convert things to something like energy, and use that energy to do things?" She ended that like a question, but it sounded plausible enough to me. "I don't really know. Sorry."

"That's ok. I mean, jeez, it's way more than I know."

She gave me a rueful smile, since we both were aware that I knew Jack and squat about anything to do with real magic before a week or two ago.

"They can affect people if they have time to prepare, too. Humans more than us, like when they sucked out the oxygen from your lungs."

That wasn't my fondest memory. I rubbed at my wrist, where Lia had burned me to save me from suffocating while surrounded by air.

"Could they be doing that again? Like, outside or to us, in here?"

Lia looked wary. "I don't think so. It takes too much time, and with the fighting-"

The guard waved his hand in a sharp, downward motion, giving a quick "Shh!" We instantly shut up. Lia startled a couple of times beside me, so I knew she could hear something I couldn't. Through the general far distant background fighting and occasional rumbles, I just couldn't pick anything specific out that was close to us.

Lia's hand got tighter and tighter on mine, and then I heard it. Clashes, faint, a yell, but definitely from the room Brielle was in, right outside our safe room.

The guard moved to us, not making a sound as he did so.

"Come stand behind me, Princess. If they breach the room, I'll try to push them out so you can get away. Get to another safe room, or get as far away as you can. Understand?"

Lia nodded and stood up, pulling me right along with her. We didn't say anything. I didn't dare to. Even though I desperately wanted to ask what the chances of them finding this room was, and then opening it, and how many of them were there, and where were the other safe rooms. How did they know where this room was? Wouldn't it be kept super secret safe for effectiveness? I know he didn't have any answers, even if I did ask, so instead I held onto Lia's hands, mine squeezing just as tight as hers.

The guard stood to the side of the entrance, just behind the drape, his sword and stick thing up at the ready, wielding one in each hand. I wondered if they could use guns against warlocks.

Something hit against the door and though I jumped, I didn't make any sound. Someone in the room outside yelled, and I wondered if it was a good guy or a bad guy. The noises were blended and I couldn't tell what was going on, just that I knew something was happening. I hoped Brielle was ok.

The door splintered and I couldn't help but cry out as the pieces blew the curtain up and shards flew past us. The guard was already swinging in toward the opening and I desperately hoped one of the good guys wasn't rushing in to help us. It connected with nothing, and the guard rushed through the door with a fierce yell.

In movies, I'd always thought it was kind of silly when the warrior screamed during their attack. Why waste such energy and hurt your throat? Why not try for stealthy sneak attack? Because, first off, they probably knew we were in here, so sneaky snake was out of the question. Secondly, it was actually scary to hear such a real scream.

I didn't know if it scared any warlocks outside of the room, but I did know that the door was currently open and I didn't want to wait for it to fill. Lia was hugging the wall, staring at the torn curtain. I tightened my grip and pulled her, moving the curtain to take a quick assessment before running to the left.

Our guard was in a fight with someone just to the

right. I could have reached out to touch him, they were that close. Purple and grey streaks whipped toward him, but he struck at them with his stick, like they were tangible things. Fully expecting to see the guard hit full on by the three bolts, I was startled when they instead shattered on contact with his short staff.

Either warlock spells were vulnerable to wooden short staffs, or those sticks had some magic of their own. After absorbing the hits, the guard swung the short staff around for a swipe at the guy's head, followed by a strike from his sword. Unfortunately, the warlock deflected the stick and fell back before the sword could connect, another swirl of energy crackling around his hand.

That was all I saw by the time we'd moved past them, at as close to a run as I could manage. I was stepping over a couple of broken chairs next to an equally broken table. One of the walls was blown out, and for a second I considered going that way, but the warlocks could have come in that way, which meant more could be coming from there, so I switched directions to a nearby closed door. More than once, one of us slipped and the other held firm to help maintain balance as we skittered across the floor.

Just in front of the door was a large mass I quickly figured to be a downed person. Don't think about it, don't think about it. Please let the door open the other way.

I hit the door, and worked the handle as soon as I

fumbled my way onto it. It swung outward and we were able to just step over the form. I stuck my head in for a moment, just to see if any forms were easily visible. Not seeing any, I went in, expecting Lia to be right behind me, but she wasn't.

Turning, I saw her staring into the room where at least two fights were still going on. I grabbed her arm, pulling and hissing, "Come on!"

She stumbled back, over the dead guy.

"But... Brielle. We could help!"

I glanced in the room as I swung the door closed. Brielle was up and swinging against two guys, one in a green bubble. With a brutal scream she swung her sword into the green shield and sparks exploded outward just as the door shut.

"We could help," Lia said again, this time as more of a plea.

"Come on," was all I said.

We weren't fighters, we weren't trained, and there was no emergency services to call. All we could do was hope to survive.

We were way too close to the fighting for me to take a time-out to discuss things with her. Instead, I fixed my grip on her and started jog-running through the room we were in. My only goal was to get far away from any fighting I could hear. There were several doors, and I chose one on the far side.

Lia didn't fight me anymore. In fact, when the door was locked, she pulled me to the left.

"Here. That door leads toward the inside of the castle."

So, we went to that one, which was thankfully not locked.

And we ran. When we saw blown up windows in one room, we went a different way. When we heard people in another, we avoided it. We ran, through rooms and hallways and up stairs.

I saw a small alcove partially hidden by elaborate draping curtain type decorations and stepped into it with Lia. We were far enough away from the fighting I felt safe enough for a breather. Both of us were breathing heavily, and while I knew I could keep going for a long time being a runner, I wasn't so sure about Lia, dragon endurance or no. She'd never gone for any sporty type of things at school.

She collapsed into a velvet chair, staring at the curtains that now shielded us. I went and moved them as together as possible so no cracks would show through before sitting next to her. She had a very blank look on her face that worried me.

"We left them..."

"The guard told us to, remember?"

Both of us instinctively were whispering, but I didn't want to stay here long.

"Brielle... We could have helped."

I grabbed her shoulders, centering her face on mine so she'd look at my eyes and not stare blankly at where we'd just come from.

"How, Lia? How could we really have helped? I can't fight warlocks and I don't think you can either, right?"

She shook her head, but I wasn't sure if it was in denial of being a fighter or in confirmation of her not being one. Or just her saying no to everything going on in general.

I needed to get her up and moving. "I don't know about you, but I couldn't do squat in there except be a distraction or a body like the one in front of the door." Ruthless, but true. That seemed to shock Lia by her expression and I pushed on. "Brielle is fighting, and kicking some serious butt from what I saw. The best thing we can do is get out of their way and let them deal with the warlocks. You with me?"

Lia nodded. A tear slid down her cheek, and we both ignored it.

We needed a plan. "So, the guard told us to get to another safe room. You know where one is?"

She nodded again. "But they're far away. One's by my parent's wing, and there's another by Westen's, but we didn't go those ways. I think there's others, but I don't know where."

"Ok, next plan is to hide. You know tons of places, where would be best for us to hole up?"

She sat there, thinking. I was getting worried she was too scared to focus, or couldn't get past the fact that we ran away from Brielle and the others.

"Come on, Lia, where?" I urged.

"I don't know!" she snapped, pulling her arms from

my hands. She returned her voice to a whisper. "This isn't like getting out of some stupid meeting, you know."

"I know, but you know tons of hiding places, and that's what we need. Someone no one else has ever thought about. You hid in the sprite circle and the broken down furnace."

"Ya, and those won't work! They're fighting outside, so getting to the sprite tree isn't exactly going to work, even though they'd probably never think of it, which sucks. And the furnace is on the opposite side of Firehold. It would take twenty minutes just to get there."

I nodded, trying to be encouraging. "Ok, so what other options are there?"

She blew out an exasperated breath and just shook her head. Now I was getting irritated. Just shaking your head at a problem wasn't going to help anything. Neither would me shaking her, which was something I was tempted to do right now.

"Fine, we could go to my cell area." It was the only place I knew besides our bedroom hall. "They wouldn't think we'd stick ourselves in there, right?"

She snorted. "Maybe, but it's down a looooong stair with no other way out, remember? Not the best option. We'd be royally screwed if they found us there."

"Ya, so, then what?" If there were any crickets left alive outside, now was the time to make some noise. "Well, where do you go?"

She raised her arms in exasperation and started listing off places. "The medical wing, the laundry, the library, the kitchen, a sitting room off the main ballroom, but they all seem way too obvious!"

"How? How are they obvious? The only obvious places I can think of would be your families' rooms and the safe rooms. Which one of those places is the closest?"

Lia was just shaking her head and I felt like slapping the defeatist attitude out of her, but she cracked the curtain the barest degree and looked out at the hall, obviously thinking of something.

"We're in the middle of the southeast wing, so probably the medical wing, but I think we should go to the library."

"Uhh, isn't the library a bit too close to your room? Wouldn't they know to look there?"

"No, not my classroom library. That hardly counts, and yes, you're right that one. But, I meant the castle's official library. It's huge and there's this one room on the side that almost never, ever gets used. The cleaners don't even get it regularly. The entrance is kind of hidden back behind a bunch of bookcases, so you have to walk along the wall to even find it."

"Sounds good to me!" I stood up, energized and ready to go. Though the zinging I felt running through me might be more from fear than energy, I ignored it. "Lead the way."

I took a quick look around the alcove for anything I might be able to use as a weapon and came up with nothing. Lia, meanwhile, was looking out the curtains, checking the hall. She held out her hand and I took it, letting her direct me while I kept an eye out for unwanted visitors.

We went partially down the hall, then entered another one perpendicular to this one. I was so hopelessly lost. The only thing I knew was that we weren't on the first floor. It didn't help that I only really knew one itty bitty hall in this whole freaking gigantic castle, but I didn't even know what direction our rooms were.

I kept seeing images of Belle riding ladders in the Beast's library as we made our way to Firehold's library, the only castle library I could compare it to, even though they probably looked nothing alike.

This trip was a lot like the last one, except instead of us blindly running away, we were now heading toward something. When we passed windows, I looked out at the massive amounts of destruction, and this wasn't even the same place I'd seen before when we went through the busted room. This was a whole new area of fighting. A giant tree was on fire, and I hoped it wasn't the sprites'. There were patches of scorched earth and little heaps littered around that I knew were dead bodies, some wearing the Firehold guard uniforms and others in robes like the one I'd stepped over earlier. I swallowed down my bile. There was nothing I could do but keep running.

Twice we backtracked because we heard noises we didn't like. We made our way through some kind of sitting room with all the curtains closed on the windows.

It made me feel safe from possible prying eyes, but I just couldn't see well enough, so I followed right behind Lia as she wound her way around chairs, tables and standing lamps. On either side of the fireplace, about five feet away, were doors. Lia led us to the one on the right.

She tested the handle lightly before opening, then immediately closed it. Confused, I gave her a "What?" scrunched face, but she grabbed my hand and started pulling me at a near run through the room. I hit a chair and almost went down, but we kept on, Lia holding me up as I stumbled to regain my feet.

Halfway through, the door opened behind us and I got a new burst of adrenaline. Instinctively we crouched down a bit, expecting magical blows to come our way. When a table burst apart just in front of us, Lia gave a high-pitched yell, but we didn't stop.

I glanced back and saw two warlocks making their way toward us, one pausing to move his hands in swirly motions. I kept glancing back, until I saw him push his hands forward, and I yanked Lia down. I wasn't sure if it helped us avoid the warlock's shot that blew a small crater into the wall, but I was glad I did it. We kept pushing on, slamming the door behind us.

There was a small decorative vase not too far from the door I started toward, but Lia pulled me back.

"It won't stop them. Come on."

I got my hand free from hers. "You go, I'll distract them."

She tried to regrab my hand, but I was dragging a

chair in front of the door. I knew it wouldn't stop them, but hopefully it would trip one of them up long enough I could hit them with the metal vase I planned on getting next.

"Don't be stupid, Dani. I am not going to leave you, now come on! They're almost here!"

"Lia! Go! They're not even after me. Get to the hiding place. Go, now!"

"Do you think they're going to just let you go? You're so-" Lia screamed as the door blew open.

I waited a second, then swung the vase around as hard as I could, holding it by the metal lip and arching it into the now empty space where I hoped one of their heads would be. I connected with something and felt the reverberation through my arms, spiking along my nerves. I couldn't keep hold of it, so I let it just fall.

Lia grabbed my still shocky arm and started running, yanking me after her. Since she wasn't going to be practical and hide, I went with her, but I pulled my arm free and kept behind her in case I needed to do more fighting.

Where was a break off room or hallway? This had to be the longest stupid hallway in the entire castle!

I kept glancing behind, seeing one of the guys make his way through the door. I felt a quick surge of satisfaction that he had to take extra time to get over the chair, but it was short lived as he raised his head and met my eyes. I was far away, but even from that distance I could tell there was no whites to them. I didn't know what dark color they might have been, but any color was scary, as was the look on his face when he saw Lia in front of me.

"Lia, run faster."

He moved his arms, his eyes still focused on Lia as a haze of power gathered around him. What I wouldn't do for one of those spell absorbing short staffs the guards had.

"Over here," she called, moving left toward a door.

Too late.

I saw him release one of those bolts I'd seen down a guard out on the grounds, and the grey energy spear went right for where Lia was about to be. I shot a burst of speed into my sprint, thankful I'd done all those running drills over the years. I knocked into her, sending her spinning off the wall, just in time to feel the bolt blow into my side, twisting me around.

I had no control of anything, and no real awareness other than the deep cold pain that paralyzed everything in me. I was on the ground with my eyes open, but I couldn't direct them or even blink.

There was a piercing shriek followed by a light so bright it obliterated everything else.

My chest was on fire. Burning, searing agony scorched everything, consuming me and I had no thought beyond the pain. When it eased the barest amount, I gasped, desperate for air. I tried to get away from the pain, I had to, but my body didn't respond to my desperate urge to move.

The pain dropped from one instant to the next. I laid there, unable to process anything. I just existed, breathing and feeling the remnants of whatever had just happened. I couldn't move anything, couldn't see anything but black, and couldn't hear anything but the rushing in my ears in time with my heart, which I realized was beating exceedingly fast, far faster than it should with me still being conscious.

Of course, maybe I wasn't conscious. It's not like I could do anything. Maybe I was in something like a cognizant coma or something.

Sound trickled past the deafening beats, and I tried to comprehend them. Shuffling, shouting, a scream. That I definitely heard, and it sounded like Lia.

My eyes popped open (which would explain why I hadn't been able to see earlier, since they were still closed) and I lolled my head to the direction of her scream. And there she was, crouching next to me, her hands up in front of her. She looked terrified. Her skin had paled, and her arms were shaking. I tried to reach up to her, but my arms were too heavy to lift.

"Run," I managed to croak out. It sounded like a 65 year-old smoker's vocal chords had switched with my own.

Her eyes immediately shot down to me and she let out a sob. "Dani, you're alive! It worked."

"Come with me, and I'll let her live."

The rough voice sounded from my right and I struggled to wiggle my head around to see who was speaking, though I could guess it was the warlock. Yup, it was. He was holding out his arms to the side, both surrounded by murky, shifting air of grey and black.

"Your cute little protection spell won't last another hit, and you know it," he sneered.

Gosh, how stereotypically bad could a guy get? Of course, he had the power to back it up, and he had taken me out with one hit...

Then my brain figured out what he was saying meant. Lia, stupid, stupid, stupid, brave Lia, had stayed by my side and was continuing to stay even though she was woefully out-skilled by the bad guy, who was mere feet from us with plenty of power ready to blast away. Hadn't I told her to leave me and run to safety before I went down? Didn't anyone ever listen to me!

"Run!" I yelled, or tried to. It came out as more of a rasp. I was able to lift one of my arms in a feeble attempt to push her away, but it fell down halfway there.

The warlock laughed and started to speak, and I'm sure it would have been some more over-the-top, but still threatening speech. However, he got interrupted when most of the hall's rather large and ornate windows were blown in.

Glass shattered across the floor and we all tried to shield ourselves. My shielding was pretty much just closing my eyes, but Lia ducked down around me, covering my head with her body. At the same time, a roar nearly burst my eardrums. At first, I thought my hearing was going out again, but then I saw Lia flinching against me and knew she could hear it too.

It stopped and Lia lifted off of me for both of us to see a large, very angry looking dragon perched precariously on the window sill.

It was Westen.

Fortunately those windows were nearly floor to high, high ceiling length, or he wouldn't have fit. As it was, Westen barely made it through. His wings snapped against the side frames, making the stone creak from the blow and the spikes on the top of his head scraping into the ceiling.

He struck his wings down into the floor, pebbles and broken glass flew up from the impact, and arched his neck in like a viper striking. His head darted forward at the warlock, who had already moved back defensively and had some kind of cloud in front of him that made Westen recoil and shake his snout clear of the stuff.

Briefly, I wondered why he didn't just light the bad guy up with flames, but then my brain reminded me that Lia and I were well within the hit zone, and he probably didn't want to roast us along with the warlock.

The warlock flipped out his hand and a grey streak shot forward, splitting into five right before it would hit Westen, who moved his neck to avoid the initial shot, but couldn't avoid them all. His head rocked upward as three of the bolts struck his neck, and he hit the ceiling, letting out another roar, this time in pain.

Someone was pulling on my shoulders. I looked up to see Lia puffing, struggling to slide me back, away from the fight. Her anchored foot slipped and she landed hard, but she made no sound even though her grimace told me she was hurt. I didn't understand. True, she wasn't the strongest, but she was a dragon in human form and I knew she could move me across the floor if she wanted to, which she clearly did. I'd once limp fished on her at the Thompson's and she'd drug me off her bed and across the whole bedroom floor, but right now she was sweating, shaking, and looking very pale.

"Lia..."

She glanced at the fight, then repositioned herself,

grabbing under my shoulders. "Don't tell me to run again, Dani!" Then she heaved backward, moving me about half a foot. She was panting.

So, I didn't tell her to run, again. Stupid, stubborn princess.

"Can't you help or something? Ugh, when did you get so heavy?"

Well, now I wanted to tell her to shove it, but since she was trying to save my life and we were in the middle of a battle, I let it go.

I tried to help as much as I could. I was slowly regaining my limbs, and I was able to push with my feet just enough to help her start our next lurch backwards. We were fairly close to the door, and if we could get through it, maybe Westen could take care of the warlock without having to worry about us becoming collateral damage.

Because I was facing outward, toward the hall, I had a pretty up close and personal view of the fight. Which was why, when the warlock turned toward us after deflecting Westen off of him, I scrambled to get out of the way, but my limbs weren't responding to my will.

"Lia, move!"

Too late.

The warlock sent multiple shots at us, a malevolent, victorious look on his face.

I screamed. Lia dropped on top of me, trying to shield me again, and I waited for the pain and darkness to take me once again.

There was a loud crack, then Westen thundered in

pain, making the ground shake. Lia looked up and we were both able to see his wing spread out in front of us, several holes sizzling in its span. I could see his head weaving near the ceiling for the barest moment, writhing in pain. Then he shifted forward, trying to get his body into the window fully.

I thought I heard someone laughing. It was the warlock. What the heck did he have to laugh about? That he'd burned a couple of holes in Westen's wing? I'm sure it hurt, like a lot, but it seemed pretty minor to me, comparatively.

Then I saw that Westen had stopped moving forward even though he was obviously trying to. He stretched out his top, then swung around, trying to shift his bottom half and being unable to do so. He was stuck in some kind of black pool that hadn't been there before. The warlock had managed to bait Westen into his trap by sucker punching at us, the bastard.

I looked past Westen as he tried to extricate himself to see the warlock holding a shaft of crystallized white light in his hand.

"Westen!" I cried out, terrified of seeing him die in front of me.

The white light expanded outward from his hand as he held it, almost as fast as one of the grey bolts flew, but somehow I just knew that this was way more powerful than a mere bolt. The light was anchored to the ground and still held by the warlock, as if it were an ever expanding spear of death. It went straight for Westen's immovable lower half.

But Westen was mostly in front of us at this point, so when he swiveled his neck around and let out a jet of flame so hot I thought my eyebrows might singe off, it was all directed down the hall, right at the warlock.

I couldn't take the brightness between the spear of light and the flame, and the heat scorched at my legs. Crying out I managed to get an arm in front of my already closed eyes to help, but it wasn't enough.

Then everything went black. I blinked, making sure my eyes weren't just closed again like before. As my eyes adjusted, the first thing I saw was Lia was doing the same thing as me, just trying to get her eyes to work again. Then I noticed Westen, laying down in front of us across the span of the hall. He seemed to be shaking, or phasing out, and a shaft of panic lit through me. He could not be dying!

"Westen," my voice cracked.

Lia heard me and shot up off the ground, stumbling over to her brother. She fell onto his enormous, scaley backside and put an ear against him.

"It's ok!" she called back, giving me a thumbs up. "He's shifting."

She came back to my side and I noticed her legs were wobbling ever so slightly.

"If he were seriously injured, he wouldn't be able to do that," she explained.

"The warlock?" I'd tried to see, but Westen took up

so much room in the hallway, and without being able to move myself, it just wasn't happening.

She grinned. "Extra crispy."

"Good. And gross." I felt a grim satisfaction knowing the guy who'd tried to kill us was taken out, and it didn't bother me at all.

Since Westen was taking his time, and I couldn't see anything else, I stared at the wall of used-to-be-windows. False dawn had started sometime during our frantic run through the castle. Beautiful reds, pinks, oranges and yellows accented the wispy clouds, and for some reason, it made me feel very peaceful.

Westen's change seemed to take forever as his form melted irregularly down, but he eventually emerged back in his human form, still laying on the ground as his dragon form had been. Lia grabbed an arm to help him get up, but he hissed and she dropped it, looking alarmed.

"Sorry."

"No, it's ok. It's just my shoulder."

Westen powered himself up with his left arm and his legs. He paused half-way up, I was guessing to catch his breath as he was heaving pretty good. He didn't look like he was in the best of shape. His right arm was held against him, his hand holding his opposite ribs. On the bright side, the black pool seemed to have lost its cementing ability. It slid off of him, mostly, as he got up.

Finally, he stood, looking very much like he was holding the pain at bay. He held out his left hand for Lia to take, and I clenched down, willing myself not to cry. I was blaming it all on the fight and the grey bolt that took me down.

"What happened to you?" Westen asked me, but Lia answered as if he'd asked her.

"She pushed me out of the way. Got hit by the energy charge he threw at me." She tilted her head back down the hall to indicate the downed warlock. "It took her out."

Lia let go of his hand and settled in behind me, lifting my head into her lap. I wasn't going to complain. It was much more comfortable than the stone floor was. Though the stone seemed to be warmer than it had before Westen roasted the hall.

Her head shot up. "What about the other one?" Lia was moving her neck this way and that to see around her brother.

Westen immediately turned and walked through the scorched out hallway like it was nothing, passing the mostly melted form without pause. There were burning bits of furniture and shattered glass everywhere he nimbly avoided, walking silent amid the wreckage. How did he do that? It was as if the knowledge of another assailant being in the area gave him a burst of heroism, the way he stealthed down the hall, his eyes moving around checking all possible danger spots. He was still favoring his arm though.

"What other one?" I asked while watching Westen

make his way. I noticed some of the broken glass had melted into little glass pools.

"The one you clobbered with that vase when he was coming through the door. I saw him coming out here to join the other one, but then Westen showed up."

Ya, I wouldn't have been able to keep track of him through that fight, either, so I didn't blame her one bit.

Westen got to the room they'd entered, still marked by the blown in door. He searched through the blackened debris around him, then went through the opening. After a few moments, he came back, shaking his head.

"There's no body. He's gone," he called out.

Lia kept looking at the door. "And he won't come back?"

I smiled at her, trying to put her at ease. "With Westen here? After what he just did to his buddy? I highly doubt it."

She gave me a wane smile. "Ya, I guess you're right."

With the fight over, I wasn't straining myself anymore and instead just tried to catch my breath.

"Our forces are routing out the last of theirs." Westen was close enough he didn't have to call out. "They should all be dead, captured, or running by now."

"Well, that's good," Lia sounded immensely relieved.

"How'd you know we were in trouble?" I asked, genuinely dumbfounded as to how he'd known to come. "And where to find us?"

"I felt Kalia's flare."

I looked up at Lia above me. "You flared?"

She grimaced.

I looked back to Westen. "And you felt it?"

He nodded. "Dragons can feel their family use magic when nearby. Flares are especially noticeable as they aren't shielded."

Westen knelt down next to me, looked at Lia, then me, then he reached over and held Lia's cheek in one hand, and put the other in my hand. He didn't feel nearly as warm as he usually did, and I gave his hand a squeeze, glad that is was actually a squeeze and not the nudge I thought it might be with how my muscles seemed to be functioning at the moment. They were getting steadily stronger. Maybe I'd be able to sit up in an hour or so.

"Oh, Kalia..." Westen sounded like he was terribly saddened, but I couldn't for the life of me figure out why.

Something wet splattered on my forehead, making me flinch. I looked up to see Lia crying above me.

"I had to, Westen. I had to!" She looked down at me, then back at him.

He rubbed his face with one hand until it settled over his mouth.

"She died."

Oh. Crap.

Not, she was dying. Not, she was unconscious. Not, she would have died.

She died.

I had died.

And Lia had done something that made me not dead.

"What did you do?" I asked. My voice sounded tiny, even to me.

Westen shielded his face with his hands for a moment, but I was too preoccupied to figure it out.

Lia smiled at me, but her eyes were filled with tears. "I gave you a part of myself."

I was confused. "I don't... I..."

Westen caught my eye, having moved his hands to steeple in front of him.

"What she means is that she gave you part of her power. Remember how she pushed some of it into you back in Montana to ward off the spell on you? It's like that, but in your core. You're permanently infused with Kalia's dragon essence. She made you Dragon Kin."

Permanently infused with Lia's dragon essence. I guess that was why it burned so much. If Lia's hand had blistered my wrist just to ward off a warlock's spell, no wonder my body couldn't function yet. It had been infused, which I suspected was a fancy word for flooded, with dragon power.

And now I was Dragon Kin, whatever that was. Then it dawned on me. Kin meant family and Westen had said this was permanent, as in, couldn't be undone.

"Ohhhhh, your mother is gonna be so pissed at you!" I exaggerated out my vowels like little kids did when taunting another for being in trouble. "You're so gonna get it!"

She swatted at me, and I started laughing. It hurt, but I couldn't stop.

"I don't care," she said proudly. "Besides, what can she do? Make me go to *more* meetings?" Her face fell slightly. "Wait, she's going to do that, isn't she?"

Westen nodded at her gravely, but I saw his mouth twitch as soon as Lia turned back to me, horror in her eyes.

"She'll have me organizing all the meals and arrangements for all incoming guests from now on, major and minor ones. I'll never get out of it."

I nodded and she groaned. So, I tried to think of something to make her feel better about the situation.

"To be fair, she was probably going to have you do that anyway."

Lia did not find this soothing. She let out a pitiful wail, causing a whole new round of laughter from me. Westen even cracked a smile, though he tried to hide it behind his hand.

"Shut up, you two. This is serious. My life is over."

"Aww, poor baby," I jeered, then had a more serious thought. "Hey, is that why she couldn't move me and is all wobbly and stuff?"

"I am not wobbly!"

Westen and I ignored her.

"Probably. She's missing a good chunk of her power."

I bit my lip. "But, she'll be ok. I mean, it won't hurt her forever, right?"

"It'd serve you right if I got sick!" Then she softened

as she saw that I wasn't in a joking mood about this subject. "I'm fine, Dani. And you're fine. Let's leave it at that."

I looked to Westen, who shook his head lightly.

"I don't know how it will affect her in the long run. Dragon Kin haven't been made for ages. It's supposed to only happen through official channels, and it hasn't been permitted in over two centuries."

"Then how did you even know how to do it?" I raised my voice at Lia.

She shrugged. "I don't know, I just did it. Hey, you're alive, remember. You should be thanking me."

"Thanking you for ignoring me when I told you to run, for risking your life while doing something against the rules. Ohhhh, your mother is really going to get you for this."

Lia slapped lightly at my shoulder. "Rude and ungrateful. That's what you are."

Westen stood up again while Lia and I made faces at each other. I noticed a distinct cradling of arm and ribs as he did so.

"Hey, you ok?" I asked, suddenly feeling somber at the reminder that Westen had gotten into a fight to the death and hadn't come away unscathed.

"You're the one that died, Dani." He almost rolled his eyes at me, ungrateful wretch.

"Gee, thanks. I'd forgotten. Seriously, though, how bad did he get you?"

He patted at his rib area once, but nearly winced with

the effort. "I'll be fine, though my wings will need time to heal. It's fairly superficial in human form. Like a bad surface bruise."

I knew all about bad bruises and their pains.

"And your shoulder?" Lia asked while getting up (I was able to set my head back down on the floor myself, yay) and like a true annoying little sister, went to inspect him herself before he could answer. She pulled his shirt, which I just now noticed was a pajama type night shirt, down to expose his left shoulder. There was a nasty looking white mark, almost as if he'd been scorched with a blow torch. The middle of it looked raw and meaty.

"Gnarly."

He gave a half-smirk of appreciation at my comment. "That, I'll have to go to a medic to see about. I don't know what he hit me with."

"Can you move it? Like rotate your arm around?" Lia went to grab his arm, most likely to do just that.

"Don't." Westen took a step back, sounding very stern and serious, which didn't affect Lia in the slightest.

"Lia, leave him alone. He said he's going to get it checked out."

Lia turned on me. "You're just trying to let him off the hook. You're going to have to go to the doctors too, you know. And I'll bet they'll keep you for observation."

She looked so smug. I didn't like doctor visits and Lia knew it. It wasn't that I didn't trust them or anything, it's just that the experiences were always negative, especially the court update ones. So, I did the only sensible and mature thing I could considering I couldn't lift myself up yet.

I stuck my tongue out at her.

And keep me for observation they did. For five days! Westen, the punk, got to leave that same day. But me, nooooooo. I had to lay there, because they wouldn't let me get up and wander around (I might get ideas or something), for five stinking days.

Some guards had found us not long after the fight had ended, and Westen made one of them go for a medical team to stretcher me to the medical bay, hospital, wing, thingy. It was pretty swanky for being out in the middle of nowhere, but that seemed to be a theme with this castle.

The doctors lost their minds at Lia and me, and immediately set up all these instruments and tests and whatnot. Mercifully, they put us in our own room, while the main triage area that reminded me of an emergency room was filled with wounded guards and other castle folk who'd been hit during the fighting.

Then her mother came, and I did my very, very best to stay out of the way, which wasn't hard considering I was bed ridden and couldn't really move much more than my fingers and toes reliably at that point.

As soon as she entered I saw Westen pull that cool, neutral mask over himself. It was like a wall slammed down on him. It was scary how good he was at switching, but I supposed that's what happens after a couple hundred years of dealing with that for a mother.

"Tell me what I heard is not true!"

"Mother," Westen started, just to get cut off with a sharp arm wave from the queen.

"Kalia, *what did you do?*"

Lia tried to pull down her own neutral façade. I saw it, but she was just too drained or weakened by everything that had happened, to be able to really pull it off like she had that night in her room.

"She died."

"And that has to do with you breaking Orindrae, how?"

Ouch. That was the equivalent of her saying, "So what?" Gee, tell us how you really feel about me...

Lia heard it, and shot up out of her bed, one of the wires attached to her pinging off and swinging around its pole wildly.

"I don't care if I broke Orindrae-"

"You should care. The Dreki Order will not-"

"Can shove it!"

"How da-"

"Mother!" Westen shouted to be heard over the two of them and stepped between them as they'd been starting to square off.

It was like watching a three player verbal tennis match where each one hit the ball harder at the next, but it was obviously Westen and Lia against their mother.

When the queen looked at him, I thought I saw surprise. She probably wasn't used to her oldest yelling at her.

"Mother," he restated, much softer. "Kalia did not technically break Orindrae."

I saw Lia visibly deflating her anger behind him. I tried to give her an encouraging smile, but she just clenched her jaw.

The queen folded her arms, her nails clenching and unclenching on her robes, which I just noticed were very fine indeed. White (mostly, where they hadn't been singed) with blue stitching throughout that seemed to emulate rain. It was quite beautiful. They had to have been her version of pajamas with the style of long loose shirt and pants, but they looked like they could masquerade at a ball they were that high of quality.

And her nails were threatening the stitching on her upper arms. "Explain."

"There is a provision for emergencies in relation to the creation of Dragon Kin, especially when there are extenuating circumstances, such as Kalia encountered."

"A skirmish with humans of grandeur is hardly an emergency."

Westen nodded. "Indeed. I was talking about Daniella dying to protect Kalia while they were under attack from two highly trained warlocks intent on either kidnapping or killing Faela herself."

Hey, I finally wasn't "the prisoner." That was nice. Baby steps of victory.

The queen's eyes narrowed, and she took a glance at me (that made me feel like a bug, which to her I probably was), then at Lia.

"Is this true?"

Lia nodded. "They threw an energy charge at me. Daniella knocked me out of the way and it hit her instead."

She turned back to Westen. "And you saw this?"

Westen readjusted his stance and that made me nervous. It seemed like the equivalent of squirming.

"At that time, I was in the south quarter fields. Once Kalia flared, I went there at once and found them cornered by the warlock."

"Then it is yet to be determined if she actually did die from that energy charge, or if it was all a set up for this human to get yet another hook in Faela. This time, a permanent, dangerous one."

Lia immediately puffed up again, I could see it. She threw an accusatory arm out at her mother, not even caring at the beeping machines freaking out at her pulling more wires loose.

"I was not tricked, Mother." She spat the last word out. "You can check all you want with the guards sent to get us, but they got overrun by warlocks, they told us to run and we did. The warlocks found us and Dani saved my life. *She saved my life*! And all you do is throw accusations at her. She died because of me."

Tears flew down her cheeks, but she ignored them. "I felt for her pulse. There was nothing. And that warlock? The one you think might be in some sort of ridiculous collusion with my best friend? Well, he had no idea who she was and he was mad that he missed me. Okay? So don't you dare say I was manipulated or whatever, because I wasn't!"

Westen put a hand on Lia's shoulder, gently pulling her back. The queen looked like she wanted to retort, but Westen started speaking first.

"Regrettably, Mother, there are no other witnesses to verify Faela's evidence. I will, of course, check with the guards assigned charge of Faela, and investigate as much as I can, but it looks like her version, and mine once I arrived, are the only ones available. And I concur with Faela's assessment that the warlock was not concerned with Daniella, and in fact, tried to kill her again after she'd been made Dragon Kin. So, unless our testimony is suspect...?"

The queen was not happy, but at least she wasn't flying off the handle or anything. She levelled Westen with a cold look.

"Domen, I counselled you about this attachment concern years ago."

I think she switched to their titles because she was feeling tetchy. Or maybe it was because Westen had started using them, but in his case, I think it was to oomph up the credibility factor in their arguments.

"Yes, Mother, but if she hadn't been there, Faela would either be dead or prisoner. Daniella saved her life either way."

The queen snorted and I imagined smoke puffing out of her nostrils. I hadn't forgotten the awesome sight of her incinerating that warlock on the field outside and then roaring in triumph. I had no doubt she'd love to do that to me.

After an age of silence, the queen went to the door and called for the doctor.

"I want to know everything, *everything,* that is going on with those two and their newfound kin connection. Understood?"

The older gentlemen in red robes bowed gravely. "Yes, Faelen."

"And you," she turned to Westen, "are to give a full report of this night's activities by the end of day. I want to know how those vermin got in here and exactly what they did."

Westen gave a short bow, in which his shoulder tremored slightly. The queen noticed. She had some intense eyes, and she flicked them between her son and daughter.

"Are you two unharmed?"

Lia waved her off. "I'm fine," she mumbled.

"I have only minor wounds, Mother. The doctors have already started treatment."

The queen gave a sharp nod, then left. I guess that was her being a concerned mother.

Westen had to leave shortly after that, once the doctors gave him his final patch up and care conditions. Apparently, he'd been blasted by some kind of reverse dark matter type of energy, and being in his dragon form had saved him from being obliterated. Though, they said it in much more doctorly type of terms.

Lia and I got the rest of the day to relax and work on me trying to get my limbs functioning again. By that night I could lift them all a couple of inches up, but it was tiring. I was able to wave at Brielle when she came to visit, sort-of. It was a weird hand wobble, but I counted it as a success.

Brielle looked pretty good for having a broken arm strapped to her chest, she said it was to keep her arm immobile. One of her eyes was swollen shut and she had a spectacular bruise to go with it. She joked about taking a sword hilt to the eye, but I didn't find that particularly funny since I could imagine it all too well. She said her eye would be fine, so there was that at least. Brielle was in good spirits overall, and it did Lia good to see her.

Lia got pulled out the next day by the doctors for individual testing. We both had to sit through them apparently. I didn't know what they were testing half the time.

Did I feel anything? No, you're not doing anything. How about now? You're still not doing anything.

I supposed they were doing something to Lia at the time. Then they prodded me, and worked on getting my muscles energized, which was painful but worth it, since it worked. By the third day I could sit up and walk a bit. They brought her in, took her out, did tests to us both. It was kind of interesting at times, but mostly boring. One time they made this magical gold glowy cloud around me that made me sneeze a whole ton. Not sure what that one was supposed to measure, but they seemed happy with their results.

I could tell something was working inside me though. My muscles might be figuring things out at a slower pace, but my bruises and scratches were all gone. The burn on my wrist had even closed and faded somewhat. I wondered if it would disappear completely, but I could still see the deformed ringlets of scar that had previously formed in the healing process.

My cheek scar even seemed smaller, but that could just be my imagination. For some reason, it just didn't bother me anymore. Dying had a way of changing your perspective on things.

On the fourth day Lia was released to return to her duties. She whined to me all about it that night. She was on light duty, which translated to her organizing things for the upcoming visiting dignitaries, but she had managed to sneak off to check on the sprites. It seemed they were far enough away from the main fighting that they'd escaped damage thank goodness, and since it was night-time, they'd just stayed in their tree, safe and sound.

Then Lia had been found, laying in her circle of sprites, and dragged back to her mother.

"It's sitting in a room with my mother and a bunch of samples. I have to just make forms of things we're going to do for the visitors. They've stopped my training because it's too physical and they don't want to push my limits with my magic still in flux. You know what that means? More time to sit and plan meals. And rooms. And color schemes."

On the fifth day, Westen showed up, looking markedly better than I'd last seen him. "Hey." I waved as he came in, with an actual wave. "What are you doing here?"

"You seem to be doing much better."

I smiled. "I am. Your doctors are miracle workers. I can even go to the bathroom on my own now. It's very exciting."

He smiled lightly, crinkling his permanent five o'clock shadow. I took his smile as a triumph. Lia would have totally laughed with me, but for Westen, a smile was just as good.

I pointed at his shoulder. "That seems better, too."

"It is, significantly." He rolled it a bit, then cringed ever so slightly. "It still has to heal some, though."

"Haha, show off. That's what you get. So, what's up?"

"I'm here to let you know that you are officially released from confinement."

I sprang up from my lounging position as quickly as my ailing body allowed. "Really? You're not kidding? Sweet!" I swung my legs over the edge and slid off, wavering a bit on landing. Westen reached out to steady me. "Let's go!"

"Hold on. Should I get a chair for you? You don't seem too steady on your feet."

"Nooooo, come on, don't do that to me," I whined. "We can go slow. I can walk. Promise."

"Here." He turned, revealing some clothes set on a counter by the door. "You get dressed and I'll go talk to the doctors."

"Deal."

He came back a few minutes later. "Good news. The doctors say that your vitals are extremely good. A bit on the high side for a human, but they expect that's the dragon essence enhancing you. Once you get over the initial burnout, you should be in better than tip top shape. You'll probably notice the effects more as time passes, which is why the doctors want you to come in daily for checkups."

"Well, that's good. I guess."

And weird. So, I was slightly superhuman? What did that mean? How would it change me? I'd already noticed I didn't get cold nearly as easily as before, which was a bonus, but again, slightly scary. I had been fundamentally changed, and I just didn't know how I felt about it. I mean, yes, happy to be alive. But scared.

"Ready to go?" Westen asked.

"You bet'cha."

Finally, we started out. Through the main room, we didn't talk. There were a few patients still in there, some sleeping. A few guards called out to Westen and he waved, addressing them all by name. One he went to his bedside and said a few words while I waited. I'd never seen him interact with the guards before really, and I was amazed at how much they seemed to care for Westen. And vice versa. I would have thought dragons were above the humans, but that didn't seem to be the case for Westen.

"So," Westen said once we cleared the hospital wing. "How are you feeling?"

He held out his arm for me to take. I eyed it a second before accepting. It felt strange to hold onto his elbow while walking, but nice. He didn't feel as innately warm as he used to. Another one of my changes probably.

I shrugged. "Fine."

"No, really."

I gave him a side glance, but he seemed genuine.

Insecure? Scared? Freaked out? I settled for, "Tired, but strong, if that makes sense."

He nodded.

"Hey, where's Lia?" I had figured on her being the one to spring me.

The corner of his mouth lifted the barest amount. "With Mother."

"Haha, awesome. Doing what?"

"Ballroom decorations planning for when the Man-vali come to visit in January."

I started laughing so hard we had to pause for me to regain my balance, though that was probably due more to my weak body than my actual laughter.

"I'm sure she'll tell you all about it later tonight."

"Naturally."

Westen glanced at me out of the corner of his eye as we walked, but I caught it.

"Are you doing alright here? At Firehold?"

I bit the inside of my lip, thinking.

"Do you miss Montana?" he continued before I could answer the first two.

"Yes and no, you know? It was the only place I've ever known, but I was prepared to leave it. Just not in quite the spectacular fashion that we did."

He nodded.

"It's just," I blurted out, feeling the need to explain the swirling thoughts of emotion that hit me from his question. "I had this plan, right? Go to college, get a job, move on. But now... It's all so weird. Everyone there thinks I'm dead. I don't even have any of my things." I gave a dry chuckle. "Except for the clothes I was in."

I forced down the sob that suddenly sprouted at the thought of losing the photo of my mother, but it was lost in the treehouse, most likely burned down with the house. Everything else could be replaced, really, but not that. Luckily, Westen didn't seem to notice the lump in my throat.

"I'm sorry it's been so problematic for you. Hopefully staying here won't be too difficult for you now that you're Dragon Kin. You can take your time deciding what your next steps will be, whether you go to college in the fall, or stay here indefinitely."

I hadn't realized I'd stopped walking until Westen pulled on my arm by stepping up onto a stair without me. He looked back, a puzzled expression on his face that quickly changed to something else when he looked at me. I didn't have brain power to figure it out, I was lost in my own spinning thoughts.

"I'm staying here? Like, your mother isn't going to kick me out as soon as they figure out what's up with the whole Dragon Kin thing?"

He stepped back down to be level with me. Though level was a strong word to use when the guy was half a foot taller than me. At least my neck wasn't so craned trying to look at him.

"Since your judgement was lifted and with you being Dragon Kin... You and Kalia are permanently linked in ways we've never experienced here. It was sort of expected that you'd stay here and continue to be observed. You'll be able to move about the castle now, have more freedom. But, you're not trapped here. You're not a prisoner. If you want to leave..."

Relief poured through me, nearly leaving me dizzy. I held onto his arm to keep from swaying I felt so giddy.

"No, no, I want to stay. I mean, at least for now. If that's ok."

I couldn't help but smile, which only widened when Westen gave me a smile in return. I had a place to live and it was going to be with Lia. I could figure everything else out along the way, with my best friend there to help me.

"Good. I'm glad."

And I believed him. It was as if the impossible were made possible in every kind of way, including with Westen. He'd always been my best friend's older, annoying, stickler of a brother. And now... Now I saw how kind, dedicated, and all around genuine he was. Even a month ago I would never have believed it possible, but here I was. My life sure had changed, in so, so, so many ways. And it looked to keep going that way.

We went by a window and my mood immediately sobered as I saw the after effects of the fight on the grounds. It had been several days and everything was cleared away, but there were gouges and scorched earth, and several burnt out trees.

"Did you suffer many casualties?" My voice was quiet, even to me.

Westen looked down at me, then out the window I was looking through. "Yes, unfortunately. Due to our training for such instances, we were able to keep it down. If the draeden had been here... well, they weren't."

His eyes had darkened, and I felt bad for making him think of such things, but I wanted to know what had happened.

"Did you ever find out how the warlocks got in?"

"No, but that isn't all that unexpected."

I was shocked. "What? Why not?"

We got to the end of the windows and I couldn't see the grounds anymore, thank goodness.

"They've known about Firehold for a long time now. With transportation and technology the way it is these last fifty years it's much harder for us to hide our bases, even with magic. They've shown themselves to be very adept at circumventing our precautions in the past, so it was a matter of time until they struck at our home."

He stared straight ahead and it was almost as if I could feel the anger rolling off of him.

I gave him the side eye. "There's something more."

He raised an eyebrow at me. "What makes you say that?"

I shrugged. "I can just tell."

"Yes, well... You're right."

"I knew it."

"Stop gloating. Do you promise not to tell anyone?"

That didn't sound like the Westen I knew, but he looked perfectly serious, so I took it as such.

"Not even Lia?"

"No, she doesn't need to worry about such things with everything going on."

I got that. She was doing really well, but she was still having a rough time of things. She put on a good face, and tried her hardest, but the death of her warden mother and the attack, everything was taking a toll on her. And since she flared and made me Dragon Kin... I was worried about how it was affecting her. She seemed so drained all the time. Not that the constant meetings and plannings helped with anything at all.

"Yes, I promise. Should we talk about it in the open?"

Westen looked around. "I think it's safe enough now. Your judgement has been suspended due to your condition, and though I'm sure Mother still has her reservations, I don't think she'll do anything about it too soon. We're busy with recovery and holding at the moment."

"Ah," was all I could think to say. I mean, it was great that my judgement was over, but being in his mother's crosshairs wasn't exactly comforting. "So what else is going on?"

"I think there's someone at the castle working with the warlocks."

Well, that was a dun-dun-dunnnnn moment if I ever heard one.

"What makes you think that?"

"Small things, and big ones. Like them breaching Firehold right when Father and the draeden were all gone."

"So, you were right that the attacks didn't add up, then? Including the first one?"

He nodded. "I think this was their ultimate plan, and the attack in Montana was a set up for it."

"If it was just to get Lia, why not just grab her there?"

"I think they meant to, but the outcome would most likely have been the same, albeit faster. I believe their goal was twofold, and Kalia was just one part of it."

We started up some stairs and I gripped his arm a bit tighter.

"And the other part?"

Westen shook his head. "I'm sorry. I can't divulge that information."

"Ok," was all I said, even though I really wanted to call bull on it. It was irritating that he wouldn't tell me, but I got it. Probably some super important inner dragon type stuff.

"But it was confirmed that they got farther into Fire-hold than originally thought."

Hmmm... interesting. I wondered what they were after.

"Did they get or do whatever it was?"

"It doesn't appear so."

"Well, that's good."

We finally reached the top of the stairs and I recognized the hallway that led to the staircase that led to Lia's hall. Whew, we were almost back. My whole body was aching slightly from the walk and I was ready to rest. What a wuss I was. Then again, I had died.

I thought of something and couldn't help but let out a single chuckle.

Westen looked at me. "What?"

"Nothing." I chuckled some more. "It's just... you sound so old right now."

He blinked. "I do?"

"Twofold, albeit, doesn't appear so... Your age is really starting to show, old man."

He stared for a moment, then gave a rueful nod. "I'll have to review my materials more. It has been a blue age since I studied."

I started laughing, a lot. So much so that we had to stop again until I was able to catch my breath.

"It's not that funny, you know," he said dryly when I started to clear up, which only threw me deeper into fits of laughter.

I tried to say, "You're the one that's funny," but every time I tried, I just couldn't work around the laughter. Westen got an annoyed look on his face, which didn't help either. Finally, I took some deep, calming breaths, centered myself, and held the laughter down.

"Ok." Another deep breath. "I got it under control." *Nope, don't smirk. Don't laugh.* "Let's go."

We were at the stairs that led to our hall, and I was excited to lay down. Pathetic as that may be, but my sides were just aching now from all the laughing.

"So, what else will you be doing?" I asked. "Besides studying up on your grammar."

"It's not grammar. It's the vernacular."

Oh my gosh, I was going to lose it again.

"And besides getting back to my regular duties, I was going to pull some of our old historical texts to see if I could learn some more about Dragon Kin, their connections, their functions, that sort of thing. Since you'll be staying here for the foreseeable future, I thought it would be prudent to get as much information on your new condition as possible, so you and Kalia could adjust to any unknown side effects. I'll see if any of the older dragons remember any kin from their younger years, though I haven't heard them ever mention it before, so that might be fruitless."

I managed to keep myself composed through "prudent" and "fruitless." Him doing research on my new condition wasn't something I expected, but I was grateful. I didn't like to dwell on it, but thinking about all the strange changes that were or could be happening because of this thing, not to mention the whole dying episode, really freaked me out. Having some kind of reference, some kind of knowledge on the whole thing, would help put me at ease.

"Do you think I could get in on some of those dragon history texts? I tried before, but Instructor Wilson wasn't very accommodating, to put it mildly, and Brielle said she couldn't. Apparently I was blacklisted or something."

Westen mouth quirked up. "Yes, Instructor Wilson is certainly nitpicky for the rules. Of course. I'll get some to you tonight, if you like."

I couldn't help the smile on my face, and not just because of Westen's old timey language. I never would have thought it, but smiling might become a regular feature for me.

"That would be great. I mean, there's only so much reading and drawing a girl can do in a pink room."

He arched an eyebrow. "Aren't you going to be reading the history texts?"

I swatted the arm I was holding with my free hand. "You know what I mean."

We started up the stairs again.

"By the way, thanks for everything, Westen."

He looked sideways at me, a question in his eyes, and I hoped the blush I felt wasn't showing.

"I mean," I tried to clarify, "from getting me that night in the woods, bringing me here, sticking up for me in the trial, getting me books and stuff to do, the whole saving us from the warlock thing... You know, everything. I, uh, am not used to people helping me so much. You know, besides Lia."

Now I really hoped the blush wasn't showing. I had to look away from him. His soft blue eyes were getting to me. .

"I hope you get used to it more. And you're very welcome."

There was my bedroom door. And I guess now it would actually be mine, and not just a room I was temporarily staying in. We stopped at it, and I stared at it for a moment. For some reason it felt like my insides were fluttering. *It's just a room, silly.*

Westen waited for me.

I held up a finger. "One more thing."

"Yes?"

"Can I paint my room something not pink?"

Carolani Day always loved escaping in a book and started writing her own stories at the age of ten. She continued reading and writing through high school, college, and beyond. She loved it so much, she went and got a Master's degree in creative writing. *The Dragon Kin* is her debut novel. She lives in central California with her husband and two girls.

Connect with Carolani Day online:
www.carolaniday.com
Twitter @CarolaniDay
Facebook: Carolani Day, Writer

Watch for *Of the Firehold*, the sequel to *The Dragon Kin*, coming soon.

If you enjoyed reading *The Dragon Kin*, consider leaving a review online. For self-publishing and indie authors, reviews are incredibly important in showing their work to potential readers. If you feel others would like the world as much as you do, please share your thoughts so they may discover *The Dragon Kin*.

CPSIA information can be obtained
at www.ICGtesting.com
Printed in the USA
LVHW050313211020
669277LV00008B/217